I0762952

this must be the place

ALSO BY KELLY QUINDLEN

She Drives Me Crazy

Late to the Party

Her Name in the Sky

this must be the place

kelly quindlen

Roaring Brook Press
New York

Published by Roaring Brook Press
Roaring Brook Press is a division of Holtzbrinck Publishing
Holdings Limited Partnership
120 Broadway, New York, NY 10271 • fiercereads.com

EU representative: Macmillan Publishers Ireland Ltd, 1st Floor, The Liffey
Trust Centre, 117–126 Sheriff Street Upper, Dublin 1, D01 YC43

Our books may be purchased in bulk for specialty retail/wholesale,
literacy, corporate/premium, educational, and subscription box use.
Please contact MacmillanSpecialMarkets@macmillan.com.

Library of Congress Cataloging-in-Publication Data

Names: Quindlen, Kelly author
Title: This must be the place / Kelly Quindlen.
Description: First edition. | New York : Roaring Brook Press, 2026. |
Audience: Ages 14–18 | Audience: Grades 10–12 |
Summary: When eighteen-year-old Louisa returns to her small Alabama
hometown for a funeral, she starts a fragile romance with Aubrey,
only to find their relationship tested by local scandals, family pressures,
and the challenge of being openly queer in a place seemingly built on secrets.
Identifiers: LCCN 2025013575 | ISBN 9781250911063 hardcover
Subjects: CYAC: Prejudices—Fiction | LGBTQ+ people—Fiction |
Lesbians—Fiction | Alabama—Fiction | LCGFT: Novels | Fiction
Classification: LCC PZ7.1.Q523 Th 20026
LC record available at https://lccn.loc.gov/2025013575

First edition, 2026
Printed in the United States of America

ISBN 978-1-250-91106-3
10 9 8 7 6 5 4 3 2 1

IN LOVING MEMORY OF HENRY,
QUEEN OF OUR HEARTS

AND FOR JOEY AND MARC,
ELDERS EXTRAORDINAIRE

1
RUSTIN

They really, truly had Uncle George entombed in a trophy case.

"I thought my father was joking," Dad said, coming to an abrupt halt in Grandma and Grandpa's foyer. We had only just walked through the front door, exhausted and hungry and ready to get this over with, but the large, imposing green urn stopped us both in our tracks. It was impossible to miss, glittering on the highest shelf of the glass display cabinet like a king atop his throne, lording above the dozens of trophies and plaques that made up his subjects. In a break from routine, Grandpa had even left the display case open, almost like he wanted to ensure we would see its newest prize. Because Grandpa, no doubt, considered his famous brother's ashes to be a prize.

Just an hour ago, Grandpa had called to ream us out for missing the wake. His sharp voice had crackled through the stereo in Dad's truck, steamrolling us when we tried to explain that we had every intention of being there, but my flight had been delayed by the thunderstorms, and Dad had waited at the Birmingham airport for two hours, and then we'd *still* had to drive the hour and fifteen minutes to Rustin, and hadn't he gotten all our texts about this?

I don't have time to check your messages! Grandpa had snapped. *I'm tending to the dead! I've got to put George with his trophies for the night!*

Dad and I had been too frazzled to take this literally.

We should have taken it literally.

I dropped my travel backpack, tied my new UConn hoodie around my waist, and stared at the elaborate urn containing all that remained of my great-uncle. "Honestly," I said, keeping my voice low, "I'm just shocked they haven't had him stuffed and mounted."

"Louisa," Dad chided, but his heart wasn't in it. He had been vacant and withdrawn the entire ride from the airport.

"What? They could have decked him out in his old football jersey and made a real show of it."

I waited for the trace of a smile to appear on Dad's face—we had always been able to bond over Grandma and Grandpa's deranged antics—but he merely sagged his shoulders and gazed upon the urn like a lost little boy. I couldn't blame him. Uncle George had been Dad's favorite person in the world, and now he wore his grief like a layer of rainwater from the storm outside.

"Let's hope it's temporary," Dad said finally. "I'm sure they'll find a better resting place after the funeral."

"Doubt it. Grandpa will probably sell tickets, set up red-carpet ropes right here in the foyer."

My grandfather had long been obsessed with his younger brother's football career. He and Uncle George had grown up right here in small-town Alabama, tussling in the backyard until the day Grandpa tore his ACL. After that, Grandpa had poured everything he had into coaching his little brother, and eventually it paid off: Uncle George became the most successful quarterback in Rustin University history and the only Rustin player to have a career in the NFL. When his NFL career ended with a knee injury, he returned to Rustin and built up a real estate empire that cemented his status as a local legend. Even when his hair turned white, people still saw him as the golden boy.

Grandpa always told the story like it was his own triumph, as if he had formed Uncle George out of clay and molded him into the exact football god he himself wanted to be. Now he curated this display cabinet to show off Uncle George's trophies, medals, newspaper clippings, and even a former uniform—all of it a testament to Grandpa's impact on his brother's success.

"That you, finally?!" a grating voice shouted. "About time!"

"Speak of the devil," Dad mumbled. He picked up the to-go bag from Tambrie's Café and followed the sound of Grandpa's voice to the kitchen.

"Literally," I whispered, because I fully expected my grandparents to give me hell about something entirely unrelated to missing Uncle George's wake. I took a deep breath and willed myself to walk to the kitchen. The collision between my old and new lives was about to begin.

The thing no one tells you about coming out as queer is that you really have to think through the logistics of it.

And believe me, I had.

My plan had been simple, strategic, and foolproof: Wait until the end of high school was in sight, ask a cute girl to prom, and post about it for everyone to see in their own time—including everyone

I'd grown up with in conservative Rustin, Alabama. Then stay in Connecticut for the summer, pick up a job at the mini-golf course, and wait for my college life to begin. If all had gone according to plan, I wouldn't have had to face anyone in Rustin until *next* summer, after my sexuality had become old news, and after I'd finished my first year of college. By then, I would surely be a blazing, confident, full-fledged lesbian, completely immune to what anyone thought of me.

But my plan hadn't accounted for Uncle George's sudden diagnosis. The cancer lay in wait like an undetected predator, then struck as fast and violent as lightning. Dad had gotten the call only last week, while he'd been in Connecticut for my graduation. I'd known it was bad when he excused himself from my party and returned twenty minutes later with a face as white as a ghost. *Collapsed on his way to the post office*, he'd told Mom and me in a shaky voice. *The doctors estimate three to six months.*

Uncle George died five days later.

For a day or two, I had debated skipping the funeral altogether. First, because Mom wasn't invited; my grandparents had erased her from the family six years ago after she'd had the audacity to ask my dad for a divorce. The fact that she moved us up north further enraged them, though I never knew whether this was because they actually missed me or because they couldn't stomach having a Yankee in the family. Second, it wasn't like I had been close with Uncle George. He was more of a peripheral figure in my life: the white-haired great-uncle who breezed into family gatherings, gave me a quick hug, and asked, *So what grade are you in now, Miss Louisa?* before trotting off to have cocktails with my grandparents. And third, because I was absolutely terrified of returning to Rustin a mere month after I'd come out. I would have to face my relatives, old neighbors, and the entire town as this new, openly queer version of myself, a version I was only just beginning to know. The only people I was guaranteed to feel safe around were my two oldest friends, Emma and Candor, whom I had grown up with and continued to visit every summer. They'd had my back since kindergarten, but even they couldn't protect me from the Rustin gossip mill.

In the end, I kept picturing Dad's ashen face when he'd gotten the call. For me, Uncle George's death was a small *ping* on my heart, like a pebble hitting a windshield. But for Dad, it was an avalanche that sent the whole car careening off the road. I didn't want him to face this sudden loss alone, especially because I knew how rotten my grandparents could be. So I made myself a promise. I would fly down just for the weekend, put on a steely resolve, and hold my dad's hand until we got through the funeral. And I would do it as my real self, even if I was still nervous and new.

Now the reality of that promise put a stone in my throat. This would be my first time seeing Grandma and Grandpa since I had come out, and my heart was beating so fast that I felt like I might pass out. I wasn't clear on the details of *how* Dad had told them about me—maybe he'd shown them my Instagram post, or maybe he'd fixed them drinks and dropped the news as delicately as he could—but I knew they knew, and that they would have something to say about it now that I'd come home.

Home. It was a complicated word for me. Connecticut had been my home for the past six years, but Rustin would always feel like my deepest, truest home, even when I was away from it, even when I was afraid of it. And now that I had unearthed a newer, truer version of myself, could that home still hold space for me?

* * *

Grandpa was bent over the old wooden dining table, sorting through a stack of papers. He had already changed out of his dress clothes and didn't bother to look up when Dad and I entered the kitchen.

"Sorry about the wake," my dad said with the air of one approaching a lion's den. "Longest I've ever waited at the airport. Lou's plane circled for an hour."

"Last I checked, those airplanes could fly through a damn rain shower just fine," Grandpa snapped.

I waited for him to look up and notice me, but he remained focused on the papers. I darted a glance at Dad, then squared my shoulders, squeezed the rainbow bracelet on my wrist, and recited my new mantra in my head: *I am gay, I am here, I am gay, I am here . . .*

"Hi, Grandpa," I said in the steadiest voice I could muster.

Grandpa finally looked up and examined me through his wire-framed glasses. I braced myself for the grand judgment, for some snarky version of *Well, if it isn't our little lesbian*, or maybe, *Don't bring your lifestyle to the funeral tomorrow*. What I got was: "The hell are you wearing? Maybe it's better you missed the wake," which, all things considered, was probably the best I could hope for.

I flinched, then tried to pretend I hadn't. These were just my airplane clothes—I had planned to change before the wake—but I still liked them. The top was from a thrift store my friend Gus and I liked to shop at; it was a vintage-washed T-shirt that said RAGE CONSUMES ME above a photo of a fluffy cat. Grandpa glared at it with the disgust he usually reserved for Democrats, goldendoodles, and men who went to therapy. I met his eyes and tried to hold fast to my promise that I would *be myself* this weekend, regardless of how anyone else made me feel. "Um," I said, clearing my throat, "I like this shirt."

"Get some nice skirts and dresses for college," Grandpa demanded, staring me down from beneath his bushy eyebrows. "If I'm paying your tuition, I want to know you're becoming a proper young lady."

I bristled but held my tongue. Dad's eyes were burning into me, begging me to play along. We both knew that if I wanted to get through college on Grandpa and Grandma's dime, then I had to walk a certain line. It remained to be seen what side of that line my queerness fell on, so for now I would have to let the little things go.

I gave my grandfather an apologetic smile and stepped forward to hug him hello. "It's nice to see you, Grandpa. I brought you a surprise." I forced another smile and pulled the corn bread box from the Tambrie's Café to-go bag. Ms. Tambrie herself had pressed it into my hands with strict instructions to tell my grandfather there was extra butter *and* peach jam inside. I could have sworn she had a crush on him. Maybe she liked comb-overs and coffee breath.

Grandpa lifted the lid and surveyed the contents. "No honey?"

"Ms. Tambrie said there was butter and jam."

"She always forgets the damn honey," he said, smacking the container aside. "And today of all days. It's been a hard enough week already."

Just then, Grandma rounded the corner, her hands aloft and her fingers pinched like something might need fixing at any moment. She had that buzz about her like she'd been hurrying from one inane chore to the next. Unlike Grandpa, she was still wearing her clothes from the wake: a formal black dress, diamond earrings, and perfectly coiffed hair the color of buttercream icing. I braced myself again, fully prepared for her to make a dig like Grandpa had, but all she said was, "Oh, Louisa, I'm glad you finally made it," as if I'd walked over from the neighbors' house instead of flying a thousand miles through a thunderstorm.

"Hi, Grandma," I said, returning her perfunctory kiss on the cheek. "You look beautiful."

She neither acknowledged nor returned the compliment. "We need to discuss the photo boards."

I had no idea what she was talking about, but that's how it always went with Grandma. She saw everyone as a potential assistant. Jesus himself could have shown up on the doorstep and she would have said, *Now, if you insist on this Last Supper, you'll have to help me set the table. Go fetch the cloth napkins.*

"They're in the living room," Grandma went on, beckoning me to follow. "Shannon and I worked on them all day yesterday."

The living room smelled overwhelmingly of flowers. There were bouquets on every surface—the coffee table, the mantel, the windowsills, even Grandma's old wooden hope chest, where she still kept her wedding dress. At family parties, usually after a glass of gin, she would fish the dress out and try it on for everyone, making sure we remarked on how well it still fit.

"People are sending flowers in droves," Grandma said. She must have realized how inappropriately pleased she sounded, because she cleared her throat and spoke more somberly. "As they should. Losing George has upended our world."

The space not taken up by flowers was covered with giant trifold photo boards like something a kid might use for a science fair project. Grandma and Aunt Shannon, my dad's younger sister, had made photo collages of Uncle George's life that spanned from infancy to his final days.

"Go have a look," Grandma ordered. "Then you can move them to the Cadillac. We'll need you to drive it to the service tomorrow."

I thought I'd misheard her. "Ma'am?"

"George's Cadillac," she said impatiently. "You'll be driving it to the funeral so we can set up the photo boards before everyone arrives."

I simply stared at her, unable to stomach the idea of driving a dead man's car. Seeing Uncle George's ashes—literally all that remained of him—had been enough of a mindfuck already.

"Oh, honey," she said, correctly reading my expression. "Don't be precious. People die every day. Doesn't mean we should waste a tank of gas."

My dad and Grandpa entered the room. Dad put a hand on my shoulder and said, "I can drive it, Lou, and you can take the truck."

Grandma tutted. "Oh, Tate, you're so soft."

Dad chose to ignore the jibe, which was his usual survival strategy with Grandma. "Louisa's had a long day. I'm starving, so I can only imagine she's ready to eat a horse. How about we eat first, then tackle the photo boards?"

Grandma rolled her eyes. She had very little patience for basic human needs like food and water. "Never mind all that. Did you get a look at these, Tate? Shannon insisted we keep the photos from your college graduation even though you had that awful ponytail."

Dad sighed in resignation and approached the collages with his hands in his pockets. "You taped the obituary up there?"

"Of course I did. Some people may not have read it yet." Grandma sniffed. "Your father worked closely with the reporter to get it just right, and I want every person in this town to appreciate it."

I looked over Dad's shoulder at the front-page copy of *The Rustin Herald*. Dad had emailed my mom the digital version, but this was my first time seeing it in print.

FOREVER OUR GEORGIE BOY

George Garridan Wade

1949–2026
THE HOMEGROWN PRINCE WHO BROUGHT GUTS AND GLORY TO OUR SMALL CORNER OF ALABAMA

George Garridan Wade, 77, of Rustin, Alabama, passed away on May 29, 2026, after a sudden cancer diagnosis. He was the son of the late Henry F. Wade and the late Kathryn (Bailey) Wade of Rustin.

I skimmed all the usual fawning over Uncle George's incredible football career, the real estate business he had started after settling back in Rustin, and his "indelible impact on our community" until I got to the small details at the bottom.

Survived by his brother Amos F. P. (Martha) Wade, nephew Tate Wade, niece Shannon (Keith) Wainwright, great-niece Louisa Wade, and great-nephews Quinn and Charlie Wainwright.

Services will be held on Saturday, June 6, 2026, at Bethel Baptist Church, at 11:00 A.M.

In lieu of flowers, the family asks that you attend a 2026 season Rustin Reckoners football game in George's honor.

"He hated that nickname," my dad muttered, brushing his finger across GEORGIE BOY.

Grandpa scoffed. "Bullshit. That nickname made his whole career, didn't it, even after football ended. How many people bragged about buying a house from Georgie Boy? How many of 'em went to his jersey retirement? How many free lunches did he get when he was palling around town?"

I glanced at Dad, who was still frowning at the obituary. I could almost feel the bitter weight of his grief. If Dad had written the obituary, it would have said things like *George ate peanut brittle by the bagful*, and *George watched* Pretty Woman *whenever he had a bad day*, and *George was the first person you'd call when your wife left you.*

"How many people are we expecting tomorrow?" I asked, already dreading the answer.

"Several hundred, maybe a thousand," Grandpa said, crossing his arms pompously.

I looked between my grandparents. I was pressing my luck, but I couldn't help myself. "Uncle George wanted something that big?"

"'Course he did. Adored in life, adored in death."

Dad caught my eye and shook his head subtly.

Unfortunately, Grandma sniffed it out like a bloodhound. "Oh, for heaven's sake, Tate, you've got to stop treating the man like a saint. George's ego was bigger than this house. He *wanted* a big sendoff."

Dad clenched his jaw and left the room without responding.

"Delusional," Grandpa said, shooting a look after my dad.

"Bless his heart," Grandma said with an exaggerated flutter. "He doesn't understand how this town needs to say goodbye to George. People deserve that closure."

And what about what Uncle George deserved? I wanted to ask. *What about what our family—what my dad—deserves?*

"Now, don't give me that look," Grandma said, correctly reading my expression again. "We've taken all of George's wishes into account. The man wanted to be cremated, so we cremated him."

Grandpa *hmph*ed. "And my mama and daddy are probably rolling in their graves. They wanted everyone in the burial plot together." He looked around, and his expression became conspiratorial. "But as you can see, I've figured that out. I'm keeping the cremains here until Martha and I pass, and then George can slide right into our plot. What the man didn't know won't hurt him."

Grandma stepped closer to the photo boards and trailed her fingertips across a series of young Uncle George in his football uniform. "He was a handsome man," she said wistfully. "All the girls were crazy about him."

Grandpa cleared his throat behind us.

"Well, then," Grandma said, coming back to herself. "I suppose we *should* eat." She turned to my grandfather. "Amos, honey, how 'bout some gin?"

We ate on the enclosed porch, where the rain hadn't managed to soak anything. The storm had finally ended but the humidity lingered like shower steam. Grandpa mixed cocktails while Grandma laid out the napkins and doily place mats. Dad settled back into himself after pouring a glass of bourbon. Then it was blessedly quiet while we dug into our fried catfish, collard greens, macaroni and cheese, and buttery biscuits.

I took a long sip of my sweet tea and realized there *were* parts of Alabama I had missed: the cooking, the magnolia trees, the trilling cicadas. Even the humidity was comforting, seeping into my skin in a way that settled my nerves like a weighted blanket. It was like my body knew I was *home*, even if I didn't want to be. Even if everything had changed.

"I'm sorry we couldn't make your graduation," Grandma said, taking a prim sip of her gin. "It's not easy to find flights up there. Might as well book a trip to Paris, the way they schedule these things."

I wanted to point out that I'd just found a flight here on the exact same route, but I held back. "No worries, Grandma. Thank you for the card and the check."

"Don't say 'check,' sweetheart, it's crass. 'Gift' is fine." Her eyes fell to my ripped jeans. "Maybe you can get some new clothes for college, hmm?"

"I said the same thing, Martha," Grandpa said through a mouthful of corn bread.

"You won't find a nice young man, looking like that," Grandma continued.

"Amen," Grandpa agreed.

My heart stuttered to a stop, then immediately started pounding with fight or flight. I cast a look at Dad—*Didn't you say you had told them?*—but he wouldn't meet my eyes. Had he lied to me? Or maybe he'd put off having that conversation because of everything going on with the funeral?

Either way, *this* was my moment: the terrifying but necessary dive into the deep end. It was time to get it over with.

"Um," I said, sitting up in my chair. My cheeks burned and my heart pounded so fast it hurt. "The thing is . . . I'm not really interested in finding a nice young man."

"That will change," Grandma said, fluttering her hand like she was brushing away a thoughtless opinion.

"No, I mean . . . I don't *like* boys." I took a deep breath. "I like girls."

I expected them to freeze, to stop eating, to start shouting, but neither one of them even bothered to look at me.

"Oh, here we go," Grandpa said, rolling his eyes and stabbing a fork into his mac and cheese.

"Now's not the time, Louisa," Grandma added, shaking the ice cubes in her gin.

I shot Dad another incredulous look, waiting for him to come to my aid. When all he did was shake his head, I looked back at my grandmother and asked, "Are you saying now's not the time for me to be a lesbian?"

Grandma clucked her tongue. "*Lesbian*," she repeated. "Everyone thinks they're a lesbian these days."

"The fuckin' mailman thinks he's a lesbian," Grandpa sneered. "Everybody wants to be *special*."

My mouth hung open. "That's—"

"Let's talk about it later, Louisa," Dad cut in.

The table fell silent. Grandpa gnawed on his food loudly and open-mouthed like a cow chewing cud. Grandma took a distinctly unladylike swig of her gin. I set my fork down and sat there numbly, feeling completely outside my own body.

For the last six years, I had divided my life in half: before the divorce, and after. Alabama, and then Connecticut. Two parents every single day, and then one parent at a time. But recently, I had subconsciously divided my life into another set of fractions: before coming out, and after. Hoping I was like everyone else, and then realizing I wasn't. Embodying the Louisa whom people assumed was a typical straight girl—and then becoming the Louisa who was very clearly *not* that.

And now I sat here, sick to my stomach, trying to hold on to the person I had become while my grandparents pretended nothing had changed at all. I had been dreading this conversation for days, playing it in my head over and over, trying to imagine the most vicious things my grandparents might throw my way. I'd braced myself for their disgust, their rage, their Bible-thumping, maybe some blistering tears; I'd even prepared for them to revoke my tuition money altogether. But I had never considered that they would be indifferent, that they would flat out *dismiss* my queerness, and that Dad would simply sit there and let them.

Was this because of Uncle George's funeral? And if it was . . . did that even matter? Uncle George had died, yes, but a new part of me had been born at the same time. Was it wrong that I wanted my family to hold space for both?

"Well, I'm full and sleepy," Dad said when he finally spoke up. "I'm sure Louisa is, too." He tossed me the keys to his truck, then turned to my grandfather. "Dad, where are those Cadillac keys?"

2
THE FUNERAL

The morning of the funeral dawned bright and sunny. Clear blue skies, whistling birds, and a strange sense of stillness in the air. Dad made good on his promise to drive the Cadillac, which was just about the only thing that endeared him to me this morning. We had barely spoken since leaving Grandma and Grandpa's house last night.

I followed behind Dad in his truck, driving barefoot because my wedge heels were too clunky on the pedals. The black A-line dress I'd borrowed from Mom fit snugly against my skin. I had taken pains to iron it last night, but it was already wrinkling from the humidity . . . or maybe from sweat. I seemed to be perspiring out of every pore in my body. If facing my grandparents had been like walking into the lion's den, then today was like walking into the Colosseum. I would be facing the whole of Rustin in everyone's favorite place to pass judgment: church.

Bethel Baptist looked the same as ever: white, stately, looming monstrously above the road. I hadn't been here since last summer, when Grandpa had insisted that the whole family pack the pews for Father's Day. My stomach had clenched uncomfortably then—I'd never felt at home in church, even when I still thought I was straight—but now it positively roiled and thrashed in protest. I half expected to burst into flames the moment I walked through the heavy front doors.

Breathe, I told myself. I blasted the air conditioner and leaned my armpits toward it, trying to dry the stubborn sweat still pooling in every crevice of my body. *I am gay, I am here, I am gay, I am here . . . and tomorrow I'll head back to safety.*

"This is unhinged," Dad said when I parked and joined him by the Cadillac. Looking around, I had to agree with him. The service wasn't set to begin for another hour, but the parking lot was already a circus. Traffic cops had been deployed to direct the swarming cars; most of them wore GEORGIE BOY buttons alongside their badges. The old church ladies were gathered out front, handing out funeral programs, paper fans, and a generous helping of judgment on people's outfit choices. And for whatever reason, the Rustin University marching band was out in full force, cycling through the fanfare music they played at football games. As Dad and I lumbered through the parking lot with the photo boards, the band paused so a lone bugler could play military taps, even though Uncle George had never been in the service.

Inside the church, the air-conditioning was running full blast and the lights had been dimmed to minimize the heat. Dad and I set up the photo boards in the atrium, then went to join the family at the front of the church. Grandma wore a snappy black pantsuit and a wide-brimmed hat with a pale pink ribbon. Grandpa was dressed in a tailored black suit with a navy-blue tie that matched Rustin's football uniforms. There were corn bread crumbs on his lapel.

"Louisa, sweetheart, come give me a hug," Aunt Shannon said gravely. She was Dad's younger sister by two years, and though Dad would never admit it, I knew he didn't like her. She wore a pantsuit that matched Grandma's, except hers was mint green and looked better suited for a Kentucky Derby party. Her hair was piled high on her head like a honeycomb. When she leaned in to hug me, I thought it might tip over.

"I'm sure you're having a tough time," Aunt Shannon said, touching my chin. "How could you not be?"

A space opened inside my heart, making room, *finally*, for someone in my family to acknowledge what I was going through—

"Losing Uncle George is hard on all of us," Aunt Shannon went on, and my heart closed right up. She tutted and plucked a stray fuzz off my dress. "But for a young person like you, I know it feels like the end of the world. It's probably the hardest thing you've ever been through."

I looked into her clueless porcelain face and bit down on what I wanted to say, which was *Oh, definitely, other than my parents' divorce and moving to a completely different part of the country and, just recently, this teeeeeeensy little thing called coming out.*

"Totally," I said instead.

"I'll be singing the communion hymn." Aunt Shannon puffed out a breath like it was a real sacrifice on her part, but I knew she'd lobbied my grandparents for the honor. Aunt Shannon thought she had an incredible singing voice. Dad thought she sang like a goat in heat.

"That will be beautiful, Aunt Shan."

"Thank you. I hope I can do Uncle Georgie proud." She turned to my dad and clucked her tongue. "Oh, sweet brother, how are you holding up?"

I dipped away and went to stand by my little cousins. Quinn, the six-year-old, clutched a Nerf gun in his hand. Charlie, the three-year-old, was eating candy from a Pokémon Pez dispenser.

"I need to blow my nose," Quinn announced.

Aunt Shannon's husband, Uncle Keith, looked around like someone might produce a tissue. When nobody did, he handed Quinn his funeral program. Quinn stared at it, then blew his nose right into the poorly cropped photo of Uncle George.

"Daddy, it scratched my nose," Quinn whined with a gob of snot stuck to his chin.

"Suck it up, Quinny. Your great-uncle just died."

Quinn shot the Nerf gun at him and ducked to hide behind me.

"That's enough fooling around!" Grandma snapped. Her hat wobbled on her tight hair. "The receiving line is starting. Get in position. Charlie, what's that in your teeth?"

We lined up single file. I was struck by the strange performance of it all: my family, fanned across the altar in a unified front, facing the whole of our town like we were about to put on a show. Grandpa was first, Grandma right next to him, both of them officious and solemn like diplomats at the White House. Aunt Shannon and Uncle Keith were next, and Dad was next to them, cracking his neck and shifting his weight nervously.

The receiving line seemed to stretch for miles. Hundreds of voices bounced off the ceiling until my ears started to ache. I twisted my toe into a burn mark on the carpet, trying to ground myself as every soul in the town came forward to pay their respects.

"Your uncle was a great guy," the people said, each face taking me in. Strange hands clasped my own: soft, sweaty, calloused, strong. "I was his barber." "George was my neighbor." "I'm with the alumni office; your uncle made our job a breeze."

Did I know them? Did I used to?

"You've turned into a pretty picture," said a local businessman whose eyes lingered too long. "You sure got tall," said one of Grandpa's old friends. "Oh, Louisa, you darling thing," said a woman drenched in cloying perfume.

"Thank you," I said, over and over, hating my fake smile.

Did they know me? *All* of me? What had they heard, and what did they think of me? And how self-involved was I to be worrying about their perceptions of me, when today was supposed to be about Uncle George? But I couldn't help feeling like I was outside of my skin, seeing myself from afar, seeing other people see me.

I am gay, I am here, I am gay, I am here . . .

Suddenly, a rush of whispers filled the room. A towering, imposing man had strutted into the church, his chest puffed out with importance, exuding so much arrogance you would have thought he was swaggering into the US Capitol Building rather than a church in Alabama. His wife lingered behind him like an afterthought, wearing a tasteful black dress and a diamond necklace.

Immediately, Grandpa dropped the hand of the woman he was talking to. He straightened up and motioned for the man to cut to the front of the receiving line.

"Amos," the man said in a deep, rumbling voice. He wore a smartly tailored suit with flashy cuff links. His hair was parted impeccably. He pumped my grandfather's hand, then kissed my grandmother on the cheek. "Martha. Such a shame about George. He was a good, God-fearing man. Our program wouldn't be what it is without him."

His words sounded rehearsed and affected, but my grandparents were eating it up. I leaned into Dad and whispered, "Who is that?"

"Rhett Calhoun," he muttered into my ear. "New head coach."

Of course. Rustin's new football dynamo, the man who stepped in last summer when Rustin's previous coach was unceremoniously fired. Coach Calhoun had revitalized the program and led the Reckoners to a winning season for the first time in four years—including a trip to a bowl game. No wonder my grandparents were looking at him like the sun shone out of his ass.

"He was a, uh . . ." Coach Calhoun clicked his tongue and looked off to the side dramatically. "Well, he was a hero of mine."

"Oh, Rhett," Grandma said, clutching her chest. I caught Dad's eye and refrained from pretending to barf.

The service went on for nearly two hours. My grandfather spoke. The minister spoke. The mayor and the university president spoke. Bert Lamott from Lamott Cadillac rambled on for fifteen minutes, collapsed into sobs, and had to be escorted off the stage by the funeral director.

Aunt Shannon warbled through "How Great Thou Art" and cracked her voice twice. Local schoolchildren laid roses on the altar, with one little boy placing a football in the middle of them. My dad held steady until the final hymn, "The Old Rugged Cross," began to play. His shoulders shook, and I buried my resentment from the night before as I wrapped my arm around him.

Then it was over, and the women were gathering their purses from the pews, and the men were loosening their ties, and somewhere to my left was the distinct sound of a beer cracking open. My body felt inordinately exhausted, like I'd just run a marathon without realizing it. I let out a long exhale and followed my dad up the center aisle and outside to the bright, blinding sunlight.

It's over, I realized with relief. I ducked away from the crowd and checked my watch: 1:15 P.M. Only twenty-six hours until my flight home. *I did it*, I thought. *I fulfilled my promise to myself. I got through the worst of this weekend.*

"Louisa!" someone called.

I turned, and there were my two oldest friends, Emma and Candor, waiting for me in the church garden. I hadn't expected them to be here, and the swell of gratitude I felt was enough to put a lump in my throat. "Guys," I said, opening my arms wide, "oh my god, you came—"

"Of course we did!" Candor trilled, launching herself at me.

"We had to see our Louisa Ebeneeza!" Emma squealed, wrapping all three of us in a hug.

It was my old nickname, the one they'd given me after our class put on *A Christmas Carol* for the fifth-grade play. Hearing it now was like a familiar balm, reminding me that I was still *me*, that I could be old and new at the same time. "You have no idea how happy I am to see you," I said, squeezing them both.

"*Same*, though," Emma said emphatically. Then she drew up short, cocking an eyebrow. "I mean, as happy as we're allowed to be at a funeral."

"We're so sorry about Uncle George," Candor said, squeezing my hands. "He was one of the good ones."

Emma leaned in conspiratorially. "But we're *not* sorry that it gave you an excuse to come home."

I grinned. "I missed y'all."

"We missed you, too," Emma said. "Do we look different? Older? Hotter?"

"Have we ma-*tured*?" Candor asked, imitating the way our old principal had pronounced the word.

I took them in: Candor with her adorable gap-toothed smile, her thick-framed purple glasses, her warm sepia skin. Her chin acne had cleared up and she wore her hair in bouncy corkscrew curls that suited her personality. Emma was still long and lanky, her summer freckles popping against her fair white skin. Her thin yellow hair was in its usual high ponytail, but the piercings running up the sides of her ears were new.

"Y'all look amazing. Couple of heartbreakers, to be honest."

"Oh, *stawwwp*," said Candor, swatting me.

"I bet you say that to all the girls," Emma said, waggling her eyebrows. "*Ayyyy.*"

I barked out a laugh. My heart started beating fast, but not in a bad way. I had come out to Emma and Candor a few weeks before my Instagram post, and they had been supportive, joyful, and full of good-natured teasing. I was grateful to know that teasing extended to seeing me in person, and that they were ready and willing to acknowledge all parts of my life. *Here* were the two people who could hold space for Uncle George and me at the same time.

"How'd it go with Amos and Martha?" Candor asked with a meaningful eyebrow raise.

"Ooof," I huffed. "I mean, they're basically pretending I never came out at all. And Dad is letting them."

"Shut the fuck up," Emma said, her jaw dropping dramatically.

"I'll kill them," Candor said, dragging a pretend knife across her throat.

"I don't know why I'm surprised anymore." I sighed and shook it off. "Whatever, it doesn't matter. I just have to make it through the rest of today, and then I'll be out of this hellhole."

My friends' smiles faltered, and I knew instantly that I'd put my foot in my mouth. Candor and Emma had their own complicated relationships with Rustin, but this was still their home, and I had just insulted it. It was a reminder of the divide that had started to grow between us since I'd moved away, no matter how hard we tried to keep up our friendship.

"Sorry," I said hastily, "I just meant—"

"No, it's okay, we get it," Candor said with an overly bright smile.

Emma nodded, but the spark was gone from her eyes. "We know it's hard for you to come back here."

"It's not—I mean, it's not that I don't love seeing you guys—" I started.

"You're still coming tonight, though, right?" Emma cut in as Candor nodded vigorously at her side. They were clearly eager to move past my misstep. "To the field party?"

They had mentioned this party a couple of times in our group text. From what I could tell, it was basically an excuse to drink, flirt, and mess around with all the kids we'd grown up with. I wasn't exactly thrilled at the idea of facing my old classmates, but I would do it for Emma and Candor's sake, especially now that I'd hurt their feelings.

"A million percent," I confirmed. "Just gotta get through this luncheon at Grandma and Grandpa's first." I paused, an idea occurring to me. "Hey, do y'all wanna come? I could use a buffer with Amos and Martha. There'll be catering from Tambrie's, and we might be able to sneak some drinks, and my dad will probably let me borrow the truck so we could go back to Em's house and get ready together . . ."

I trailed off at the looks on their faces: matching expressions that said they weren't sure how to let me down easy.

"What?" I asked. "What's wrong?"

"Oh, no, nothing!" Candor said. "It's just . . . Aubrey got a new car. And we're supposed to test-drive it with her."

Aubrey. A name that landed like a bucket of ice water on my head. I had completely forgotten about their new best friend, the one they'd been raving about since last August. After their first day of senior year at Rustin Preparatory Academy—a full three weeks before I'd started in Connecticut—Emma and Candor had FaceTimed to drop the news that not only was Coach Calhoun's daughter enrolled in their school, but she had sat at *their* lunch table.

She's so nice and pretty, Candor had said wistfully, *it's like hanging out with a really down-to-earth celebrity*.

Dude, she offered us box tickets for the Rustin home opener! Emma had raved later, as if she'd forgotten the time we got box tickets through Uncle George.

It feels like we've known her our whole lives! Candor had texted after their first group sleepover.

A thousand miles away, I'd felt the ugly twist of jealousy in my stomach. It had only ever been Emma, Candor, and me. Even after I'd moved away, we had talked every day, and they had *never* let anyone else into the trio. How was a fourth person going to fit into our dynamic? And what if they liked her better than me?

"It's a brand-new Audi," Emma said impressively. "Her dad is doing, like, a promotion with the local dealership."

"A *convertible*," Candor added. "And she offered to drive us all tonight!"

"Wow," I said, hoping I sounded enthusiastic. It was clear they wanted me to share in their excitement. "No, that's . . . that's awesome. You should definitely test-drive it."

"Sorry," Candor said, biting her lip.

"We made the plan a couple of weeks ago," Emma said apologetically.

"No, guys, it's cool. I get it. I'll just see you for the party."

There was a lingering moment of awkwardness as the sun beat down on the three of us.

"Well, good luck with the luncheon!" Candor said, squeezing my hand again. "We can't wait to have you all to ourselves later!"

I resisted the urge to point out that *all to ourselves* shouldn't include their new best friend. "I'll be there," I promised.

The luncheon felt almost as crowded as the service had been, even though I knew there couldn't have been more than fifty people present. Grandma put me to work setting up extra card tables in the backyard, complete with linen tablecloths, sunflower bouquets, and cloth napkins.

"Are you sure you don't wanna use paper napkins, Mom?" my dad asked. "I'd hate for you to wash all these later."

Grandma tutted with her hands on her hips. "Good lord, Tate, what would people think, that we've gone to the poorhouse? I raised you better than that."

In the dining room, Ms. Tambrie herself had assembled a buffet that could feed the entire Rustin football team: crispy mountains of fried chicken, steaming pans of collard greens and macaroni and cheese, vats of potato salad, and a tub of banana pudding nearly as big as my suitcase. Her corn bread had a place of honor on its own table, complete with serving bowls of butter, jam, and honey.

"Another piece, Amos?" Ms. Tambrie asked sweetly.

"Amos Wade, you get over here and greet our guests!" Grandma barked from the foyer. She was fussing over the photo boards with Aunt Shannon, who had finally, sensibly, taken her hair down.

Grandpa grumbled and quickly took the plate of corn bread. Then he hooked me by the elbow on his way out of the dining room. "Go find out that fella's name," he ordered, tipping his chin toward the corner. "He keeps saying hi like he knows me or something. Got a voice like a baby choking on its own spit."

I frowned, glancing at the man with the cloud of curly red hair. "That's Uncle Keith's brother, Jeff. You played gin rummy with him at Aunt Shannon's barbecue last summer." I hesitated, then gave in to my impulse. "You drank five martinis and called him Ronald McDonald all night."

Grandpa didn't seem to notice my cheek. "Pfft," he said, rolling his eyes. "How am I supposed to remember that?"

It went on like that for hours: Grandma and Grandpa pulling me in different directions, Ms. Tambrie fussing at me to refill the sweet tea, random people stopping to chat about how nice the service had been or how ungodly hot the summer was shaping up to be. Each time another neighbor or distant relative pulled me aside, my heart stuck in my throat as I worried, *This could be it*, this could be the person who asked intrusive questions about me coming out, or offered to pray for me, or said, *But are you sure, honey? Maybe you just haven't met the right guy—*

But nobody said a word about it, even though I could tell they knew. Their voices were too pleasant, too casual, while their eyes bored into me in a salacious, voyeuristic way. All I could think about was blowing off steam with Emma and Candor later, then flying home tomorrow and leaving this all behind. *Twenty-two hours till I'm free*, I told myself as I checked my watch again.

"Louisa," Dad said a while later, resting a hand on my shoulder. He leaned in and spoke softly into my ear. "Go take a break. I know it's been a long day. We've got one last thing to get through and then we can go home."

I frowned, trying to imagine what this *one last thing* could be. "You mean we've got to get through cleanup?"

Dad blinked a little too fast. "No. The attorney's coming. For the reading of the will."

This was welcome news, because it meant my grandparents would be sequestered away for a while, no doubt grabbing for every last dime of Uncle George's money. "Sounds good. I'll stay out of the way."

Dad's mouth hung open. "Er . . . no. We'll need you there, too."

My pulse quickened. "What? Why?"

Dad hesitated. I knew he was the executor of Uncle George's estate, and that he'd already seen the will, so did that mean . . . ?

"Wait, am I in the will?" I asked incredulously.

Dad cleared his throat and squeezed my shoulder, already turning away. "Just. Go have a moment to yourself."

I stared after him, but then Grandma rounded the corner with that taskmaster look in her eyes, and I bolted up the stairs before she could notice me. I shut myself in the study, away from the barrage of voices and chores, and tried to calm my racing heart.

I can't be in the will. No chance. Dad just wants me there for emotional support while he deals with Grandma and Grandpa. I just have to get through this one last thing, and then I'm free to let loose with my friends tonight.

The room was blissfully quiet. The curtains were open to the late afternoon sun, and dust motes floated idly across the air. The desk surface was covered by one of Grandpa's WADE ELECTRIC blueprints, this one showing the layout of a local dentist's office. Yet another victim Grandpa had tricked into giving him business, probably by capitalizing on the Wade name. He would probably leech even more clients now that he was sure to inherit Uncle George's real estate empire.

I found the desk drawer where Grandpa hid his stash of

MoonPies, opened one, and savored the sugary taste. Then I plopped myself on the old brown leather couch, stretched my legs, and fell asleep before I'd even wiped the sugar from my mouth.

An hour later, after the guests had gone home and my little cousins had taken my place in the study, the family gathered around the old oak table in Grandma and Grandpa's dining room.

"Louisa, this is Mr. Otis Penny," Dad said. "Uncle George's attorney."

Otis Penny rose from his chair. He was a portly middle-aged Black man dressed impeccably in a tailored Italian suit, topped off with an emerald silk ascot. He studied me through a pair of horn-rimmed glasses that magnified his keen, yellowing eyes.

"You're the great-niece?" he asked in a baritone voice.

"Yes, sir."

"Hmm." He frowned like I had failed a test. I glanced at my dad, but he was making a show of shuffling his papers, carefully avoiding my eyes.

"Let's get to it," Grandpa barked.

There was a scuffle as seven chairs scraped the wooden floor. Grandpa leaned back at the head of the table, one leg across his knee like he was settling in for a report from his inferiors. Grandma sniffed and tapped her manicured nails on the polished table. Aunt Shannon sat with her hands folded primly like a schoolgirl, no doubt trying to model appropriate behavior for the rest of us, while Uncle Keith sat there looking like he wasn't quite sure what to do with his face. I sat next to Dad, twisting my hands in my lap, my heart pounding with anticipation.

I expected to start with pleasantries, maybe platitudes about how sorry Mr. Penny was for our loss, but he was having none of that. He jumped right into the will with a dry, legalistic focus, droning on about "If you'll look at page four, point three . . ." Every minute or so, he stopped to mop his sweating forehead with a monogrammed handkerchief. After the third go-round of this, Grandma hissed at me to bring him an iced tea.

When I returned with the cold sweet tea in my hands, Otis Penny was finally getting to the goods. "To my nephew, Tate Charles Wade," he droned, "I leave my primary residence on Moreland Road."

Dad visibly swallowed, clearly choked up.

"To my niece, Shannon Wade Wainwright, I leave a trust to be used for the purposes of educating her children, as well as my piano, to be used for her own enjoyment."

Aunt Shannon made a show of closing her hands over her mouth as if she was going to cry, but her eyes remained completely dry.

"To my brother, Amos F. P. Wade, and my sister-in-law, Martha Mills Wade, I leave my painting of dogs playing poker, which they always treasured—"

Grandma made a face like she was smelling a steaming pile of horse manure.

"—and my entire portfolio of real estate holdings—"

Grandpa bounced his leg over his knee, looking smug.

"—with the exception of one property."

There was silence as each of us waited for that dangling exception. Otis Penny seemed oblivious, licking his thumb pad to turn the page with an agonizing slowness. He scanned the next line with his finger, those keen eyes narrowing.

And then Otis Penny nearly shook me out of my chair.

"To my great-niece, Louisa Jean Wade, I leave my ownership stake in the Frisky Cricket."

There was a ringing, palpable silence.

The what? I thought, looking around for someone to explain, but no one met my eyes. Grandpa had gone eerily still, his eyes narrowed on Otis Penny. Dad was looking intently at his papers and seemed immune to my pressing stare.

It was Grandma who broke the silence. "You're being funny, Otis," she said in a sharp voice that implied nothing whatsoever was funny.

"I've never been very funny," Mr. Penny said matter-of-factly.

A booming *thump* rattled the table. Grandpa had slammed his fist down, his face going splotchy red. "Have you lost your mind?" he snarled. "How the hell can an underage girl inherit a goddamn bar?"

"A bar?" I repeated. My mind wasn't working fast enough, and for some bizarre reason, I could only picture a metal crowbar.

"When was the last time George revised his will?" Grandpa demanded.

"May 25th of this year," Otis Penny said firmly.

"*Four days before he died?!*" Grandpa roared. "And you're actually taking that seriously? You know as well as I do that George wasn't in his right mind at the end—painkillers addling his brain—he earmarked the other properties for me and he clearly meant for me to get this one, too. Fix the damn paperwork, Otis."

Otis Penny stretched back in his chair. He seemed entirely unperturbed by Grandpa's tantrum. "I'm afraid there's nothing to fix."

Grandpa looked ready to throttle him, but before he could argue, Aunt Shannon cut in. "Can't she just sell it to some poor sap and make a few bucks to add to the family pot? Even if she's underage, she should still be able to—"

"Louisa is eighteen," my dad interrupted. His neck had turned red, but he spoke with unusual authority. "She's a legal adult who has legally inherited the bar."

Grandpa pounded the table again. "So what if she's eighteen?! She doesn't live here, she has no real-world experience, she's about to ship off to the University of Rhode Island—"

"The University of Connecticut," my dad corrected. He glared at his father and sister. "And you can stop saying 'she.' Louisa's sitting right next to me, so let's do her the courtesy of using her name when—"

"You watch your tone, boy! I've got half a mind to skin you alive, carrying out these ridiculous bequests, inviting this kook into my home to say the things you're not man enough to say—"

"I had no control over how George structured his will," my dad said evenly.

"Ohhhh, poor little Tate," my grandfather said in a cruel, mocking voice. "Helpless little executor, tossed about by the winds, too weak to make your own decisions. It's no wonder you couldn't hack it as a quarterback."

My father's face burned. He sat slowly back in his chair, and in a flash, I saw him as a humiliated little boy at the dinner table, trying to find his place in this godforsaken family. His whole life, he'd found solace in Uncle George, his oldest and greatest protector—but now that protection was gone. And suddenly, I understood why Otis Penny was here: to be the buffer Uncle George could no longer be. Dad had predicted his family's behavior, and he'd called in reinforcements in the form of a dry attorney who had no skin in the game.

Otis Penny took advantage of the withering silence. "I believe selling the bar *was* George's intention, actually. Before the diagnosis, he was in the process of negotiating with the university. They've been making a land grab for quite a while now. It's my understanding that George hoped Louisa would follow through on the sale and pocket the proceeds."

There was another ringing silence. Then:

"The *university*?!" Aunt Shannon shrieked, leaning across the table. There was a gleam of greed in her eyes; she clearly considered the university to be a completely different ball game than *some poor sap*.

"How much are they offering?" Grandpa asked with eyes as sharp as a hunter's.

"Is it more than Quinn and Charlie are getting?" Uncle Keith added.

"Otis, you *must* fix the paperwork!" Grandma said shrilly.

"Will everyone *please* calm down—" Dad interjected.

I barely heard any of them. My brain was stuck on Otis Penny's words:

George hoped Louisa would follow through . . .

George hoped . . .

Uncle George had thought about me. Uncle George had *hoped* for me. Had he loved me more than I realized? A lump settled in my throat as I pictured him in his final days, taking pains to think of me, to leave me a piece of his life . . .

But *why* had he left it to me? If he wanted me to have the money, couldn't he have just designated a fund like he had for my cousins?

"Excuse me," I interrupted, and for the first time, everyone stopped and acknowledged me. "Mr. Penny, could you please explain a little more? What is this bar? Where is it?"

Mr. Penny gave me a small smile, almost like he'd been waiting for me to ask. "Miss Wade, you have inherited George's full ownership stake in a bar called the Frisky Cricket, down on the south side of Rustin, off Route 29. Been in business about twenty years now, mortgage paid off, no debts to speak of. Couple of years in the red, but decent sales over the last few. It's under the radar, but George seemed to prefer it that way." He paused as if a thought had just occurred to him. "Damn good Moscow Mules, if you ask me."

"We're not asking you, Otis," Grandpa snapped.

"Okay," I said, taking this in. I knew Uncle George had owned a lot of real estate, but I'd never heard him or anyone else in the family mention a bar. "So is this like a sports bar, or a nightclub, or . . . ?"

There was a sudden shift around the table. A moment ago, everyone had been pouncing for information; now they went suspiciously quiet. Aunt Shannon glanced at the ceiling, Grandma rubbed her fingers against her throat, and Grandpa's neck turned a mottled shade of purple. Dad touched my leg as if to steady me for something, but he wouldn't meet my eyes.

Mr. Penny scanned the table. He seemed to be waiting for something, but the silence hung so heavy that I could hear Uncle Keith's knuckles crack. When no one bothered to answer me, Mr. Penny let out a long, weary sigh.

"Miss Wade." He leaned forward and looked straight into my eyes. "I have to assume these fine folks"—he gestured airily at my family members in a way that meant he did not consider them *fine* at all—"have had their hearing compromised, so I'll be the one to tell you."

I waited. Something deep in my bones started to rattle.

"The Frisky Cricket is a gay bar," Mr. Penny said matter-of-factly.

I stared into his yellowing eyes and had the strange sensation that I was falling through space with nothing to keep me tethered.

a gay bar

a gay bar

a gay bar

I couldn't move. I couldn't process. Uncle George had left me a *gay* bar? A gay bar he had owned for twenty years? Why the hell had he owned a gay bar? *Unless—*

A rush of heat swept through my entire body. *No way*, I thought. *I would have known. Someone would have told me.*

"It's a bar that happens to serve *some* gays," Grandpa said forcefully, "and George only bought that land to diversify his portfolio. He was a visionary that way, always knew you had to be strategic about buying up low-value properties on the Monopoly board—"

"Dad," I said quietly, turning to him. "Did Uncle George—was he—?"

"It doesn't matter!" Grandpa shouted, rising from his seat. "You will *not* be inheriting this bar! I'll be damned if you even set foot in it!"

White-hot fire raged against my sternum. I forgot about my tuition money, my desire to rescue Dad, my plan to hold quietly to my true self until I left town tomorrow. My emotions were boiling over and I was so, *so* tired of this fucking family. "Why not?" I challenged, my heart pounding in my ears. "Because it *serves some gays*? Is that what you're having a conniption about?"

"DO NOT SPEAK TO ME LIKE THAT, YOUNG LADY—"

"*I'm* gay!" I yelled, smacking my hands on the table. "I am a proud, terrified, *raging* homosexual, and I have spent the last twenty-four hours waiting for you to acknowledge that, and now I'm finding out that Uncle George was the *only* person to honor this part of me by designating this specific gift, and you're all sitting here throwing a fit because you don't want me to have it? Is that because you're greedy, or because you're a bunch of ignorant homophobes, or both?"

"Enough!"

It was my grandmother who shouted this time. She had gotten to her feet, her skinny, arthritic fingers twitching against her pantsuit. Her fierce green eyes—my eyes—glinted across the table.

"You will *not* speak to us like that, Louisa Jean," she said, quivering with fury.

The sharp silence pressed everywhere. Grandma and Grandpa and I stood on opposite sides of the table. Everyone else sat frozen. My heart was still hammering and my skin felt hot to the touch.

"Tell me," I demanded, my own voice surprising me.

Grandma blinked rapidly. "Tell you what?"

"Was Uncle George gay?"

Grandma set her jaw, those glinting eyes fixed on me. Next to her, Grandpa's chest heaved with rage.

"Louisa," Dad said under his breath.

"No, Dad, someone needs to answer me." I looked between my grandparents, then across the table at Aunt Shannon, who flushed and looked away. When a full thirty seconds had passed and nothing had been said, I backed my chair away from the table and squeezed my fists at my sides.

"Louisa," Dad whispered again.

"I'm out of here," I said, trying in vain to control my trembling hands. "I'm done." I turned to Mr. Penny. "Thank you for being the only person decent enough to tell me the truth."

Mr. Penny inclined his head. He seemed entirely disgusted by the situation. "I'll be on my way, then," he said to the table at large.

"Thank you for this . . . *meeting of the minds*. It went as well as I expected."

He rose to his feet, sorted his papers into his old-fashioned leather briefcase, and left the room without further ado. I sent one final glare to my grandparents, then to my dad, before I followed him.

"Mr. Penny! Wait!" I yelled, chasing him down the driveway. He turned around with an expression of mild surprise as I drew to a stop in front of him. "The Frisky Cricket—you've been there, right? Moscow Mules? Can you take me?"

Otis Penny blinked. Then he laughed a quiet chuckle that startled me in its resonance. "Sweetheart, *no*. I'm sorry about your family, but my work here is done. I'm not about to drive a teenage client to a bar. That's a case study in liability." He laughed at his own joke, then looked around like there might be other lawyers present to appreciate it.

"Mr. Penny, please. I *have* to see this bar."

"Have you heard of Google Maps?" Chuckling again, he spun on his heel and stepped out to the street.

I deliberated for a moment, gripping my hair as I stood sweating in the evening heat. There was no way I was going back into that house, even if I had been given strict orders to stick around and clean up. No, I *had* to go to the Frisky Cricket. Uncle George had left it to me for a reason, and I felt a visceral, primal pull to find out what that reason was.

Emma and Candor, said a voice in my head. Shit. I was supposed to go to the field party with them tonight. Could I convince them to crash the Frisky Cricket instead?

No, my inner voice said, *you want—need—to do this by yourself. And besides, they're with their new best friend right now.*

I pulled out my phone. I felt guilty blowing them off, but in my defense, I hadn't known all this was going to happen when I had agreed to the field party. Maybe I could take them to breakfast tomorrow and tell them about it. That way I could still see them before I left, and maybe twelve hours would be enough to turn everything I learned tonight into a funny story.

Me: So sorry y'all, something came up and I can't make it. Brunch tomorrow to fill you in? My treat?

I darted into the foyer and stole Dad's keys off the credenza. Uncle George's emerald urn was back on the top shelf of the display cabinet, but this time, I wasn't repulsed by the sight; if anything, it felt like the spirit of Uncle George was urging me on. I turned off my phone location settings, backed the truck out of the driveway, and sped off into the night without a second thought.

Uncle George had left me a gift. I had no choice but to open it.

3
THE FRISKY CRICKET

There it was: an old, shabby, completely unremarkable building. It had cracks in the cinder block, a sun-stained awning draped across the entrance, and neon beer signs lighting up the windows. It might have been a filling station back in the day, a roadside oasis where weary travelers stopped in to replenish their gas tanks and grab a Coca-Cola from the ice chest. It was easy to overlook if you were just driving by, and yet two beacons confirmed I was in the right place: a weathered old Pride flag flying by the front door, and a faded sign of a cartoon cricket wearing a bow tie.

I loved it immediately.

I had followed my GPS to the edge of town, where strip malls and apartment buildings gave way to farmland. Then I pulled Dad's truck into the parking lot, stepped out onto uneven gravel, and breathed in the sight of my inheritance.

Inheritance.

The word danced around my brain, old-timey and fanciful like something out of a Dickens novel. It was impossible to process the idea that this shabby little secret now belonged to *me*, all because Uncle George had signed a piece of paper that made it so.

The front door banged open, music and laughter spilling into the quiet night. Two older men strode out, ribbing each other about a joke I didn't catch, one of them raking a hand through his thinning hair. The other paused beneath the building's overhang and lit up a cigarette while his companion looked on. Their dynamic was flirtatious, playful but cautious, like two schoolboys finding each other for the first time.

Was Uncle George—had he been—? I wondered again.

I was still working up the nerve to go inside when something brushed against my legs. I jumped, nearly tripping in my funeral heels, and looked down to find a skinny black cat winding her way between my legs. She had white markings across her mouth and a long, languid tail. I reached down to pet her, but she scampered toward the door.

Okay, I thought, *I hear you.*

I took a deep breath and followed her.

When I was seven years old, I fell head over heels for the Disney cartoon movie *Robin Hood*. I watched it every day, stretched on my stomach in front of the TV, wishing I could be one of those anthropomorphic foxes or rabbits or bears who made a home in Sherwood Forest. The one scene I played over and over was when Robin Hood led Maid Marian behind a waterfall, through a cave, and into a secret clearing where his band of outlaws threw an impromptu party. I was enchanted by their songs, their lutes and barrel drums, their joyful dancing, but above all, by the open secret of it all, this idea that you merely had to duck behind the right waterfall to find your people.

I had been looking for that waterfall all my life, and here it was.

People were drinking, laughing, twirling each other across the floor, their faces ruddy, their eyes bright. They were young and old, scraggly and polished, dressed with flair and blandness, of every color and body type. The logical part of me understood these were just ordinary human beings, but the instinctual part of me chimed with recognition, with belonging, with kinship, because these were *queer* people, people like *me*, right here in Rustin, dancing behind the waterfall. All I wanted to do was join them, to step into their glow and hope they recognized me as one of their own, to call this place home as surely as they did.

Uncle George, I thought. *Does this exist because of you?*

The obvious place to go was the actual bar top in the left corner, so that's where I went, squaring my shoulders to appear confident. I set my hands on the scratched wooden counter and waited for the bartender to catch my eye. When he did, I gave him a casual chin nod the way I imagined a regular customer might.

"What are you having?" he asked, flipping a dishrag over his shoulder. He was a short Filipino guy with the swoopy hair of a nineties teen heartthrob. He wore a fitted black T-shirt with a shiny trans flag pin on the collar.

"Beer," I blurted out. I glanced at the taps and chose something at random. "Er—Abita Amber. Please."

"Sure. Can I see your ID?"

I had hoped this was the kind of place that wouldn't card me, but at least I had my fake ID to get by. I made a mental note to thank my friend Gus not only for convincing me to get one, but also for helping me to choose a fake name. I didn't want this bartender to see *Wade*, guess that I was related to Uncle George, and start asking questions. No, tonight I wanted to be anonymous and alone, just a random person stumbling upon the waterfall and soaking up the joy. No baggage, no shitty homophobic family, no complicated relationship to this town.

I fished the fake ID out of my wallet and handed it across the counter, trying to seem like I was used to the whole routine.

The bartender's eyes flicked over it. "South Dakota, huh?" A note of doubt crept into his voice. "That's a long way from here."

I smiled casually and pretended I got this comment all the time. "Moved there a few years ago for college, but I grew up here. It's always nice to come back. Grounds me, you know?"

He peered carefully at me, then seemed to decide I was telling the truth. He nodded and stepped away to grab a pint glass, and I exhaled in relief, grateful I hadn't drawn any attention.

Behind the bar was a wall of decorations, layered in a way that told me they had been added over time. Most of the top corner was covered by a Progress Pride flag, but kitschy little gems could be found across the rest of the space. The sign directly in front of my eyeline read:

GAY OWNED

GAY OPERATED

SO HAVE A GAY OLE TIME!!!

"Gay owned," I said under my breath. *Uncle George*. Was this proof of what my family wouldn't tell me?

The bartender handed over my beer. "Leave it open, or close out?"

I could hardly process the question. My brain was still stuck on *Gay owned*. "Hey, do you know the owner?"

"Which one?"

I stared at him. "Huh?"

"Which one?" he repeated. Then his face paled, and his eyes went unfocused like something had just occurred to him.

"What?" I asked.

The bartender shook his head. "Sorry—I, uh. I guess you haven't heard. One of our owners died last week." He gestured around the crowded bar. "That's why everyone's here tonight. To celebrate him." He lowered his eyes. "I keep forgetting it's real."

One of our owners. Did Uncle George have a business partner? I deflated, realizing my grandfather might have been telling the truth about Uncle George investing in multiple properties that bore no reflection of his own identity. Maybe it was the other owner, or owners, who was actually gay. Maybe this bartender could tell me more. "I'm so sorry to hear that. Who was it?"

"George Wade. You know, the famous football guy? He was a big deal around here."

I swallowed. "Was he—um—" I steeled myself. "Was he, like—" I gestured between the bartender and myself, hoping he would understand.

The bartender gave me nothing, but his posture tightened. "Was he what?" he asked, and there was an edge to his tone now.

"Was he queer?"

The bartender gave me a hard, searching look. He looked torn about something, like he wasn't sure whether to show his cards. "Who wants to know?"

We stared at each other, and then I looked away. "Sorry—never mind. It's none of my business."

I put a $10 bill down and slipped away without looking back, carrying my beer to the opposite side of the room. I busied myself with studying the décor on the wood-paneled walls. Dozens of crinkled dollar bills were pinned there in what seemed to be a customer ritual. On one of them, someone had drawn long hair and makeup on George Washington's face and written *Washingtina* in scratchy handwriting. There were framed photographs, too: bowling teams from decades before, a gaggle of drag queens posing with books, and a parade of women on motorcycles. A photo booth strip of two young men kissing was stapled next to a Polaroid of an interracial lesbian couple with their arms around each other. A more recent picture frame showed a small group of Rustin University students marching behind a banner that said STAND UP FOR TRANS RIGHTS, upon which someone had stuck a Post-it note that read *trans people are hotter than you!!!*

The whole thing was a neighborhood shrine that told the story of people like me. I was riveted. I also felt like I hadn't earned the right to be here. It was as if I'd stumbled upon a beautiful banquet that other people had prepared, lovingly cooking the food and setting the table and lighting the candles, and it didn't feel right to simply sit down and eat without having contributed. And shouldn't I be contributing?

The minutes slipped by. I finished my drink and thought about ordering another. The crowd was growing larger, rowdier, but somehow more intimate. There were shouts of recognition each time the door opened to admit someone new. People here *knew* each other. Maybe that's why I felt eyes on me, trying to figure out who I was, how I'd ended up here in their communal home.

Two women in particular kept glancing at me. Were they checking me out? But no, they were clearly older than me, and their expressions were full of concern. When I dared to look back at them, the blond one cocked her head and gave me a challenging look, almost like she could see right through me. My heart started beating faster. Did she know who I was? Did she know I was underage? I hastily turned away and crossed back to the other side of the room.

"Back for more?" the swoopy-haired bartender asked.

"Yeah. Can I have another one of those beers, please?"

"Coming right up."

I leaned my elbows on the bar top and waited, but then—

Someone put a hand on my shoulder. I turned around, startled, to find the blond woman standing much too close.

"Yeah, hi there," she said breezily, as if we were continuing a previous conversation. "Do you mind if I ask your name?"

She was maybe in her early thirties, dressed in a black blazer and skinny jeans, her blue eyes sharp and discerning as they bored into mine. She crossed her arms and stared me down with unmistakable teacher energy, as if she could sniff out teenage mischief like a bloodhound.

She's onto me. My heart beat even faster and my palms started to sweat. I tried to appear pleasantly confused as I met her piercing stare. "Excuse me?"

She smiled like she could see right through my performance. "I asked your name."

I cleared my throat and squared my shoulders, trying to match her steely resolve with a smile of my own. "Are you hitting on me?"

The question seemed to bounce right off her. "I'm not going to dignify that with a response," she said, still smiling like I was completely transparent. "I'm asking your name because I'm pretty certain I already know who you are, and if I'm right, that makes you underage." She grimaced in a performative way. "So I'm gonna need to see your ID."

My pulse skyrocketed. *I know who you are. Underage.* I had never seen this woman in my life, so how could she possibly know me?

"I—I already showed my ID. And besides, I'm twenty-one. Promise."

"Great comeback," she said dryly. She leaned forward and lowered her voice. "I'm not trying to embarrass you, Louisa." My neck prickled at the sound of my name. "But we both know you shouldn't be in this bar. ID, please."

Wordlessly, I dug into my back pocket and pulled out the fake. My face burned as I handed it to her.

She looked it over with a frown. "Louisa River," she read under her breath. She snorted. "Clever."

I closed my hanging jaw and considered my next move. The woman didn't seem too angry, but she certainly wasn't pleased. Was she going to throw me out? Maybe even call the police?

She pocketed my ID and turned back to me. "I'm gonna give you a piece of advice, Louisa. Next time you get a fake, choose a state that sounds reasonable. No one lives in South Dakota."

I stared at her, bracing for my fate.

"Follow me," she said, nodding toward the back of the room. She didn't even wait to see if I listened, just wove her way toward the back hallway. I watched her catch the eye of the woman she had been talking to earlier and nod again. Then she led me into a small office and gestured for me to sit down.

"Explain," she ordered, leaning against the wall.

Before I could even open my mouth, there was a quick knock at the door and the other woman slipped inside. She was strikingly pretty, with olive skin, dark brown hair, and kind eyes. She glanced at me, then looked at her friend. They seemed to be having a wordless conversation.

"I'll get some water," the second woman said, backing out and shutting the door behind her.

The first woman, the blonde, turned to me and sighed. "So."

"How'd you know who I was?" I asked.

For the first time, the trace of a smile appeared on her face. She pointed at something behind me, and I turned around to find my own senior portrait pinned to a bulletin board. The shock of it left me speechless.

"George talked about you all the time," the woman said. Her arms were still crossed, but her voice had softened.

The door opened and the second woman reentered. She smiled warmly at me, handed over a glass of water, and settled into an upholstered chair like a therapist preparing for a session with a particularly tender client.

"Well, Louisa?" the blonde prompted from her spot against the wall.

"Are you okay?" the brunette asked.

I looked from one woman to the other. "Am I getting arrested? Is this, like, good-cop-bad-cop or something?"

The blond woman snorted. She gave the brunette a knowing look. "Why does everyone assume I'm the bad one?"

"I've been trying to tell you," the brunette teased.

"No, Louisa, you're not in trouble, but you *do* need to explain yourself. What are you doing here?"

I breathed, trying to decide if I believed them.

"You're safe," the brunette reassured me. "We're just concerned. Underage kids don't often show up to gay bars alone, and if they do, there's usually a reason."

I looked between them again, trying to see myself the way they saw me. Did they think I was a runaway? A lost soul? That I had been kicked out of the house?

"It's nothing like that," I said. "I just . . . wanted to see this place."

There was silence as they appraised me again.

"Drink your water, Louisa," the blonde said finally.

"Can you stop saying my name? I don't even know yours." I paused, and a flare of the anger I'd felt earlier returned. "Should I embarrass you with a big show of asking for *your* ID?"

The blonde didn't flinch. She seemed completely unfazed, almost bored by my insolence. But the brunette was suddenly biting down a smile, as if she was distinctly amused by the whole exchange.

The blonde huffed and dragged her hands down her face. "Okay, this wasn't supposed to be all weird and dramatic. Can we try again? Louisa, *hi*. I'm Hannah, and this is Baker. We knew your uncle very well, and we don't want you drinking underage in his bar, especially on an emotional day like today." She paused and gave me a softer look. "Baker was right to ask the important question: Are you okay?"

Are you okay. It was such a simple question, but this was the first time anyone—particularly an adult—had taken the time to ask me since I had set foot on Alabama soil. And they weren't asking for the sake of it. I could tell by their expressions that they wanted to know the real answer.

"Why are you being nice to me?" I asked, trying to steady my voice.

Baker frowned. "What do you mean?"

"You don't even know me."

"Do we have to know you to be nice to you?"

I bit the inside of my cheek. "You could have just thrown me out of the bar."

"I still might," Hannah said, but she was smirking, and I could tell she was trying to put me at ease. "Listen, forgive me if I'm being presumptuous, but I know you came out recently. George showed me your Instagram post. Then he up and died, and now you're in his bar with that starving look in your eyes that every queer person has when they find a queer space for the first time. So we're putting two and two together and checking to make sure you're all right."

I met her earnest expression, but all I could say was, "Uncle George had Instagram?"

"God no. He was terrible with his phone. He showed me a really bad screenshot someone else had taken of your post."

Dad.

"He showed me a few of your pictures over the years," Hannah went on. "I recognized you at the funeral, too." She twisted her mouth like she was tasting something sour. "If we can call that spectacle a funeral."

Outside of my dad, this was the first time I'd heard someone express disdain about Uncle George's funeral. "You were there?"

Hannah gestured beyond the wall, indicating the bar at large. "We all were." She and Baker shared a meaningful look, and her tone became sharper. "In the back, of course. But still."

I read between the lines of what she was saying. For the first time, it occurred to me how many people in the bar had been dressed in black. Had all of them gone to the funeral? Had *all* of them known Uncle George?

"Can I ask you something?" I asked with my heart pounding.

"Of course," Baker said softly.

"Was my uncle . . . was he, like . . ." I gestured between us the same way I had done with the swoopy-haired bartender.

"Go ahead," Hannah encouraged. Her expression was both kind and defiant, like she was telling me I could do this.

I took a deep breath. "Was Uncle George gay?"

Hannah and Baker shared a loaded look, one that I couldn't parse apart. "What makes you ask?"

More frustration came over me. It was predictable that my family had been cagey about this, but now I was here at this gay bar, searching for an answer that seemed obvious, and both the bartender and these women were still dancing around the truth?

"Why won't anyone give me a straight answer?" I asked, trying to control my shaking voice.

"Straight isn't exactly our thing," Hannah said with a wry smile. She was clearly trying to loosen me up, but I didn't have the energy to fake a laugh. She must have seen my frustration spilling over, because she sighed and came over to sit on the desk, a mere foot from me. "I'm not trying to be evasive. I'm just wondering how much your family has told you."

"Nothing," I said immediately. "My family is obsessed with Uncle George's football career and nothing else. I just found out the Frisky Cricket exists, like, an hour ago. None of them ever mentioned it."

"And they never talked to you about George's personal life?" She paused and asked the next question like she hoped she was mistaken. "George himself never told you?"

I shook my head.

"Jesus," Hannah said, pinching the bridge of her nose, as Baker clucked her tongue with sympathy. "Louisa, I'm so sorry. That's inexcusable."

I chewed the inside of my cheek, waiting. I felt small and foolish and embarrassed, the same way I had felt when I first moved to

Connecticut and every seventh-grade girl except me was invited to Bree Shatter's thirteenth birthday party. It was excruciating to be the only person left out.

Hannah looked directly into my eyes. "Yes, George was gay."

George was gay

George was gay

George was gay

There it was: the explicit confirmation. I breathed deep and moved the air through my belly, trying to anchor myself, to grasp onto this paradigm-shifting truth. *Uncle George was gay. I had a gay relative. I'm not alone.*

"He was gay," I said aloud, tasting the words.

"So gay," Hannah said.

"Super, super gay," Baker added.

"Like, constantly-checking-out-the-delivery-guys gay."

"I . . ." Suddenly, my throat felt thick. "I wish I'd known. I came out, like, a month before he died. I never got to talk to him about it." My eyes found the copy of my senior portrait pinned to the bulletin board. *Dad showed him. Dad made sure he knew.* A warm spring of affection broke through the anger I felt from earlier.

"He told me about you coming out," Hannah said gently. "He told both of us, actually."

"He was so excited," Baker said. "So very proud of you."

"He kept saying, 'My niece is in the family!' and we were like, 'Yeah, George, she's your blood—'"

"And he was like, 'No, I mean she's *in the family*!'"

In the family. It was such a simple way to say it. I felt overcome with pride, and affirmation, and belonging, and this warm, expansive, sunlit feeling that Uncle George had not only known but embraced my real self.

"I just wish I'd known about him," I said thickly.

Hannah sighed in a defeated way. "Yeah. George kind of struggled with . . . well . . ."

"Integrating all parts of himself," Baker finished.

There was something deep and knowing in the look Hannah gave her. "Exactly. He was a master compartmentalizer. When he was George Wade the football star, it was like his private life didn't exist. When he was here, all the 'Georgie Boy' stuff faded into the background. And with his family, well . . ." She winced at me. "I think he felt there were certain expectations."

"So . . . he . . . he basically led a double life?" I asked.

Hannah gave me a sad smile. "I'd say it was a . . . layered life. He brought different parts of himself to different situations."

"And nobody else knew? Like, people in Rustin? People in football?"

Hannah sighed. "I think the proof was there if they wanted to look for it, but how many of them wanted to look for it? The people who knew, knew. And the ones who didn't seemed to like it that way."

"People see what they want to see," Baker clarified.

"And they profit off how things are seen, too," Hannah said meaningfully.

I understood what she was saying. How many people had benefited from the image of Uncle George as a red-blooded, macho, inherently *straight* quarterback? My grandparents. The Rustin Football machine. The First Baptist minister, the mayor, the university president . . . Uncle George's barber and his neighbors and all the people he met in real estate . . . How many of them had known the truth? How many had suspected? How many refused to see? Had *I* refused to see?

The world kept spinning. Music pulsed through the wall. Hannah and Baker watched me carefully, their concerned expressions verging on pity.

"Do you both work here?" I asked eventually.

"I do," Hannah said. "Full-time in the summers, and some part-time shifts during the school year. I'm a school counselor."

"Yeah, I figured."

Hannah gave me a quizzical look. "What do you mean?"

"You've got major teacher energy. Bossy and nosy and very, like, *I can relate to you*."

Baker burst out laughing, clutching her stomach in delight. Hannah's mouth fell open like she couldn't believe what she was hearing. "I . . . don't know how to respond to that."

I shrugged. "You clocked me right away. I clocked you, too."

Baker laughed even harder. She seemed utterly delighted, and I swelled with satisfaction.

"This is George's fault," Hannah grumbled, pointing vaguely skyward. "He sent you here to fuck with me."

"And it's delicious," Baker said, wiping tears of laughter. "I think you've met your match, Han."

Hannah tutted. "Don't compare me to this insolent child."

"You deserve this. It's exactly what you were like at eighteen."

"Whose side are you on?"

"Currently Louisa's."

"You can forget about that back scratch later," Hannah pretend-snarked.

They were momentarily in their own world, their eyes bright and smiles intimate. It was like they had completely forgotten I was sitting across from them.

"So . . . ," I said. "Y'all are—like—?"

"Roomies?" Hannah asked dryly.

"Yes, we're together," Baker confirmed with the air of someone who frequently had to translate Hannah's humor.

In the same smooth motion, they held up their left hands. Small, sparkling diamonds glittered on their matching silver bands.

"Fiancées," Hannah clarified. "But I'm really just looking for a tax break."

"Shut up," Baker said in a routine way.

"Cool," I said, genuinely thrilled to see a future version of myself in them. I had a few queer friends back in Connecticut—Gus and some other people we'd gone to prom with—and I was peripherally aware of a few queer teachers at my school, but this was the first time I'd had a genuine conversation with someone who had it all figured out. "I've never had, like, lesbian elders."

Hannah practically choked. "*Elders*? We are thirty-two years old!"

Baker laughed good-naturedly. "I am okay with being an elder. We worked hard for it."

I grinned at them. The entire moment felt surreal. It wasn't lost on me that I had spent the last twenty-four hours wishing desperately to get back to Connecticut, where I felt like I could be my whole queer self, but now here I was, in small-town Alabama, truly engaging with older queer people for the first time in a gay bar that made me feel like I *belonged*.

"This is probably going to sound stupid," I started, looking between them, "but—being here tonight, and meeting you, and learning about Uncle George—it's the first time it's occurred to me that—well—that there are people like *me* in Rustin."

Baker smiled softly. Hannah's eyes twinkled as she said, "Well, yeah. We are everywhere."

"It's easy to assume we're not. I somehow missed this part of Rustin even though it's been right here in front of me." I recited Baker's earlier words. "People see what they want to see."

Hannah smiled wryly. "Very good, grasshopper. These elders hardly need to impart any wisdom at all."

"It's late, though, and these elders need to get home," Baker said pointedly. "Can we give you a ride, Louisa?"

"Oh, no thank you, I'm good. I have my dad's truck."

Hannah leveled me with a look. "You've been drinking."

"I had *one* beer."

"Yeah, and you're young and still new to alcohol, and for all I know, that could have been your first ever drink. We don't know how it affects you."

"We're taking you home," Baker said decisively.

I hesitated, feeling preemptive grief at the thought of leaving the Frisky Cricket already. "Could we just go back out there for a few minutes?"

Hannah gave me an amused, knowing look. "You get three songs."

"Deal," I said, and we went back out to the waterfall, and my hungry heart took it all in.

4
HATCH

It was close to midnight when I slipped through the front door, and for just a moment, I thought I'd gone completely under the radar.

But the back porch light was on, and I could see Dad's head slumped against the window, where he was clearly waiting for me to come home. He was probably worried—and angry. I could either face this now or face it in the morning.

"Louisa," he said, shooting forward in his wicker chair when I stepped onto the porch. He cleared his throat like he hadn't spoken in hours. "Where have you been? You left without saying anything, you didn't answer your phone, do you know how worried I've been?"

It was jarring to be standing in front of him after being at the Frisky Cricket all night. I felt like I had just binge-watched an amazing fantasy show and then turned off the TV to realize it was all a dream.

"Why didn't you tell me Uncle George was gay?" It was the

only thing I could manage to say. My voice cracked in the late night heat.

Dad blinked up at me. He had changed out of his funeral clothes and was now dressed in his usual PFG fishing shirt. He held a cigarette in one hand and a glass of whiskey in the other, and based on his bleary eyes and tousled hair, I could tell they were hitting him. "Where were you, Louisa?" he asked again.

I reached into my dress pocket and pulled out a matchbook with the Frisky Cricket's branding on it. I tossed it roughly to Dad and watched the realization dawn on his face.

"Honey . . ."

"You never told me," I said, trying to steady my shaking voice.

"Jellybean," Dad said tiredly, using the old nickname. "You know how this family is. Nobody ever talked about it, not even Uncle George himself."

"But this is you and me, Dad, not the rest of the family. *You* could have told me, especially after I came out to you. You could have told me *today*." I paused, hating myself the slightest bit when I realized I was about to echo Grandpa. "Instead, you let Otis Penny do your dirty work."

Dad hung his head. He had the grace to look ashamed. "I know. And I'm sorry."

"Didn't you think—I mean, that day I called you from Connecticut and told you I was gay—didn't you think it might help me to know about Uncle George? That I wasn't the first one to navigate this?"

Dad gave me a pained look. Then he patted the empty chair next to him. "Will you sit down for a minute?"

I couldn't bring myself to do it. My emotions were threatening to spill over for the umpteenth time today, and the thought of sitting next to the source of a lot of those emotions was unbearable. Instead, I slid down to sit on the floor, my back jutting into the screen door.

Dad looked crestfallen, but he didn't push me on it. He nodded, slouched back in his chair, and took a drag of his Marlboro. "Louisa," he began, "after that phone call in April, when you told me how your heart worked . . . I started doing some research."

It was the last thing I expected to come out of his mouth. I sat completely still, waiting for more.

"I didn't really know what I was looking for. I just wanted to understand you better. So I looked some things up online. I found a couple of parent support groups. There are lots of good articles, stories, vocabulary guides, that kind of thing. I even sent your mom a few of 'em. The more I learned, the more I thought to myself, I should have done this years ago. It could have helped me connect with Uncle George on a whole 'nother level." He paused. "See, you've got to understand that Uncle George was from a different time. He never talked about his lifestyle—"

I bristled at the word *lifestyle*, but I didn't want to interrupt and risk derailing the conversation. I needed the truth too badly.

"—and nobody else did, either," Dad went on. "It's not like your grandparents sat me down and told me, and I knew better than to ask. I can't even remember how old I was when I first realized it. It was something that just . . . *was*." He flicked the ash off his cigarette and screwed up his mouth like he was trying to articulate something. "When you came out to me, I thought, well, here's my courageous daughter bringing something into the sunlight. Maybe it'll nudge George to speak openly, at least to me. So I showed him your Instagram and—and he got this look in his eyes, I'll never forget it . . ."

Dad swallowed and blinked very quickly. He was clearly struggling to keep talking, but I could hardly bring myself to feel sympathy. Why had my "courageous" choice to come out prompted him to worry about Uncle George rather than *me*? Why couldn't he have called *me* and talked through all the things he'd learned? And where had this support been last night, when I'd tried talking to my grandparents about my sexuality and Dad had shut me down?

"We still couldn't bridge that gap," Dad continued, "but I decided I'd keep researching, keep learning, and someday soon I'd sit him down and get up the guts to ask him about it." He sniffed, and I knew what the next words would be. "But then he got sick."

Dad started to cry. I lowered my head, trying to give him a moment. Internally, I was still warring between my hot, pulsing anger and the age-old urge to comfort him. Was I punishing him by withholding sympathy? Was I a terrible person for expecting things from someone who was hurting so deeply?

"Sorry," Dad said, pawing at his eyes. "Anyway, I . . . I haven't known what to do since then. I wanted to tell you about Uncle George but I just . . . I wasn't sure how to bring it up, or even if I *should*. I read all these things about making sure you don't out somebody, respecting a person's privacy and timeline, that kind of thing. I didn't know what the respectful thing was, especially knowing how private Uncle George could be . . ."

"But he's *gone*, Dad," I said, trying to rein in my anger. "He's gone, and I'm *right here*."

Dad gave me an anguished look. "I know, honey, and I'm sorry. The past couple weeks, just getting out of bed every day has been like scraping the bottom of the barrel. But I'm gonna do better. I'll help you navigate this sale, and we'll get you that money, and you'll never have to rely on Grandpa again."

Navigate this sale. In all my excitement about discovering the Frisky Cricket, I had completely forgotten that Uncle George had been in the process of selling it. That he had *hoped I would follow through*. It was like a trickle of ice water running down my spine.

"I'm tired," I said abruptly. Then I got to my feet and left Dad sitting on the porch.

I couldn't sleep.

After an hour of tossing and turning, I crept out of bed and onto the porch again. The stars were bright and the bullfrogs croaked their steady rhythm. I placed my hands on my stomach, took a deep breath, and tried to exhale the restlessness from my body.

Uncle George was gay.

Breathe.

He built a safe space for queer people.

Breathe.

There's a place for me in Rustin.

I stopped breathing.

All weekend, I'd been counting down the hours until my return flight to Connecticut. That countdown had been my port in a storm, but now it caused a wave of anxiety to crash over me. Was I supposed to just hop on a plane tomorrow and go home to my regular life as if this weekend had never happened? Sign away the bar without ever setting foot in it again? Forget Hannah and Baker and the kindness they'd shown me, as if they were mere shadows that had danced across my vision? Forget Uncle George and his complicated legacy and this precious gift he had left me, which I had only just scratched the surface of understanding?

And what was *home*, anyway? This stolen nighttime moment with its humid air and summer noises was as much my home as anything. Long before my parents' marriage had dissolved, before I'd tamped down my Southern accent to fit in with the kids up north, before I'd realized I was gay . . . before any of that, I had been formed by Rustin. Sprung from the soil, cradled by the tree line. I had always thought Rustin would be part of my past but never my future. But now? Now possibilities were opening before me like the blue sky after a cloudy day. There was a specific place for me here. There were *people like me* here, in the first home I'd ever had, in the very place where I didn't think people like me existed.

Something was churning in my gut, and I knew—even if it didn't make sense—that I was about to do something that scared the hell out of me, and that it was too late to tiptoe back into the summer I'd planned on having.

Can you help me? I found myself asking. It was a prayer, but it took me a second to realize it wasn't God I was pleading with.

Uncle George, I wish you could have shown me your whole self. Was it terrifying, especially back then? How did you hide it? How did you breathe?

Yesterday I'd thought no one in Rustin cared about me coming out, at least not in a positive way. And yet Uncle George cared. He saw himself in me. He left his legacy in my hands. How could someone have such faith in me? And why did I have to lose him before I even knew him?

"Are you sure this is the right place?" the Uber driver asked. He was an older man, skinny as a reed with a long, scraggly beard. Pictures of his grandchildren were clipped to the sun visor. It had taken almost fifteen minutes for my app to match with him, which probably wasn't uncommon for small-town Alabama, especially at seven o'clock on a Sunday morning.

"Yep, this is it," I said, already wrenching the door open.

"Are you *sure*?" He stared suspiciously at the Pride flag. His car hovered on the edge of the parking lot, like he was afraid to get too close.

I didn't answer, simply got out of the car and shut the door with a crisp snap. I hurried to Dad's truck and pretended to be getting into it. Once I was satisfied that the man had driven away, I relaxed my shoulders and turned around.

The first thing my eyes landed on was the sign I had missed last night:

FOR SALE

The shock of it, the hard reality, was another trickle of ice water down my back. *This* was the plan everyone expected me to follow. It was a plan that made sense, now that I could see the Frisky Cricket in the light of day. The cracks in the foundation were bigger than I'd realized. Shingles were missing from the roof. The front door was grimy and needed a good scrub.

But it was still my waterfall.

I approached the front door and tugged its long metal handle, but as expected, it was locked. Glancing up, I could see there were no security cameras, so I began searching for a spare key. I checked beneath the floor mat, inside the potted shrubs, and above the doorway, but there was nothing.

Then something brushed across my calves. It was the black cat from last night, staring up at me with those vivid green eyes. She mewed as I bent down to pet her.

"Hi, friend," I said quietly. "Are you hungry? If you can lead me to a key, maybe I can find you some food."

She curled against my legs and let me rub her back until she purred. It soothed me somehow. Maybe she was a sign from Uncle George, a sign to keep going.

"Let's check the back, okay?" I *psspsspss*ed for her to follow me and we eased our way around the building to the back of the property. It was larger than I expected—vast, empty land that stretched to an ancient tree line. The sunlight spilling over the treetops nearly took my breath away, and I wondered if Uncle George had ever come here in the early morning, and if it had dazzled him, too.

I found the back service door and tried it: also locked. This door, however, was less secure than the front one, with a simple key entry that looked easy to pick, at least based on what Emma had taught me a few summers ago. I fished in my pocket for the bobby pins I'd brought along, then worked one into the door handle and began to fiddle with it. I had just heard a promising *click* when—

"What the hell do you think you're doing?"

I jumped and spun around. The bobby pins scattered across the wooden steps. The black cat hissed and ran away.

An old man was glaring at me from the garden plot along the perimeter. His wide-brimmed sun hat couldn't hide the furious expression on his face. My eyes darted to the large metal shears in his hands.

"We're not open yet," the man barked in a high, grizzled voice.

My heart was racing, but I seized on that telling pronoun: *We*. Was this another employee, like Hannah?

"You work here, sir?"

"'Work' is one way to describe it," the man huffed. "You gonna tell me what you're doing?"

I stepped into the sunlight and raised a friendly hand. I would have preferred to stay incognito, but considering it looked like I was breaking and entering, I figured I needed to come clean.

"Sorry to scare you. I'm Louisa Wade." I paused to make sure he felt the weight of my next words. "George's niece."

The gardener gave me a long, hard look. "I know that. Still doesn't explain what the hell you're doing."

I blinked at him. This man *also* knew who I was? Had he recognized me from Uncle George's bulletin board just like Hannah had? Even if he knew me, what were the chances he would believe me when I said this next part?

"This probably sounds like I'm making it up, but I actually own this place now." I let the words hang in the air as a thrill raced down my spine. "Uncle George left it to me, but I don't have a key yet, so I was trying to find another way inside."

The gardener continued to stare at me. Then he let out a short, sputtering laugh. "You're gonna need to try that again, sweetheart, because that didn't make a lick of sense."

I recoiled at the use of *sweetheart* but tried to give him the benefit of the doubt. Maybe this man worked as a contractor who didn't stop by very often, which meant I would have to be the bearer of bad news.

"You know the owner, George Wade?" I tried in a soft, placating voice. "I'm sorry to tell you, but he died recently." I paused to watch the gardener's expression, but it was immovable. "He left me this bar in his will."

The gardener gave me a long, appraising look—and then bolted toward me with a speed I hadn't expected, brandishing the gardening shears like a weapon. My heart jumped into my throat and I backed away, reaching wildly for my phone—

The gardener came to an abrupt halt. He seemed to have

forgotten he was holding the shears, because when he saw me staring at them in horror, he rolled his eyes and tossed them into the dirt. "For Christ's sake, Louisa, I'm not gonna *hurt* you," he growled.

I believed him. Not only because he dropped the shears and kept his distance, but because something in my subconscious told me this man was familiar, like a face I'd seen in a dream. "Do I know you?"

He crossed his arms over his protruding belly. "You did, once." His keen eyes raked over me. "Hmph. You've got the Wade hairline. Widow's peak."

I nodded tentatively, wondering what that had to do with anything. "Okay. Who are *you*?"

The shadow of a smile crossed his face, almost like he was deeply amused by the whole exchange. "Marion Hatchet. The *actual* owner of this ugly old money pit."

My heart skipped a beat. "What?"

"If you wanna see it that badly, come back when we're open and I'll give you the tour. You don't have to cook up some story and bust your way in."

"No—but—I thought Uncle George owned this place."

"He did. Alongside me."

My mind started buzzing, putting the pieces together. I remembered last night, asking the bartender if he knew the owner, and how his response had been, *Which one?* I remembered Otis Penny's voice reading the dry, legalistic language about my inheritance . . .

"Oh my god," I said under my breath. "He left me *half* a bar."

"I beg your pardon?" the gardener asked, tightening his arms over his belly.

"'Full ownership stake,'" I recited. "That's what Otis Penny said. He meant the fifty percent that Uncle George owned, didn't he?"

The gardener went eerily still. "You talked to Otis Penny about this?"

For the first time, I realized I had the upper hand. I looked into the gardener's scowling face and took my time answering. "Yes, *sweetheart*, Otis Penny came to my grandparents' house yesterday for the reading of the will. He named every person my uncle left something to. When it got to me, he said Uncle George had left me his 'full ownership stake' in the Frisky Cricket."

All the color drained from the gardener's face. He stared me down again, but this time it seemed like he was praying for the punch line to the joke.

"Well," he said finally, more to himself than me. "Well."

He fished his phone out of his pocket and held it a good two feet in front of his face, searching through it. Then he dialed whomever he was calling. From my spot on the steps, I heard a tinny voice pick up.

"No, it's damn well not," the gardener said, irritation once again lacing his grizzled voice. "A certain Miss *Louisa Wade*"—he glowered up at me—"is down here at the Cricket claiming she owns the place." Pause. "Yes, I think I know who I'm looking at. Uh-huh. Why don't you check, then?" Pause. "Uh-huh. You'd better come down here."

He hung up without a goodbye.

"Who was that?" I asked.

The gardener ignored me and took his time putting his phone back in his pocket. He gestured for me to sit on the steps. "Might as well pick up those bobby pins while you wait. Don't wanna leave evidence of your *breaking and entering*." He threw me a final glare and skulked off to the garden without another word.

I hovered on the steps, trying to decide what to do. My pulse tripped with the possibility that this man had called the police, in which case I should get out of here until I could secure a copy of the will to prove my legitimacy. But the tone he had used was a familiar one, not like he was reporting a crime. It was more likely he had called someone he knew, someone who had a stake in what was going on here. Maybe it was Otis Penny, who would no doubt clear up the situation and might even give me a key.

It was worth waiting around to find out. I eased myself onto the steps and gathered up the bobby pins as discreetly as possible, refusing to let the gardener think he could boss me around.

Fifteen minutes later, my dad rushed into the backyard.

"Dad!" I called, relieved to see a familiar face. I forgot that I was still angry with him—I was just thankful to have an ally right now. "How'd you know I was here?"

Dad's clothes were rumpled like he'd just rolled out of bed. "Louisa—" he said, eyes lighting on me. "What're you—"

"Dad, that man over there doesn't believe me about—"

But Dad looked past me and locked eyes with the gardener. He marched toward him, and the gardener did the same, and for one wild second, I thought my dad was going to throw a punch.

But he *hugged* him.

"Hatch," my dad said scratchily, clapping him on the back. "You look good."

"You wanna explain all this to me, Tate?" the gardener—*Hatch*—asked. He flapped a soiled glove around like that covered the whole situation.

"Wait," I said, something clicking in my brain. "You called my *dad*?"

Hatch ignored me, staring expectantly at my father.

"She's not lying, Hatch," Dad said.

Hatch widened his eyes almost comically. He took a step back and looked around like an invisible audience might come to his defense. When no one did, he crossed his arms and gave my dad the same intense stare he'd been giving me. "Want to fill me in on the details here, Tate?"

"The details are hazy, but from what Otis tells me, it sounds like they revised the will last minute. George called him the day after he got diagnosed."

"No, he didn't."

"He did."

"He would have told me if he'd changed the will."

"Hatch . . ." My dad ran a hand through his messy hair and shrugged in a way that suggested this was above his pay grade. Then he reached into his pocket and pulled out a copy of the will.

Hatch read the document slowly, painstakingly, until the truth finally registered. Then he turned away and rubbed his hands down his face like a man waking up in the morning. "He changed it," he said in a low voice, meant only for him to hear, for him to process. "He changed it."

My dad looked pained. "For what it's worth, this wasn't the only change. Otis said he designated some new charities and earmarked a few things for the Rustin endowment fund."

"This wasn't part of the plan," Hatch said in that same far away voice.

"It doesn't change anything," my dad said placatingly. "The sale will still go through." He hesitated. "Only difference is that George's slice of the pie goes to Louisa now."

It was the wrong thing to say. Hatch snapped into sharp focus again, his blistering eyes swinging from Dad to me. "Which means I have to navigate a sale with a teenager who doesn't even remember me."

Dad seemed surprised. He turned around and gave me an expectant look. "Louisa, you don't remember Hatch?"

I stared suspiciously at the ornery old man. "I think I'd remember someone with such a *sparkling* personality."

Dad was still searching me with that expectant look, like maybe I would suddenly remember. "Honey, you knew Hatch when you were little. He was Uncle George's, uh . . ."

"Partner," Hatch said gruffly.

The word seemed to come from far away. I stood speechless, staring between my father and this crabby old man. First I'd learned Uncle George was gay, now it turned out he had a romantic partner? A partner I'd met when I was younger? Where had this man been in the intervening years? Why wasn't he mentioned in the obituary?

"'Was' being the operative word. We broke up years ago," Hatch went on. He paused, and his voice turned to acid. "George was too damn selfish to have a real partner. If I wasn't sure of that before, I am now."

Dad swallowed. "I don't think he was trying to screw you, Hatch."

"Course he was. This was one last ego trip for him and he's using your kid as the pawn. Reaching beyond the grave to let me down one more time."

A fresh rush of anger swept through me. Why did Hatch assume Uncle George's bequest had anything to do with *him*?

"Hatch, I'm sorry," my dad said heavily. "Look, I'll make this as easy as I can. I'll guide Louisa through the preliminary paperwork, and when it's time for closing, I'll fly her back down to sign—"

"Don't speak for me," I snapped, surprised at the volume of my voice.

Both men turned around, finally giving me their full attention.

"Uncle George left this bar to *me*. He wanted me to see it, he wanted me to know it, and he wanted me to decide what to do with it." I paused and took a deep breath. "And I've decided not to sell it."

There was a loaded silence. Then Hatch let out another bitter laugh. "Excuse me?"

"I don't want to sell it," I repeated.

"Well, that's too bad, because the plan's already in motion, darling. Has been since long before you set your shiny little sneakers on Alabama soil."

"Don't talk to her like that," my dad said sharply. Hatch raised his eyebrows, but Dad held his ground. "I mean it. At least hear her out, Hatch."

My heart bloomed the tiniest bit. I wasn't sure if Dad actually wanted to hear my two cents, or if he was just trying to make up for our conversation last night, but either way, I was grateful.

Hatch turned to square off with me. "All right, Louisa, I'll humor you. Say we don't sell the bar. Are you planning to move here and run it? 'Cause last I heard, you're starting college in the fall."

I tried to match his steely gaze. "Exactly. The fall. That gives me the whole summer."

"Then what? You go off to be a big-time college girl and leave me here to do everything? Call me once in a while to check in on sales?"

I hadn't exactly worked this part out yet, and I could tell from Hatch's smirk that he knew that. I could either bullshit him, or I could say what was on my heart and hope it resonated with the man my uncle had once loved. "Look," I said, thinking quickly and doing my best to sound respectful, "finding this place last night—it—it was like a lifeline. Walking through that door was like nothing I've never experienced before. I can't just up and leave without giving it a fair shake." Hatch puffed up, ready to interrupt, and I rushed on. "For better or worse, you and I are chained together now, and we can't move forward until we agree. So just—just give me thirty days. That's it. If you still want to sell at the end of those thirty days, I won't stop you."

Hatch scrubbed a hand through his bristly white beard. He looked at me the way Hannah had last night, like he was trying to see beneath the surface.

"Hatch," my dad said. His voice had gone soft. "George wanted to let her in."

Hatch clenched his jaw. "It's too little, too late."

"Maybe it's not. At least give her the chance to see what you built together."

Hatch sniffed and cleared his throat. I watched his expression change and knew he was going to relent. "You wanna stay here and flit around for thirty days, fine," he told me. He was still trying to sound tough, but he mostly sounded exhausted. "But if you're here, you're working. And I'm not paying you. You can keep your tips, but no hourly rate. I'm not teaching you, I'm not asking your opinions, and I'm not giving you money to spend on crazy whims. You might fancy yourself an owner, but I'm still the boss, and as far as I'm concerned, it's business as usual until the sale goes through."

I gave him a small smile. "You have a deal."

Hatch reached out and clasped my palm for the briefest second. "You're as stubborn as he was," he grumbled. In a strange way, it seemed to be a compliment.

"Maybe it runs in the family," I replied.

5
AUBREY CALHOUN

Milkshake slooooots

Me: so . . . I have some interesting news??
Me: spoiler alert: I canceled my flight!!
Me: instead of brunch, how about I bring y'all Zaxby's?

Candor McDaniel: What!!!

Emma Donarski: OMG THIS IS THE BEST NEWS

Candor McDaniel: I'm so intrigued

Emma Donarski: YES ZAXBYS. We're at my house!!

Me: Be there in 30!

Emma's house hadn't changed a wink—the same old brick town house with spindly black railings. The Rustin U garden flag was still planted off the front walk, weathered and sun faded from time. I parked in the open driveway and made my way to the door in the golden evening light.

Candor was the one to answer. "Louisa Ebeneezaaaaa!" she singsonged, swinging the door wide. She was barefoot in yoga pants and a tank top, and I knew it was likely that she hadn't been home since before the party yesterday. She and Emma tended to flit between each other's houses so often that they never knew where they left their AirPods or favorite sweatshirt.

"I can't believe you're still here!" Emma shouted from the hallway. She slid over in her socks and hip checked Candor out of the way. "*Why* are you still here? Please tell me you've come to your senses and are ready to matriculate to RU with us."

"With *you*," Candor said pointedly. There was a note of pride in her voice, like she wanted us to remember that she was going to Spelman, her mom's alma mater.

I laughed and shifted my way inside. "No, I'm not going to Rustin . . . but I'm here for an entire month! I extended my trip!"

Their screeches were so loud that I had to cover my ears. I fought the urge to tell them that if I had things my way, I'd be here for even more than a month.

"The coven will be at peak strength once more!" Candor said. She put a hand on my shoulder as if to hold me in place. "Say more, but not yet. I need that Big Zax Snack."

We ate in the family room, spread around the coffee table with our fried chicken, Texas toast, seasoned fries, and dipping sauces. I had missed the tangy Zaxby's sauce more than I'd realized, and when I plowed through my own too quickly, I switched to dunking my fries into Emma's. She was entirely oblivious, too busy making love to her Texas toast.

"Is it true," Emma asked with her mouth full, "that people up north don't do sweet tea?"

"It's true," I said solemnly. I took a sip of my own tea and let out a satisfied *ahhhh*. "If you ask for it, they'll give you this really scared look and come back with regular iced tea and a bunch of sugar packets."

"That's so sad," Candor said seriously.

"You're so brave," Emma added.

"Listen." I sat up and finished chewing. "I'm really sorry about last night. I promise I wasn't trying to ditch you."

Emma waved off the apology, but she wouldn't quite meet my eyes. "You're fine, Lou."

"We figured something came up," Candor said, shrugging a bit too quickly.

I bit my lip. Neither Emma nor Candor was the type to hold a grudge, but I could tell I *had* hurt their feelings, even if I hadn't meant to. My gut twisted with remorse, but I reasoned it would pass in a moment, because my friends would understand once I told them about Uncle George's bequest.

"Something *did* come up," I started. "It turns out Uncle George—"

But I never got to finish the sentence, because the front door burst open and a new girl swept into the room.

"AHHH!" Emma and Candor squealed, leaping to their feet as if Taylor Swift had just walked through the door. They jumped all over the girl, showering her with even more hugs than they had given me. The spark in their eyes—the one that had faded when I'd brought up last night—was now back in full force.

The new girl smiled brightly and squeezed my old friends with an easy tenderness. "I missed y'all! Who took my parking spot?"

And immediately, I absolutely *hated* this girl.

First, because she had interrupted my apology-slash-inheritance-announcement at the worst possible moment. Second, because my best friends were throwing themselves at her like she made the sun come up every morning. Third, because she had the audacity to call it *her* parking spot as if she came over here every fucking day, as if Emma and Candor were *her* friends and no one else's. And lastly, and most infuriatingly of all, because she was *stupid* hot.

She was close to my height, fair skinned, with shiny russet hair gathered into a high ponytail. She had striking blue eyes and smooth, sun-kissed cheeks that I just *knew* would be as soft as a fucking kitten. But mostly, it was the way she carried herself: blazing into the room with a fierce, easy confidence, like she was ready to confront anyone and anything in her path, like she might shove you off a mountain and then assure you, with a smile on her face, that it was your own damn fault.

"I did," I said, squaring up to face her. "Who are *you*?"

I asked even though I knew who she was, because of course Candor and Emma had talked about her all year. But I wasn't about to make this easy for her, not when she had breezed through the door like she was entitled to the whole world and everything in it, including my two best friends. I had just been through the strangest, most surprising, most uncomfortable days of my life, and I wasn't about to roll over for yet another person who made me feel like I didn't belong here.

The easy grin slid off the girl's face. She gave me a bemused once-over, like she was confronting a particularly heinous goblin, and glanced between Emma and Candor. "So this is the famous Louisa?"

Candor made a valiant effort to pretend like I wasn't being an asshole. "The one and only!"

"Louisa Ebeneeza!" Emma added, her smile faltering.

"Lovely to meet you," the girl said in the same way my grandmother said *Bless your heart*. "I'm Aubrey." She paused, and her steely gaze locked on mine. "But I think you already knew that."

I clenched my jaw and stared her down, refusing to let her see that she had gotten under my skin so quickly. The polite part of me said, *Apologize. Tell her this was a misunderstanding*. But the exhausted, tenuous part of me said, *I can't deal with one more person who makes me feel invisible*.

"Um—here!" Candor said, leading Aubrey to her Zaxby's bag on the coffee table. "You can have some of my fries! We were just talking about Lou's plans to stay for the summer. We can finally all hang out!"

The unspoken plea was obvious: *Everyone, please be friends.* Reluctantly, I sat back on the floor and dug into the Zax sauce, determined to get my emotions under control. Emma and Candor launched into small talk, both of them talking fast and high-pitched, clearly trying to smooth over the awkward introduction. Aubrey settled herself on the couch and crossed her legs imperiously, refusing to partake in Candor's fries.

"Anyway," Candor said after a long monologue about the current phase of the moon, "what were you gonna tell us, Lou?"

I hesitated. I had been so excited to tell my friends about the bar, but how could I do that now that this girl had infiltrated? I didn't want to share this precious new piece of myself with *her*.

"Um . . . ," I began. "So the thing is, Uncle George . . ."

Aubrey interrupted. "George Wade?"

I threw her an impatient glare. Did she honestly think she was part of this conversation? "Yes, obviously."

She hiked her eyebrows like I was unstable. "Sorry, didn't realize that was *obvious*."

"I would think that Coach Calhoun's daughter, who apparently considers herself besties with *my* best friends, would know very well that I'm in town because my uncle George died."

"So you *do* know who I am," Aubrey snipped.

"Did y'all know it's a quarter moon tonight?" Candor interrupted loudly. "It's actually my favorite phase because—"

"Uncle George left me a bar," I blurted out, focusing only on Emma and Candor.

There was a shimmering moment of silence. Emma and Candor cocked their heads in unison, both of them staring like I'd spoken in tongues.

"I'm sorry, what?" Emma said.

"A bar! He left me a bar! Like, a physical space that sells alcohol!"

They shrieked. Candor jumped off the couch and Emma jumped off the floor. Suddenly the three of us were grabbing each other's hands and dancing in a circle like a group of sugared-up kindergartners playing ring-around-the-rosy.

"Uncle George left you a *bar*!" Candor yelled.

"You're *rich*!" Emma screamed.

"I own a bar!" I hollered at the ceiling, squeezing my best friends' hands.

Emma turned to Candor with a delighted gleam in her eyes. "Do you realize what has happened?!"

Candor gasped and grabbed Emma's shoulders. "Oh my god. The *manifestation*."

Now I was the one to cock my head. "Excuse me?"

"We've been manifesting since graduation!" Emma exclaimed. "For our first real night out! We've tried everything—fake IDs, hitting up Candor's cousin, we even tried to crash a bachelorette party a few weeks ago—and now you show up and tell us we have a ready-made bar where we can drink and dance and make out with people!"

"Hold on, hold on, hold on," I said, laughing with my whole body. "I don't have a carte blanche for partying."

Emma furrowed her brow. "Louisa, you know I don't speak Spanish."

"It's French," Aubrey said from the couch, and we all turned to her, suddenly remembering she was there.

"She *knows* that," I snapped. "It's her way of being funny."

"Okay, but what's the bar?" Candor asked. She backed away from Emma and me to create space for Aubrey to join the conversation. "Where is it?"

"Get this," I said, holding up my hands like I was about to do a magic trick. "It's a gay bar!"

Emma and Candor shrieked again. Aubrey shifted on the couch behind them.

"Wait, did he know you were gay?" Candor asked.

"Wait . . . was *he* gay?" Emma asked.

I drew up short. "Um—" And truly, how was I supposed to explain this part? I had reasoned earlier today that it was fine to tell my best friends the truth about Uncle George, but how could I tell them now that Aubrey was here? Not only was she a stranger to me, but she was also the daughter of Coach Calhoun. She had a direct line to the same Rustin Football machine that had long profited off Uncle George being *straight*. But did that even matter anymore, now that Uncle George was dead and gone?

This is how Dad felt when he wanted to tell you, said a small voice in my head.

"You know, I'm not sure," I said finally, pretending like the possibility had only just occurred to me. And then I recited my grandpa's line, absolutely hating myself but rationalizing that there was no other way to get through this. "Apparently he owned a lot of different properties."

"What's it called?" Candor asked.

I breathed a sigh of relief that no one had pushed me on the question of Uncle George's sexuality. "The Frisky Cricket."

"Oh my god, that's so cute," Emma said, clapping her hands.

Aubrey shook her head. "They're selling that place."

It was like a balloon popped. Our giddiness evaporated as quickly as it had started. Candor and Emma gave me a baffled look, waiting for me to explain, and I felt embarrassed that I had to share the caveat of the sale on Aubrey's terms instead of mine.

I glared at her. "How would *you* know that?"

She stared at me like I was being intentionally difficult. "Everyone knows that. The university has been scouting for over a year, especially down in South Rustin, where that bar is."

Where that bar is. Her casual disregard set my teeth on edge. "It's not 'that bar.' It's called the Frisky Cricket, and I own it."

"Okay . . . ," she said, as if she didn't believe me. "Well, you won't own it for long, based on what I've heard."

"Do you make it a point to keep up with local real estate?"

She blinked as if I was dense. "The university is buying that land for the new football complex."

There was a sharp pause. My stomach bottomed out as the weight of her words hit me. "What football complex?" I asked, trying to keep my voice even.

"Their new state-of-the-art facility. Multiple practice fields, weight rooms, a film room . . . It's all part of their 'vision' for growing the program. That's part of the reason my dad got the job here, because he was aligned with them on taking Rustin Football to the next level." She shrugged like the whole thing was completely rational. "Didn't Uncle George tell you all that?"

"Don't call him *Uncle George*," I snapped. "You didn't know him."

She held up her hands in a gesture of surrender. "Sorry," she said in a tone that meant she was the exact opposite of sorry.

"And your dad is involved in this?" I pressed, my voice rising dangerously. "Doesn't he know about the Cricket?"

She shrugged like that was neither here nor there. "I don't know."

"Well, now you can go home and tell him," I said, trying not to shake with anger. "Tell him it's an incredible, irreplaceable miracle of a place and we're not selling it for some stupid football complex."

"Yeah, sure, I'll tell him," Aubrey said dryly. "*Hey, Daddy, I met this rude, combative girl today and she said to stay away from her plaything*. That will go over *so* well."

"It's not my *plaything*."

"You don't even live here."

"I've lived here longer than *you*."

She let out a tinkling little laugh. "I'm sorry, are you for real right now? What, you want to hang out for a few weeks, learn overnight how to run a bar, take on the university like some kind of David versus Goliath?"

"Yes," I said clearly.

"That's delusional."

"Aubrey," Candor hissed.

But I had heard enough. "Okay, you know what? I'm out of here." I clambered up from the floor and gathered my Zaxby's trash. "Em, Candie, love y'all. Let me know when you want to hang out *alone*."

And before they could do more than call my name, I was out the door and in my uncle's Cadillac, reversing out of the spot that Aubrey thought belonged to her.

6
THE BAR BUSINESS

"This is so gross," I mumbled under my breath.

"There's nothing romantic about the service industry," Hannah replied. She cocked her head to get a better look at the toilet. "Some might say it's *shitty*. Ba-dum-chhh."

"Real clever," I huffed, digging the toilet brush back into the bowl.

"Thanks, I'll be here all week. And you missed a spot near the rim."

Today was my first full day of working at the Frisky Cricket. I had woken up buzzing with energy like a kid on the first day of school, picked out the only clean shirt I had left (Mom was mailing a box of clothes down, thank goodness), and slid gently into the Cadillac, no longer afraid of it. It was a beautiful, blue-sky day, and I had a whole month to fall in love.

Hannah had been waiting for me, dressed casually in a gray Emory muscle shirt with a flannel tied around her waist. With a smirk, she had relayed Hatch's first task: to clean both bathrooms top to bottom. Either Hatch was punishing me, or he was trying to get me to quit already. But he'd have to try harder, because cleaning the bathroom didn't faze me—especially when the graffiti was so entertaining.

David is a bitch, said the current message I was reading on the stall door.

Below it, in faded red lipstick, was the reply *YES I AM*.

"So what else did he say?" Hannah asked, restocking the free tampons in the supply caddy.

"Didn't he give you the rundown already?"

"No, Hatch is bad with drama. He doesn't understand that the real treat is in the details."

Drama. Did Hannah think my decision to stay was dramatic? Did she, like Hatch, view me as a temporary problem, an irritating roadblock? Or worse, did she agree with Aubrey that I was "delusional"?

I wiped my sweaty brow with the back of my forearm and backed away from the toilet. "He gave me a whole list of ways he won't accommodate me," I said neutrally. "Teach me, coddle me, forgive me, pay me . . ."

"Yeah, he loves a good litany of the saints."

"Is he always grumpy? Or just with me?"

"Uh-huh," Hannah answered.

We finished the bathroom and returned to the bar top, where our lone patron, a skinny, balding white man in a bow tie, was nursing a Manhattan and poring over a stack of papers. He muttered something to himself and seemed oblivious that we'd walked back into the room.

"All right, the day's worst chore is done," Hannah said to me. "Let's move on to the important stuff. First things first, you need to meet the cat." She looked across the bar top at the man with the bow tie. "Edge, I'm giving the new kid a tour. Don't steal anything."

The man called Edge surfaced from his pile of papers. "Steal?" he repeated in a nervous, absent voice. "No, no, I should think not."

"Good man," Hannah said routinely.

Outside in the blinding sunlight, I hovered by the door while Hannah called for the cat, shaking the kibble bag with a *Psspsspss*. We were about to give up when the skinny black cat finally appeared from beneath the porch, slinking toward us imperiously like it was her own idea to eat.

"Sweet girl," Hannah said, bending down to caress her. "Louisa, may I introduce our favorite employee: RuPaw."

I laughed in surprise. "Incredible. Who named her?"

"Hatch, of course," Hannah replied, as if it was obvious that Hatch's personality went beyond the textbook definition of *curmudgeon*. She trailed her fingers along the cat's spine, then scooped her up and held her like a baby. "Come on, Ru, help me with the tour."

Hannah led me around the parking lot, pointing out various patrons' favorite spaces to park, warning me to avoid the spot with the pothole, and recounting the time her own car—a blue Subaru with a faded Louisiana plate—had gotten stuck in the mud after a late evening storm.

"I thought it was hopeless, that I'd have to call Baker and ask her to come get me, but then the most glorious thing happened." She paused for dramatic effect. "The *lesbians* appeared. They came rushing out of the bar like a swarm of worker bees, and Claudia started directing everyone like an air traffic controller, and Lindsey and Katie were lifting the trunk like a couple of Navy SEALs, and Allison got her pliers out for absolutely no reason—"

On and on she went, looping me around the parking lot, cradling RuPaw in her arms. The cat seemed entirely at ease, like she was used to Hannah's storytelling.

"That was George's favorite spot," Hannah said, pointing under the tree where my dad had parked yesterday. "The last few years, he kept saying he wanted a special sign placed there so everyone would know it was his spot, as if we didn't all know that already. He wanted it to say *Proprietor*, but when we asked him to spell that, he couldn't. Hatch got a real kick out of that. I threatened to get a sign that said *Queen Mother*, but somehow I never got around to it."

Her voice went slack. She cleared her throat and shook her head. I lowered my eyes, not sure how to comfort someone who had known my uncle better than I had.

"Anyway, that's enough of the parking lot. Come around back and I'll show you the delivery entrance."

She turned around, but my eyes lingered on the FOR SALE sign. I debated asking her what she thought about it all: the sale, the football complex, Hatch's determination to shut the bar down. But I wasn't sure I had earned her confidence yet. Hannah was warm and inviting, but there was also an edge to her that made me feel like I had to prove myself. Plus, I wasn't sure how close she was with Hatch. I held my tongue and followed her to the back of the property.

Within half an hour, Hannah had given me a tour of the whole place, which was not saying much; I'd seen most of it on my first night. Still, I learned about the back office, the safe, the utility closet, and the hallway where surplus inventory was kept. It was a haphazard, finicky old building and every little crevice had a story or a disclaimer. "You have to jiggle that spigot for a few seconds," Hannah pointed out, "and there's uneven flooring here, so watch your step, and the fire alarm trips every few days, but I'll write down the code for you—"

"You know everything," I marveled. I was starting to feel like I had bitten off more than I could chew, but I didn't want her to pick up on that and possibly relay it to Hatch. I was *in* this now, and I was going to learn as much as she had.

By this point, more patrons had trickled in. One of them caught Hannah's eye and gave a subtle nod of the chin, and Hannah turned to me.

"Claudia wants a White Russian," she said, leading me toward the bar top. "Ready to play with Kahlúa?"

If I'd thought learning the physical space was overwhelming, then learning how to make cocktails was going to be my downfall. Hannah zipped through the White Russian instructions, then mixed up an old-fashioned and a gin and tonic for another patron and their friend. Everything was a whirl of shakers and garnishes and proportions, and there seemed to be a shorthand for everything. Plus, making the drinks was only step one. Step two was learning how to ring them up on the register.

"Don't worry," Hannah said when she saw the look on my face. "We'll take it one drink at a time. I don't expect you to master any of this, especially not in thirty days."

So Hatch *had* told her that detail. It lit a fire in me, propelling me to pick up a clean glass and attempt a White Russian of my own. Hannah crossed her arms as she watched me eyeball the vodka measurement. When I handed the finished drink to her, she shook the ice cubes and took a thoughtful drink.

"Not bad," she said, giving me an appreciative grin. "Ru, what do you think?" She held it out toward the cat, who was sitting atop the bar counter in what I was pretty sure was a health code violation. RuPaw sniffed the drink for a moment before scampering off like she had better places to be.

"Can I try it?" I asked.

Hannah hesitated, gripping the glass as she leveled me with a look. "You can have a *sip*," she said quietly, trying not to let the patrons hear, "but only because I'm here. Hatch doesn't want you drinking, and I agree with him."

I bit down on my childish retort of *But I own this place*. I didn't want to seem like a brat in front of Hannah, plus I didn't want her to tell Hatch I was being difficult. "Understood."

Hannah handed the glass over. I took a sip and smacked my lips, tasting the chocolate milk–esque cocktail. "Mm. Yeah, I like it."

Hannah raised her eyebrows. "Well, from now on, you can like it in *theory*. Remember, freshman: No drinking, or I'll kill you."

A few hours later, after I'd successfully poured a couple of beers under Hannah's tutelage, the swoopy-haired bartender who'd served me the other night arrived.

"I'm *heeeeeeere*," he sang as he zipped in. He crashed a huge aluminum water bottle covered with stickers onto the counter, unzipped a bicycling helmet, and shook his sweaty hair out of his eyes.

"Midas," Hannah said with the air of a cat tracking a canary. "So glad you've joined us. We have something to discuss."

Midas looked up dopily from where he'd been clocking in at the register. When he saw me, the color left his face.

"I believe you've met Louisa," Hannah said. "Did you know she's only eighteen?"

Midas's eyes darted back and forth from Hannah to me. After a pause, he settled his shoulders and said with forced bravado, "What's up, South Dakota?"

I burned with embarrassment.

"Midas, we've talked about spotting fakes," Hannah said sternly.

"Hers looked legit!" he protested.

"I highly doubt that."

"Why is she here? Shit, am I going to jail? I have a race tomorrow."

"Can you reschedule the race for after you go to jail?"

Midas deflated. "For real?"

"No, not for real," Hannah said impatiently. "But Midas, come on. This is the second time this has happened. Do you want to give the county an easy reason to shut us down?"

"That's a *little* dramatic, Hannah, even for you. We're on a sinking ship here."

"And we're gonna run the ship as well as we can until it's time to jump overboard," Hannah said pointedly.

A sinking ship. Was that really how they felt about the Cricket's future? The idea of a sinking ship was so fatalistic, so inevitable, but I couldn't understand why that should be the case with the Cricket. Otis Penny had said there were decent sales over the last few years, and from what I had seen, there were plenty of patrons who were thrilled to call this place home. So why did Midas and Hannah think the bar was doomed? Was this Hatch's negative influence? Surely Uncle George didn't think all was lost, or he wouldn't have left the bar to me . . .

"All right, all right, I'm sorry," Midas said, bringing me back to the moment at hand. "I just didn't want to insult her! She looked like she could've been of age, and how am I supposed to know what a South Dakota ID looks like?"

"That should have been your first clue. Who the hell comes to Alabama from South Dakota? And this kid looks like she's fifteen—"

"Rude," I interjected.

"*Hannah*," Midas said with the air of explaining something to an alien visitor, "it's insulting to question someone's age. Do you know how many of my relatives look younger than they are? Like yeah, we're short, I get it, but I'd get my ass whooped if I carded one of my older cousins. Just because *you* clearly look like you could be forty, doesn't mean—"

"I don't look like I'm forty!"

"See? So insulting." Midas held up his palms, the picture of innocence. "I'm an easygoing guy, and I'm in the habit of believing people."

Hannah shook her head like she had run out of steam for this conversation. "Fucking himbo," she grumbled.

"Crotchety lesbian," he shot back.

Hannah took her dishrag and smacked him across the ass.

"HR!" Midas yelped, running away from her. "HR violation!"

"So that's Midas," Hannah said easily, as if they hadn't just bickered like a preteen brother and sister. "You'll never forget his name, because if you do, he'll use his classic line about being 'the king with the golden touch.'"

I stared after him. "Do we *have* HR?"

She snorted. "No. We have Hatch."

I bit my lip. "You didn't have to put me on the spot with Midas. I was gonna apologize to him about the other night."

"Go ahead, you still can. He's probably scampered off to fix his hair."

Before I could start in Midas's direction, however, the back door slammed and heavy footfalls plodded down the hallway.

"Oof, Papa Bear's here, and he sounds pissed," Hannah said with the air of someone commenting on the weather. "I don't have the energy for this. Louisa, you can update Hatch on how the day's been so far."

She zipped off without another word. Before I could do more than move to stand by the register, intending to look busy, Hatch stormed into the room.

Now that I knew who he was, I felt the great physicality of his presence. He reminded me of a polar bear: big and imposing, with piercing blue eyes and shocks of white in his short, careful beard and close-cut hair. Gone was the gardening hat and outdoor clothes; today he wore a maroon polo shirt that stretched over his belly and tucked into his dark jeans. A carabiner of brass keys hung from his belt loop, more than twenty of them jangling together so that when he walked around the bar to glare at me, he both looked and sounded like the Sheriff of Nottingham.

When his eyes fell on me, he stopped abruptly and sized me up. There was a long silence while we stared at each other, Hatch burying his fists into his jeans pockets.

"So you're really doing this," he said finally.

I squared my shoulders and tried to sound matter-of-fact. "I am."

He dug his tongue between his teeth. Waited.

"Hannah taught me how to make a few drinks," I offered.

The words may as well have bounced right off him. He continued to stare at me, those ice-blue eyes ripping through me. "I'm not paying you," he repeated.

"I don't need you to." His intense eyes were starting to make me nervous, so I turned to the register and pretended I was in the middle of doing something. "Besides, that pay affects *my* bottom line, too."

He snorted, and I looked up despite my commitment to playing it cool. I hadn't been trying to sound funny.

"Do you even know what a bottom line is, Louisa?"

I glared at him. "I know it's essentially the money you're left with once costs have been taken out."

Hatch raised his eyebrows comically, like I was telling a joke to a whole audience of people only he could see. "Look at that. A business savant."

I scowled at him. "I don't have to understand 'business' to know what this place means to people."

Hatch hiked his eyebrows again. "Do you think I *don't* know what it means to people?"

"I know you're ready to sell out to the university," I said angrily. "That you're fine with giving up this safe space so the precious football program can have one more freaking thing." I hadn't meant to reveal this knowledge yet—I'd wanted to see how long it would take Hatch to tell me—but he was getting under my skin, and I wanted to get under his, too.

Hatch blinked slowly. His hands remained in his pockets like he was having a pleasant chat at the grocery store. "You weren't this smart-mouthed when you were little," he said finally.

I set my jaw. "That was a long time ago."

An indecipherable expression passed over Hatch's face. "Yes, it was."

Just then, Hannah breezed back in. She stopped between us, looking from one to the other, before she rolled her eyes theatrically. "Hatch, give it a rest. The kid is one of us."

Hatch was about to respond when the front door banged open. We all turned to look.

Standing there in the sunlight, looking for all the world like he'd just stepped off a cruise ship, was Otis Penny.

"Uh-oh," Hannah said, not looking the least bit worried.

Hatch leaned aggressively against the bar top, putting all his weight on his palms. He forgot about tearing into me and set his sights on Otis instead. The scowl on his face could have stopped a preacher. "You can walk right out that door," he growled. "In this establishment, we serve friends, not traitors."

Otis seemed completely unperturbed. "Come on now, Hatch, I did what was asked of me." He took off his Panama hat, spun it in his hands, and waltzed right up to the bar. "I'll take a Moscow Mule."

"Did you not hear what I just said?"

Otis sat himself on a stool, plopping his hat down on the counter. "I'll take extra ice, too."

"You're trying my patience, Otis."

"And you're trying mine. I've been running around in the heat all morning, so I'd like that Mule sooner than later, thank you."

Hatch doubled down onto his palms, leaning forward to stare Otis Penny in the eyes. "I thought you and I had an understanding."

"We do," Otis said coolly. "Part of that understanding is about the man we were dealing with. You know better than anyone how he could be." Unfazed, Otis smacked his lips and looked around to Hannah and me. "I don't suppose one of y'all could whip up that drink for me?"

"I've got you, Otis," Hannah said. She breezed behind Hatch, who threw a half-assed scowl at her that she completely ignored.

"Thank you, darling," Otis said. "Now, Hatch, do you wanna speak about this in private? Or is this part of the show for customers now?"

Hatch looked around at the scattered patrons, who were all blatantly watching the exchange. He cleared his throat and waved a hand around. "Mind your business, y'all. Just some foreplay between two old friends."

Otis cracked a laugh that seemed genuine. "You should only be so lucky."

"You're not my type anyway," Hatch shot back.

Otis stood up from his barstool and accepted the fresh Moscow Mule from Hannah. "Thank you, doll." He looked at Hatch. "Well?"

"My office," Hatch grunted. He turned to go, but stopped and tossed a look back at me. "And as for you . . ."

I waited.

"If you really wanna keep this place running, then here's your first real assignment: Call that awful grandfather of yours and remind him the electrician is overdue. Oh, and clean RuPaw's litter box. Every day. Twice a day." He smirked in a self-satisfied way and prowled back to his office without checking to see if Otis followed him.

"Best of luck, Lou-anna," Otis said, shuffling past me with a wink.

I waited for the office door to snap shut before I turned to Hannah. "What did Mr. Penny call me?"

"He doesn't know anyone's name. I'm always 'sweetheart' or 'darling' or 'Blue Eyes.' Rumor has it his secretary prints out his clients' names in fat green ink, all caps, size sixty, before he takes a meeting."

"At least he's nicer than Hatch."

"Don't take it personally," Hannah said. "Hatch is like an old street cat. Needs to feel people out. That's why he and RuPaw get along so well."

I stared her down, trying to appear more assertive than I felt. "You didn't have to dump him on me. That's the second time you've hung me out to dry today."

Hannah's eyes sparkled with amusement. "It's good for you, darling. Welcome to the family."

7
THE HOME TEAM

After three days of grueling work, Hannah insisted I take a day off. This should have been welcome news to me—a chance to sleep in, to get myself better situated at Dad's house, to restock my toiletries—but when I woke up that morning, I felt strangely bereft.

"I need your help with an errand," Dad announced, poking his head into my room. "We'll leave in ten minutes. Wear something comfortable."

"What? *Now?*"

"Do you have something else going on?"

"What if I have to work today?"

"You don't," Dad said shortly.

"How do you know that?"

He walked away without answering. Dad and I had barely crossed paths since I'd started working at the Cricket, but I got the feeling he'd been checking in with Hatch to see how I was doing. I wasn't sure whether that comforted or irritated me.

Reluctantly, I rolled out of bed and went to brush my teeth in the hallway bathroom. When I met Dad in the kitchen a few minutes later, dressed in my recently washed RAGE CONSUMES ME shirt, he handed me a travel mug.

"Wasn't sure how you take it," he said, chuckling awkwardly. "But there's nothing like a nice cup of coffee for a morning drive."

"Oh," I said, surprised. "Black is fine. Thank you. Where are we going?"

Dad turned to leave, throwing the answer over his shoulder. "George's house."

We took Route 29, the hometown highway, past the tractor supply outlet and the original Methodist church. We trundled down Main Street, past the barbecue joint and the local tourist shop, Rust. And then, right on the outskirts of Rustin University, we came upon a giant billboard:

WADE ELECTRIC

POWERING THE HOME TEAM SINCE 1983

It featured a larger-than-life picture of Coach Calhoun standing with his hands at his waist like Superman. Next to him was a chiseled Black guy in a Rustin uniform, holding a football outward like it might burst through the billboard.

"Forgot to warn you about that," Dad muttered. "Grandpa spent big bucks on this new campaign. He sees Coach Calhoun's tenure as a chance to gain more business."

"He already has, like, *everybody's* business," I replied. For years, Grandpa had lobbied Uncle George to appear on billboards and in commercials for Wade Electric, and it worked: Pretty much half the town ran on Wade Electric. "I mean, he even has the Frisky Cricket's business." My stomach squirmed uncomfortably, remembering the assignment Hatch had given me on Monday—an assignment I still had not completed.

"He only has that because of George," Dad said. "Hatch would have switched providers years ago if he could have. I think he'd have done it first thing after the funeral, if it wasn't for the sale."

I looked at him. "Did you know he's selling so the university can build a new football practice facility?"

Dad startled and looked over at me. "You're kidding."

I studied his face. "Uncle George didn't tell you?"

"No. I didn't even know about the sale until he died." He shook his head. "A new practice facility, Jesus. Like they haven't spent millions already." Dad jerked a thumb at the billboard we had just passed. "I'll tell you what, that's gotta be Rhett Calhoun's doing. Everywhere he looks, that man sees an opportunity to further his influence. He's more like a politician than a coach."

I remembered what Aubrey had said the other night about her dad's "vision" for an expanded football program aligning with the university's. The land grab for the Cricket was starting to feel more and more like a threat, and Hatch's reticence to mention the details was starting to feel more calculated.

"You know . . . ," I said, deciding to share my theory, "I think Hatch was the one pushing for the sale, and Uncle George was just going along with it, but then he got sick and realized his legacy was more important than money. I think that's why he left the Cricket to me: so I could stop Hatch from selling out."

Dad clucked his tongue. "Louisa . . ."

"No, Dad, you don't get it. The Cricket, it's like . . . it's a soft place to land for anyone who's ever felt different in this town, anyone who hasn't fit into that football-player-and-cheerleader cookie-cutter norm. And I think Uncle George understood that. I think his realest, truest self came alive when he was there. He wouldn't just give it up for some stupid football field."

"Honey, you heard Otis Penny: George *wanted* you to follow through on the sale."

"He said he 'hoped' I would, but maybe he meant a different sale. Maybe he wanted me to buy out Hatch, or to find another buyer who would take over the Cricket and keep it running, or—"

"Louisa, listen to yourself. You're talking nonsense. What, you're gonna buy out Hatch and run the bar from Connecticut? That dog won't hunt, jellybean."

"I don't need you to poke holes in my logic, Dad, I just need you to get what I'm saying. The Cricket is *special*, but Hatch walks around like he can't see any of it, like he's just gearing up to sell a lumpy old dump—"

"Honey, you don't *know* Hatch."

"I know he's bitter. I know he's given up. I know Uncle George broke up with him for a reason."

Dad shook his head and let his silence speak for him. He swung the truck into Golden Hills, the wealthiest residential community in town, and the gate attendant waved us in without stopping to check Dad's ID. We rolled past imposing mansions with perfectly manicured lawns, and I found myself wondering how Uncle George felt coming back here each night after a rousing time at the Cricket. There was a stark contrast between the dingy, sweaty, louder-than-life bar and this pristine, isolated oasis . . . but only one of them felt like home to me, and I suspected Uncle George had probably felt the same.

"Look right there," Dad said, pointing up ahead. "Coach Calhoun's fancy mansion."

He slowed down so I could take in the magnificent farmhouse-style estate with its grand windows, gabled roof, and wraparound porch. The front lawn was so perfectly green you could have played golf on it. A water feature bubbled serenely near the front walk.

"Damn," I said, forgetting to be annoyed with Dad.

"He bought it from a retired oil magnate. Had some Silicon Valley tech company install security cameras everywhere."

"Kind of paranoid, don't you think?"

Dad snorted. "Not for a politician in the making."

We turned onto Uncle George's street and the old Victorian came into view. I'd only been there a handful of times, usually when my dad was scooping up Uncle George for a family gathering. Uncle George had rarely invited anyone inside. Was that because he was private, or because he didn't want anyone to know his real self? Did he have pictures of Hatch lining the walls? Oscar Wilde books lying on the coffee table? Shania Twain CDs gathering dust in the corner? Was his house the one place, other than the Cricket, where he could feel safe in his skin?

Dad parked in the driveway next to a familiar tan Lincoln. I turned to him and scowled, fully annoyed with him again. "You didn't tell me Grandma and Grandpa would be here, too. They're gonna fuss at me for storming out the other night."

"They probably will," Dad agreed, "but you can handle it. You own a bar now." From the wry way he said it, I could tell he was annoyed with me, too. He cut the engine and turned to give me his full attention. "Speaking of, let's not bring up your arrangement with Hatch. The less they're involved, the better."

"Wait, don't they like Hatch, either?" I asked, stunned to find something in common with my grandparents.

"They like him about as much as he likes them," Dad said, already climbing out of the truck.

It was hot and stuffy inside the house. Grandma and Grandpa were already upending the kitchen and the living room like a couple of bandits searching for jewelry. I waited for their inevitable berating about the other night, but they pulled a different strategy from the playbook: passive-aggressively punishing me with a never-ending list of stupid demands.

"Clean that grout 'round the kitchen tile," Grandpa said, handing me an old toothbrush, "and make sure to get under the fridge, too."

"Sort the china plates into expensive versus cheap," Grandma said, expecting me to intuit the difference, "and sell the expensive ones on the Facebook Marketplace."

"Find out how much this painting is worth."

"Wipe the baseboards."

"Unclog that drain."

I piled books into boxes, threw out expired items from the pantry, and was dispatched to pick up lunch before my grandparents even stopped to ask why I was still in town ("For the vibes," I said with a deranged smile; "So we can spend more time together," my dad cut over me). We worked our way from room to room, sorting and cleaning and quibbling over what was worth saving, and all the while I looked for evidence of Uncle George's real life—and found nothing except proof that he was a messy pack rat who favored David Baldacci mysteries. There wasn't a single photo, greeting card, or weathered gardening hat to suggest that Hatch had been part of Uncle George's orbit at all.

"Should we tackle the bedroom next?" Dad asked, wiping sweat from his brow.

Grandpa twisted up his face. "I'm not going in *there*," he sneered.

My dad blinked, clearly confused, but I suspected what was coming.

"He might have *weird* stuff in there," Grandpa went on. "I don't want to see that."

"I agree, Grandpa," I said in a would-be-innocent voice. "I mean, I wouldn't want you to find Uncle George's leather collection."

My cheek earned me the added task of scrubbing the bathtub.

Around five o'clock, Dad took pity on me and suggested I start loading the cars. It gave me a break from my grandparents' presence and came with the added bonus of playing on my phone when no one was looking. It was still ungodly hot outside, and I sweated from every crevice as I shoved a bag of couch cushions into the trunk of Grandma and Grandpa's Lincoln.

"It must feel strange, going through his things," said a voice.

I spun around to find Aubrey Calhoun standing at the top of the driveway, holding the leash of a golden retriever who clearly wanted to keep walking. *Great.* I had escaped my grandparents only to be ambushed by this Stepford wife in training. Out of the frying pan and into the fire.

"Why are you here?" I asked loudly, not caring how rude I sounded. It had been a long day, and I couldn't tell whether I smelled of sweat or mothballs, and Candor and Emma weren't here to play nice in front of.

"I live here," she said pointedly, gesturing down the street.

"Oh. Right."

There was a pause.

"George was always nice," Aubrey went on. "He used to throw

the tennis ball for Magnolia sometimes." She petted the retriever's head. "I think she misses him."

"Well, I'm sorry for her loss."

Aubrey wasn't put off by my snark. She continued to stand there, watching me play Tetris with the contents of Grandpa's trunk. "Do y'all need any help?"

I peered suspiciously at her. What was she angling for?

She seemed to read my mind, because she slipped into a disbelieving laugh. "Oh, come on, have you lost *all* your Southern niceties? It's standard practice to ask if your neighbor needs help."

"Even if you don't mean it?"

She raised her eyebrows. "Maybe I do mean it."

I wasn't sure what to make of that. What did she want? Why was she lingering? Why did she look infuriatingly pretty in that pink racerback top?

"I saw Daddy's billboard," I said, trying to get under her skin. "Must be fun to drive past that every day."

The lightest patch of color flared on her cheeks, and I felt entirely too pleased that I'd put it there. "Isn't it *your* family's billboard?" she shot back.

Before I could answer, another voice joined the fray. "Who's this, now?"

Grandpa had stepped outside, carrying a toaster with the cord dangling dangerously near his feet. "Are you raffling off George's stuff to the neighbors, Louisa?" He chuckled like it was a clever joke, and I prayed for that cord to dangle just a *little* bit closer to his foot.

"No, Grandpa, we were just talking."

"Hi, Mr. Wade, I'm Aubrey Calhoun," Aubrey said brightly,

raising a palm in greeting. She tugged the golden retriever's leash. "And this is Magnolia."

Grandpa lumbered down the steps and down the driveway. "Well, can't say I like dogs much, but it's nice to meet a good human. You're Rhett's daughter?"

"Yes, sir."

"Good man," Grandpa declared. "Building a good program. I'm sure you're proud of him."

"Yes, sir." Aubrey's smile didn't reach her eyes, which didn't make sense to me. She had seemed to gloat about her dad at Emma's house the other night.

"In fact," Grandpa said, swaggering closer like we'd asked him to be the star of our conversation, "let me find something for your father. George had some neat memorabilia from his years as—"

"Oh, Mr. Wade, that is very generous of you, but don't worry about it."

"No, no, I insist," Grandpa said with a dismissive wave. "I'll be right back." He shoved the toaster at me and lumbered back up the driveway.

"He's nice," Aubrey offered.

I gave her an impatient look. "He's a jerk."

She narrowed her eyes. "You really don't do pleasantries, huh?"

"Not unless they're actually pleasant."

A beat of silence passed. "Look," Aubrey said bracingly, as if we had finally cut past the bullshit, "I'm sorry you didn't know about the football complex. You know, at . . . at the Frisky Cricket. And I'm sorry you had to hear it from me. I know what it's like to learn things about your own life from other people, especially someone you dislike."

I studied her, trying to see beneath the layers. Who in Aubrey's life was telling her truths about herself? Was it her dad? The Rustin gossip mill?

"I never said I disliked you," I replied.

"You're not exactly hard to read," she said flatly. "Candor has always described you as 'earnest.'" She paused. "Which I took to mean *kind*, but I guess that was my mistake."

I faltered. I *knew* I was being mean to this girl, but it was another thing to hear it stated explicitly. For just a moment, I wanted to say, *I'm really sorry. I'm going through something and I haven't shown you the best side of me—*

"How 'bout this, then?" Grandpa called, reappearing on the front steps. He brought Aubrey a framed photograph of the old Rustin football stadium. A generous person would have described it as vintage, given the age and faded color. To Grandpa, I knew it was trash.

"Oh, my dad will love this," Aubrey replied, and I couldn't tell if she was lying or not. I got the sense Grandpa could have handed her an old toenail and she would have fawned over it.

"You tell him we sent it along," Grandpa told her.

"I will, Mr. Wade, thank you."

"Well, Louisa, there's more to be done," Grandpa said, clapping me on the shoulder as if he'd read a pamphlet entitled *How to Feign Affection in Front of Strangers*. "Grandma needs your help scrubbing the oven." He turned back to Aubrey with a gleam in his eyes, as if he couldn't wait for her to tell her dad how magnanimous he had been. "Lovely meeting you, Miss Calhoun. You make sure you tell your parents we said hello."

"I will, sir. Good luck with the clean out."

Grandpa nodded and ambled back up the driveway. I sighed,

opened the trunk to fit the toaster inside, and slammed it shut. When I turned back around, Aubrey was watching me closely.

"What?" I asked.

She shrugged. "Nothing." Her eyes darted up to Uncle George's house. "It's a nice home. I hope you had lots of happy memories with him here."

I wasn't sure if she intended *him* to mean my grandfather or Uncle George. She couldn't have known that neither assumption was correct, though for entirely different reasons.

"Yeah," I said vaguely. "I mean . . . it's no mansion, like your house."

The look on her face was impossible to read. "Mansions have a lot of empty space," she said finally. "Come on, Magnolia, let's go."

She tugged the dog's leash and continued her walk without looking back at me, and I watched her go with a confusing stab of guilt in my stomach.

8
FRISKY FRIDAY

By the end of the week, I felt like a tried-and-true employee of the Frisky Cricket. I knew how to ring up drinks on the register, how to jiggle the vacuum's power cord so it would work properly, and how to card a patron with authority. I also knew some of the regulars by now: the man called Edge was Professor Edgerton, who taught at Rustin's music school and was supposedly a leading authority on Dolly Parton's entire catalogue; Claudia, who favored White Russians, was a middle-aged Black woman with short hair and faded tattoos, who often fixed things around the bar and whose wife, Melanie, talked extensively about their three French bulldogs; Midas's roommate, Rook, was a fellow grad student who sometimes wore a cape to the bar for no apparent reason, and who changed their drink order every time they dropped in.

Hannah had taught me how to mix a variety of drinks: gin and tonic, whiskey sour, vodka cran . . . and of course, Otis's preferred Moscow Mule. I'd learned how to pour a beer without foaming the top, and I'd memorized our small selection of "local" beers, which was really just anything brewed in the South: Hannah favored Abita from her native Louisiana, but there was also Lazy Magnolia, Terrapin, Creature Comforts, and Orpheus. Under her very controlled direction, Hannah even let me taste-test a few of the drinks so I would know what I was talking about.

"But if you tell anyone I let you sip, I'll deny it," she said, giving me the unnerving stare she probably used on her students. "And I'll have you shipped off to boarding school in Switzerland."

I frowned. "Isn't that a line from *The Parent Trap*?"

She stalked off without answering me.

So there we were on Friday night, buzzing around to prepare for the weekly "Frisky Friday," which was, from what I could gather, a raucous night of line dancing paired with $1 off drinks for anyone who brought a friend. Hannah and Midas acted like it was the same old boring routine, but I was enchanted. Tonight would be my first time working the bar on a weekend. I imagined it would feel like last Saturday night, crowded and thrumming and *alive*, except I would be on the other side of the bar this time.

"This music is giving me hives," Midas griped as he changed out the Bud Light keg. "Why are you playing *oldies*?"

"This is Vanessa Carlton, you irreverent little prick," Hannah said with another towel swat to Midas's hip.

Hatch arrived around six o'clock, giving no explanation for why he was late. He hovered over everyone, micromanaging our assignments as if we couldn't be trusted to handle things on our own.

"You need to cut those lemons smaller," he said after I'd already cut up a dozen wedges for drink garnishes.

"How could they possibly be smaller?"

"No one wants a dentures-sized lemon with their drink."

"How about you pop yours out and we'll compare?"

Hannah and Midas snorted, then pretended they hadn't been listening. Hatch ignored them and turned to me with narrowed eyes. I expected another critique of my garnishing skills, but he changed tactics and caught me off guard. "Did you call the electrician yet?"

That shut me right up. Blood rushed into my face as I tried to come up with an excuse for why I hadn't followed through on such an easy task. The truth was somewhere between *I forgot* and *I don't want to deal with Grandpa's company*.

"That's what I thought," Hatch growled, his eyes flashing. He turned his whole body to address Hannah and Midas. "Keep an eye on her tonight. Don't let her screw up another simple assignment."

I burned with embarrassment and refused to look at the others. Hatch gave me a final scathing look before stomping off to the back office to "manage payroll."

"That means he's drinking a martini from his personal stash," Midas said, trying to lighten the moment, "and whining about paperwork and taxes."

I nodded and went back to the lemon wedges, making no effort to cut them smaller.

By eight o'clock, patrons had started filtering in—and most of them made sure they were noticed. Professor Edgerton wore a three-piece suit with a purple ascot and a floral lapel pin. He asked me to store his old leather briefcase behind the bar in his usual hiding spot. Claudia showed up in wide-leg silk trousers with a matching vest, clutching Melanie's hand like they were about to walk the red carpet. A few of Hannah's friends trickled in, Baker among them, all wearing outfits they seemed to have ordered from a femme chic catalogue. Even Otis Penny was there, wearing a breezy linen shirt and suede smoking slippers. He patted me genially on the shoulder and said, "Marvelous to see you, Lucilla."

"Am I underdressed?" I asked Hannah anxiously, nodding toward my striped baseball tee and baggy jeans.

Hannah shot a look around the room as if she hadn't clocked everyone's outfits already. "Compared to these flashy bastards? Yes." Then she gestured to her messy bun and ratty old LIVE LAUGH LESBIAN cotton T-shirt. "Compared to your fellow barmaid who fully expects to go home with stains and spills this evening? No."

I nodded vigorously like that might help me believe her. "Okay. But, like . . . a lot of people look *hot*."

"I mean, my fiancée certainly does, but that's par for the course." Hannah grinned and shook my shoulders. "Get out of your head, freshman. This is what you signed up for. And it's *fun*."

"It's fun," I repeated, trying to internalize the words.

"It's fun!" Hannah said emphatically, smacking a hand on the bar top. "Midas, play some dance tunes. Louisa needs to loosen up."

"One step ahead of you," Midas said, and a second later "Pink Pony Club" blasted through the ceiling speakers.

When Hannah disappeared to the back hallway, Midas knocked me with his elbow. "Hey, South Dakota." He slipped me a shot of whiskey. "For the nerves."

"Oh, I don't know if I should—"

"I can't hear you!" he singsonged, throwing his own whiskey shot back. "Haghhh! Fuck a duck, it burns *every* time." He shook his floppy hair like a dog shaking water from its ears, then looked at me sincerely. "Do what you want, darling, but it's my understanding that *Hannah and Hatch* are not supposed to let you drink. No one has said a thing about *me* letting you."

I smiled genuinely. "Even though I got you in trouble last time?"

"Psshh, Hannah doesn't scare me. She's all bark and no bite. And besides, last time, you were a customer. Tonight, you're part *owner*." He winked and danced his way back to the counter, where a handsome person wearing a checkered button-down was waiting to order a drink.

"Bottoms up," I whispered to myself, and shot the whiskey back with my eyes closed.

The evening passed in a blur of pop songs and dancing. I served a few drinks but mostly assisted Hannah and Midas as a barback. If Hannah suspected Midas had let me drink, she didn't say anything about it, or perhaps she was just too busy to care. We were swarmed with patrons and discount requests and music suggestions. I urgently had to pee, but every time I tried to slip away, another customer needed something. It wasn't until Hannah got into a tiff with a pair of emo lesbians visiting from Knoxville that I was finally able to slip off to the bathroom.

"But I don't understand," one of the emo lesbians grumbled as I passed by, "why can't you play just *one* Evanescence song?"

"That's really not the vibe tonight," Hannah explained for the third time.

By the time the line dancing started, everyone was liquored up and ready to play. It was mostly older folks who participated, with Claudia and Melanie taking the lead, but several younger people joined in as well. The group of them moved like one mass, taking up an entire side of the room as they slid and shuffled and kicked up their shoes. I distinctly heard Rook yell, "Yee-haw!" as

I maneuvered past them—nearly tripping on their cape—to grab more napkins from the storage hallway.

Hatch had been in and out of his office a few times now, seemingly more relaxed, which I suspected had to do with the secret martinis. But for the last forty-five minutes, he'd been holed up with the door shut, even as the music pulsed louder and the roar of voices reached a fever pitch. When a wave of college students showed up and swelled our numbers to the max, Hannah pulled me over and instructed me to fetch Hatch.

"*Me?*" I protested. "Can't you or Midas—"

"We're up to our necks in drink requests and Midas and I will serve them much faster than you," she said shortly. "Put your big girl pants on and grab the boss."

I sighed, squared my shoulders, and went to Hatch's office. When I knocked on the door, a full verse of music passed before Hatch answered with a gruff "Come in."

I nudged the door open and wedged my way inside. It was blessedly quiet in here, a world away from the thumping energy on the other side of the walls. Hatch was reclining in his chair with his feet kicked up on the desk, looking intently at something in his hands. When he saw me, he hurriedly stuffed it away.

"What?" he asked aggressively.

I crossed my arms. "We need backup. It's getting pretty crowded out there."

"I'll be right out," he said, making no effort to move.

I hesitated. I didn't want to drag this out any more than I needed to, but I knew our capacity had reached a tipping point and Hannah would kill me if I came back without Hatch in tow. "Um . . . It's kind of urgent, though. We're slammed. Midas is mixing so many drinks that he's threatening to sue us for carpal tunnel."

Hatch heaved a deep sigh, jumped up with his usual surprising speed, and pushed past me into the hallway.

I lingered behind, eyeing the desk drawer he'd shoved something inside just a moment ago. I knew it was wrong to snoop, but I didn't understand this man, and I definitely didn't trust him. What if he was looking over deal paperwork from the university? What if he was plotting to cut me out of it? I reasoned I had just as much of a right to know what was going on as he did. Like Midas had said, I was an owner now.

Quietly, I tiptoed to Hatch's desk. It was covered in stacks of papers, most of which appeared to be bills, all of them addressed to Marion Hatchet. I pulled the drawer open one painstaking inch at a time. The paper he'd been holding was right on top. I grabbed it and turned my back to the door to hide what I was doing.

Before I flipped it over, I realized I wasn't holding a piece of paper. It was a photograph. An old Kodak print with a laminate back and faded pink numbers. *This isn't deal paperwork*, my inner voice said. *Put it back and get out of here.*

I didn't listen. Instead, I flipped the photo over, knowing in my bones what it would be.

Uncle George.

He was younger, probably in his fifties, with bristly salt-and-pepper hair and an impressive mustache. He wore a classic white T-shirt tucked into blue jeans, and he was leaning on a fence post with a crowd of people behind him. The crooked grin on his face matched the twinkle of mirth in his eyes. It was exactly how I remembered him—his very essence—except he looked happier, less guarded. He looked like his truest self.

And Hatch had been sitting here for who knows how long, simply looking at this photo. Had he been the one to take it? Had they been on vacation together? Was this how he liked to remember George? My throat was suddenly thick, but my brain couldn't make sense of how to process anything.

Then:

"What the hell are you doing?!" a voice roared behind me. I spun around, clutching the photograph to my chest. Hatch was frozen in the doorway, his body impossibly large, his face blotchy with rage. His glare went through me like an ice pick.

"I'm sorry—I was—I just—"

"GET OUT!"

My entire body surged with adrenaline. I hurriedly placed the photo on the desk, face down, as if that would make my sin less egregious. I scuttled to the door and around Hatch's imposing body, my shame so powerful that I couldn't even look him in the eye.

The door slammed shut behind me. It was so loud that a couple of patrons actually jumped. I stood paralyzed as the adrenaline rush worked through me, my breath coming so fast it was like I had sprinted from the parking lot. I hustled through the crowd and ducked behind the bar top to join Hannah and Midas.

"Where did Hatch go?" Hannah asked from the register, brushing her fallen hair out of her eyes.

I focused intently on pouring a draft beer. "Don't know."

I was so discombobulated that I mixed a whiskey-Coke instead of a whiskey ginger, then rang someone up for ten beers instead of one. Midas touched my arm, forcing me to stop and look at him.

"Take five, freshman," he said kindly. "Get your head on straight. Or gay. Or whatever."

I didn't need him to tell me twice. I dipped away from the bar top and wove through the hot, sticky bodies until I reached the back exit door. I shoved it open and pushed myself into the clear night air, putting my hands on my knees while I took several deep breaths.

"Louisa," said Hannah's voice.

I turned around to find her closing the door. I knew by the look on her face that she had talked to Hatch.

"I didn't do it on purpose," I said quickly.

"I'm not here to lecture you." She met my disbelieving stare. "Okay, maybe a little. But mostly I wanted to check if you're okay." She came toward me, put a steadying hand on my back, and gestured for me to sit on the same steps where I'd first met Hatch. "Tell me what happened."

I explained about the paper he'd been holding, and my suspicions about him hiding information about the sale, and even about the wave of emotion that had come over me when I'd seen the photograph.

"Why would you think Hatch is hiding information from you?" Hannah asked.

"Because he never told me about the football facility. I had to find out from someone else."

"Did you *ask* him?"

"No, but . . . can't you tell that he doesn't care about this place? We're going to lose something precious all because he's ready to wash his hands of everything Uncle George built here—"

"That is categorically untrue, Louisa."

"Hannah, you don't get it. I've never had a place like this before. I didn't even know there were queer people in Rustin, or that they—*we*—had a place to go. I can't understand how anyone would give up on that."

Hannah turned toward me, suddenly sharp. "You think I don't

get it?" She laughed hollowly. "You think Baker doesn't get it? And Midas? And Edge and Claudia and—"

"No, no, I know *you* guys get it, but—"

"Hatch gets it, too, Louisa. Every queer person does. We've all needed a place to go at some point. You are not unique or misunderstood or exceptional for feeling the way you do about the Cricket. But before you get up on your high horse about saving this place, you need to learn what it has meant to the people who've come before you, especially Hatch. You don't know what it cost him."

"What do you mean, what it cost him?"

Hannah drew up short. She bit her lip like she had said too much.

"What does that mean?" I pressed.

Hannah blew out a breath like she was furious about something. "It means I loved George dearly, but he didn't always do right by Hatch."

I waited for the beat to drop. When it didn't, I asked tentatively, "Have you ever been to Uncle George's house?"

"No," she answered impatiently. "Why?"

I faltered, not knowing how much to share. "It's just . . . I was helping my dad and grandparents clean out his house this week . . . and there were all these personal effects and like, pieces of his life . . . but not a sign of Hatch *anywhere*. No pictures, no birthday cards, nothing. But then I come here and everyone's like, *Oh, Hatch is grieving George, Hatch is trying to move on, this place was Hatch and George's baby* . . . and it's like, is that really the truth?"

Hannah took a deep breath. "There wasn't a single picture of Hatch?"

"Not one, Hannah."

"That breaks my heart."

"I know. It's like Hatch is pining for someone who didn't want him back."

Hannah's brow furrowed. "No, I mean it breaks my heart that George couldn't even feel safe in his own home."

I stared at her. "What do you mean?"

"Louisa, George and Hatch were deeply in love. Flawed love, yeah, but it was love nonetheless. The fact that George has no evidence of Hatch in his own home—it just goes to show how far he compartmentalized his life."

"I don't understand."

Hannah searched my face. "Literally *no one* in your family has told you about their relationship?"

"My dad said they used to be partners. That's it."

Hannah dragged a weary hand down her face. "Listen. I am telling you this not because I want to get into their personal business, but to help you understand where Hatch is coming from, and why it hurts so much for him to have you here." She took a centering breath. "George got into the bar business because of Hatch. This was like twenty years ago, and Hatch had just moved to Rustin from . . . I don't even know, it doesn't matter. But Hatch worked for a restaurant concessions group and had always dreamed of opening his own bar. He met George, they started dating—secretly, of course—and George agreed to go into business with him, as long as he could be a silent partner."

"For a gay bar?"

"For a gay bar," Hannah confirmed. "Which is why George insisted on the silent partner part. The way Hatch tells it, George figured he could use his businessman façade to invest in whatever kind of real estate he wanted, and if people asked questions, George could justify it as being open-minded, a good ally, willing to take a chance, what have you."

I remembered Grandpa's words: *He was diversifying his portfolio.*

"Supposedly the deal was they would run the bar together—with George behind the scenes, of course—until they had made enough money to move away and officially start their life together. Hatch wanted to get married, live openly, do the whole white-picket-fence thing."

I waited breathlessly, already suspecting where this was going. Bile started to rise in my throat.

"But years passed, and George couldn't do it. He was too attached to the life he'd cultivated here." She paused, and her next words were drenched in sadness. "He was too attached to that Golden Boy persona. He couldn't let it go."

I remembered standing in my grandparents' living room last weekend, reading the obituary, agreeing with Dad that Uncle George wouldn't have wanted a big sendoff. Grandma's words echoed in my head. *George's ego was bigger than this house.*

"So what happened?" I asked, the words coming from some scraped-out pit inside of me.

"They broke up." Hannah shrugged like there was no way around it.

"But they continued working together?"

"Business is business," she said simply. She hesitated. "And I don't think they ever fell out of love, even if they couldn't make it work."

I pictured the old photo of Uncle George—the crinkly smile, the sun-browned skin. I pictured Hatch on the other side of the camera, trying to capture the man he loved. To my great embarrassment, I felt tears prick my eyes.

Hannah didn't seem fazed by my crying; if anything, it was like she expected it. Wordlessly, she wrapped me in a hug and squeezed, and I only cried harder.

"You're all right," Hannah cooed.

I pulled back and sniffled, wiping my eyes. "I'm sorry. I don't know why I'm so emotional lately."

"Maybe because your uncle died, and he never told you he was gay, and he left you this giant-ass rainbow bar, and his ex-lover is being mean to you?"

I let out a watery laugh. "Yeah, maybe. I'm sorry, I don't usually cry all over people."

"Louisa, I'm a school counselor. My whole job is to let you little urchins cry all over me." She paused like another punch line was coming. "Personally, I *never* cried in high school."

I laughed again. "Yeah, I call bullshit."

Hannah released me. She handed me a bar rag like I might use it to dry my tears, and we both laughed.

"Where will you go?" I asked. "If the sale goes through?"

She gave me a quizzical smile. "I won't go anywhere. I have a full-time job for most of the year, remember?"

"Yeah, but . . . won't you be sad?"

"Of course I will be," she said like it was the easiest thing in the world. "But that's just how life goes. Some things end, others begin. I'm getting married in the fall. That's my main focus."

I smiled. "You and Baker will be really pretty brides."

"I know," she deadpanned. "Listen, I'm sending you home for the night. You need a break."

"No, no, I can help—"

"No offense, freshman, but your absence won't make or break us." She stood up and pulled me to my feet. "Don't you have anyone to hang out with other than us 'elders'? Go call your friends. Make bad decisions. Do whatever the young people do." She leveled me with one of her trademark looks. "You have twenty-five days left in your bargain with Hatch. Think carefully about how you'll use them."

And then, to my shock, she called for RuPaw, who had been hiding under the back steps the entire time. The cat slinked past me with an air of *She sure told you*, her tail held high as she followed Hannah back inside.

9
THE FIELD PARTY

Milkshake slooooots

Me: Please tell me y'all are out tonight

Emma Donarski: you know it
Emma Donarski: Waldron boys' farm.
We have alcohol . . . take an Uber!!

It was like Emma had read my mind. I wanted nothing more than to get drunk and forget this emotionally exhausting night. I called an Uber and left the Caddy in the bar parking lot, not even caring about how I would get back here tomorrow.

The Uber took me down the one-lane hometown highway until we turned onto the dirt road that led to the Waldron boys' farm. I lowered the window without asking as we rolled closer to the sound of voices and the smell of bonfire smoke.

"This all right?" the driver, a plump middle-aged woman with a kind face, asked.

"Perfect. Thank you, ma'am."

"Be safe, honey."

It was a clear, cobalt night dotted with stars. The bonfire crackled in the middle of the field, sending plumes of smoke into the vast sky. I recognized a few of the distant faces, kids I grew up with whose names were forever seared in my mind. I hadn't seen some of them in years. Maybe they remembered me, maybe they didn't. I wondered how many of them had heard I'd come out, and what they thought about it, and whether I cared. Anxiety nipped at my stomach, taking me back to the feelings I'd had when I'd first set foot in Alabama last weekend.

I thought of Uncle George walking into a space like this one—a heteronormative space, filled with the people he'd grown up with, where everyone was assumed to be straight. The kind of space where he would have to compartmentalize his life. The kind of space where Hatch couldn't follow—even if he had wanted to.

How had Uncle George done it for so many years? How had he withheld such an intrinsic part of himself, especially when it affected the person he loved most? I imagined trying to do so and felt my windpipe instantly clog. The whole sky couldn't hold enough air for me.

I am gay, I am here, I am gay, I am here . . .

"Louisa!" someone shouted, breaking through my fog. A moment later, Candor knocked into me with the force of a small cannon. Emma was right behind her, practically tackling both of us to the ground.

"Oof," I said, trying to catch my breath.

"Louisa Ebeneeza!" Emma shouted. "You made it!"

"Welcome to the party!" Candor said loudly. "It's not our party but it's a fun party!"

Their eyes were gleaming and unfocused. I hadn't seen them drunk in a while, not since last summer when we'd snuck off with a case of Mr. Donarski's beer. "Hi, you two," I laughed, grateful to be pulled out of my heavy thoughts. I threw my arms around their shoulders and squeezed. "Are you having fun?"

"We been drankin'," Emma said.

"Drankin'!" Candor repeated.

Another silhouette approached us, and I exhaled tiredly, already knowing who it would be. I didn't have the energy to deal with this girl tonight. All I wanted was the comfort of my old friends and the pull of a bottle to help me forget Uncle George.

"Well," Aubrey said, "look who it is. Nice of you to show up this time." She gave me a pointed look, as if to remind everyone that I hadn't shown up for last weekend's party. Unlike Emma and Candor, she sounded perfectly sober, or she was at least doing a good job of hiding her alcohol.

Her dig about me *showing up* put a spark of hot anger back in my blood, which was a welcome change from the melancholy I'd been feeling a moment ago. I squeezed my arms tighter around my friends and met Aubrey's glare with one of my own. "Lucky me, running into you two days in a row," I said sardonically. "Do you have to follow my friends *everywhere*?"

Emma wriggled out of my hold and tapped me on the nose like a midcentury nanny. "Louisa 'Beneeza," she said, hiccupping, "be nice."

"Yeah, Scrooge, be nice," Aubrey said with a smirk. She turned to Emma and Candor. "They just started passing the moonshine around, if you still wanted some?"

"Yes!" my friends said in unison, and without further ado, Candor grabbed my hand and tugged me along behind them.

We reached the bonfire just as one of the Waldron boys started playing a fresh song on his guitar. There were more people here than I'd realized, and I became acutely aware of many sets of eyes on me as I found a place to squeeze in with my friends. Without meaning to, I leaned closer into Candor.

"It's mostly Rustin Prep kids," Candor whispered, sensing my anxiety. "A few County High people, too. They're all nice, I promise."

And they *did* seem nice. "Hi, Louisa," a few of my old classmates said, while some nodded and others simply stared like they were trying to place me from a dream. I noticed a few telltale whispers and side-eyes, but people mostly left me alone.

If anything, they seemed more intrigued by my proximity to Aubrey. It was clear that her presence rippled through the crowd like a breeze you could feel on your skin. People watched her with stars in their eyes, wanting desperately to be noticed, to be seen, to become part of her sparkling orbit. Candor and Emma seemed thrilled by the secondhand shine. I couldn't help but roll my eyes, because it's not like Aubrey had *done* anything to earn this attention. People were just enchanted by the fact that she was Coach Calhoun's daughter.

"Hi, Aubrey," said a big, jocky guy with long sideburns. I recognized him immediately: Asa Waldron, the middle brother. He'd once tricked me into making a dirty joke on the playground when we were eight years old. I'd repeated it to my grandmother and had my mouth scrubbed with Palmolive. Asa may have gotten older, taller, and better looking, but I couldn't look at him without tasting dish soap.

Asa handed Aubrey a bottle of Ole Smoky moonshine. "Heard you were lookin' for this," he said pompously, like he was handing over the holy grail.

Aubrey's eyes danced as she took the bottle from him. "You heard right. Thank you." She gestured to Emma and Candor, but not me. "Mind to get us some chasers?"

"Comin' right up," Asa grinned, stepping away.

As soon as his back was turned, Emma and Candor collapsed into giggles. "Oh my god," Candor said giddily, "he's got it bad for you."

Aubrey didn't reply. The flirtatious smile vanished from her face, and she became all business as she shoved the bottle at Emma and started riffling through her purse.

"I don't need a chaser," I said, impatient to taste the blackberry moonshine. I reached for the bottle, but Aubrey smacked my hand away.

"Ow!" I yelped, cradling my stinging hand.

"We're doing this properly," she said, pulling rubber shot glasses from her purse.

"You carry shot glasses in your *purse*?"

Aubrey sighed like I was truly testing her patience. "As my mother says, a lady should always be prepared."

"A lady," I repeated, snorting. "God, you're like a fucking cotillion class."

Aubrey smiled in a faux-sweet way. "I have some wet wipes, too, if you want to clean out that filthy mouth of yours?"

"Sure, as long as I can borrow your stick, too?"

Aubrey frowned. "What stick?"

I gestured behind her. "You know, the one up your ass?"

"Y'all, *enough*," Emma pleaded, grabbing our hands. "We've been all"—she hiccupped—"excited for you to meet each other"—another hiccup—"but now you're just"—hiccup—"angry lil puppies that make me want to cry."

"Me too," Candor said drunkenly, rocking on her heels. "My bes' friends hate each other and it's so *sad*."

It was the first time I'd heard Candor or Emma extend the term *best friend* to someone other than me. Aubrey must have registered it, because she shot me a triumphant look that seemed to say *See?* I couldn't look back at her. As childish as it was, my feelings were hurt. I felt left out and left behind. What would have happened if I had never moved away from Rustin? Would there have been no need for Aubrey's presence in the friend group? Or would she have become my friend, too?

"Can we just drink our moonshine?" Emma pleaded.

Aubrey nodded and poured three shots with a steady hand. She handed one to Candor, one to Emma, and the last one to me.

"Aren't you—?" I started to ask.

"I'm not drinking," she said firmly.

I blinked. She didn't drink, but she still brought three shot glasses? Was that so she could feel part of the ritual, or had she anticipated that I might be there? And why did that make me feel strange?

"Cheers!" Emma shouted, clinking our glasses together. She shot hers back while Candor took hers in two small pulls. Aubrey looked expectantly at me, so I downed mine and handed the shot glass back to her with a mumbled thank-you.

"You're welcome," she said without looking at me. She pulled a paper towel from her purse and dried the lip of the shot glass before tucking it away.

We fell into a better rhythm after that. Aubrey and I weren't exactly *nice*, but it seemed we had reached an unspoken agreement to leave each other alone. Besides, she was too caught up with Asa. He had returned with Coca-Colas for each of us and was now stuck to Aubrey like tree sap. Emma and Candor couldn't stop giggling about it, both of them talking to Asa with fluttery eyes and sparkling smiles. I felt like I was on the outside looking in, not only because I no longer understood their in-jokes about school, but also because I couldn't relate to mooning over a boy like that. It made me ache for the comfort of the Frisky Cricket, even after the difficult night I'd had earlier.

"Louisa Wade," Asa said eventually, turning toward me like a spotlight. "Long time no see."

My heart started pounding. I held steady and gave him a curt nod. "Hey, Asa."

"Rumor is you like girls now," he said with a leering grin.

Emma and Candor froze. Aubrey's back went rigid, her mouth falling open like she wanted to say something but wasn't sure what.

My heart pounded away, but I dug my sneakers into the soil and held my head high. *I am gay . . . I am here . . .* "Actually, I've always liked girls," I said evenly. "It's just that other people know now."

"Right, right." The leering grin spread across his face again. "See any hot ones tonight? What's your type?"

My mouth was going dry. I took a long sip of my Coke before answering him. "I don't really care to have this conversation with you, Asa."

"Oh, come on, I'm an ally," he said, puffing out his chest. "Isn't that what y'all call it?"

I turned away from him and looked squarely at Emma and Candor. "Where's the bathroom?"

It was Aubrey who answered. "I'll show you."

"What? No," I said, shaking her off.

"I could use a break," she insisted, and was it my imagination, or was she sending me a pointed look?

I rolled my eyes up into my head. "*Fine.*"

We left the others to their own devices, with Aubrey bossily insisting that Emma and Candor drink some water. Then she led me up to the Waldrons' house, marching five paces in front of me like a deranged tour guide.

"It's right through here," she called over her shoulder, "and the bathroom is—"

"I'm sure I'll find it, thanks. Most of them resemble each other."

She scowled and took off ahead of me. I bristled again, annoyed that she was trying to beat me to the bathroom, but the moonshine sat pleasantly in my stomach and it didn't seem to matter all that much who got to use the bathroom first. The important thing was that I was away from Asa.

When I reached the house, though, the hallway bathroom was empty. *Whatever*, I thought, *she's probably decided she can't settle for less than an en-suite bath.* I shut myself inside and did my business, grateful to have a moment alone.

When I came out, I heard voices. I turned the corner to find Aubrey in the kitchen—talking to none other than Asa. *What the fuck.* Had he followed us up here? Could I sneak away without them seeing me?

". . . I mean, if you wanted to," Asa was saying, leaning into Aubrey's space. "Maybe just dinner."

Aubrey stood against the sink, smiling indulgently with one hand in her dress pocket. "Thank you," she said with all the practice of a society debutante, "but I'm actually seeing someone right now."

Asa went silent. "Oh," he said, sounding genuinely crestfallen. He quickly recovered and gave her a winning grin. "Well, your boyfriend is a lucky guy."

She gave him a prim, tight-lipped smile, the kind she probably used when people asked probing questions about her dad. "Thanks."

Asa nodded, then caught me watching them. He cleared his throat and pushed past me and out of the house. Aubrey ignored me, but it didn't escape my notice that her posture had gone rigid again. Bizarrely, she turned to the sink and started rinsing glasses.

"What are you doing?" I asked.

She shot me a look like *I* was the weird one. "What? It's filthy in here. You can tell it's a house full of boys."

"I thought you had to pee."

"I never said that."

"So you just came up here to wash dishes?"

"Do you dissect *every* little thing people do?" she snapped. "I just needed a five-minute break, and even that was interrupted."

"We have very different definitions of what constitutes a 'break.'"

"Oh, I'm sure we have different definitions of *many* things," she said dryly. "Like manners, and showing up for your friends when you say you're going to, and—"

Anger flared in my chest. "Don't you dare comment on my friendship with Emma and Candor. That was a weird fucking night for me, and the two of them didn't care that I had to—"

"Are you serious?" She laughed a loud, bitter laugh, the most unladylike I had seen her. "Of course they cared. They hadn't seen you for a year. They were borderline *excited* when your uncle died because it meant you'd be coming home for the funeral. They talked all week about Louisa-this, Louisa-that, and how we'd all hang out, and how I'd finally get to see how *awesome* you are. And then you ghosted them without an explanation."

My stomach hollowed out just like it had done during Hannah's lecture earlier. I ignored it and focused on the fury I felt toward her. "Don't start yelling at *me* just because you can't shake some annoying asshole guy," I shot back. "Here's an idea: Maybe instead of inventing a boyfriend, you should just *tell* him you're not fucking interested."

"How would *you* know I'm inventing a boyfriend?" she asked, swelling with indignation. "You keep acting like you know me, like you're allowed to hate me based on the few isolated encounters we've had, but you *don't* know me, Louisa. I think you're too fucking self-involved to truly know *anyone*."

She stormed past me, knocking into my shoulder as she went, and I reeled as much from her swearing as I did from the shock of tears in her eyes.

Aubrey drove us home in her brand-new Audi, which Emma insisted on calling "the Rowdy" despite everyone's pleas that she stop. Aubrey put the top down as if to remind us we were in a fancy convertible, and I sat in the backseat and watched her graduation tassel fly from the rearview mirror while I tried to stop seething from our confrontation in the kitchen.

"I don't want to drop y'all straight home," Aubrey said as we came upon a lone stoplight. "Emma is trashed."

"Your mom's trashed," Emma said, and collapsed into a snort of laughter. She and Candor seemed oblivious to the simmering tension between Aubrey and me; they were too intoxicated from both moonshine and boys. Aubrey and I had returned to the bonfire to find them chatting with a couple of guys from County High, who had seemed sincerely devastated when we'd announced we were leaving.

"I'm thinking we hit the Popeyes drive-through," Aubrey went on, and Candor gasped with delight. "Sober everyone up with some chicken and carbs."

Twenty minutes later, we sat in a corner of the brightly lit Popeyes parking lot, none of us speaking because our mouths were full of fried chicken and mashed potatoes. The whole car stank of fried batter even with the top down. I tried to take a sip of my Coke without leaving a trail of grease on the cup, but it was impossible. The upside was that indulging my drunk munchies helped to soften the anger I was feeling. I leaned back against the headrest and closed my eyes against the nighttime breeze.

"Damn, I was ravenous," Emma said through a mouthful of food. She *had* somewhat sobered up over the last half an hour, though I refused to give Aubrey credit for that. "I feel like someone in the Middle Ages rolling up to King Arthur's table for the big feast. Look at this chicken leg. Just look. This is straight out of a medieval cartoon. This is like, medieval porn."

"You're flicking chicken skin on me, Em," Candor said, licking her lips. "Shut up and give this porn your full attention."

"Delicious porn," Aubrey mused, attacking her mashed potatoes with a plastic fork. "I don't know how they do it, but somehow they always get the pepper just right."

"Are you allowed to say 'porn'?" I asked, unable to resist poking the bear.

"Did you want to walk home, Scrooge?" she said testily.

"Whatever, Cotillion."

We slipped into silence again, our bellies full and weighed down. Emma slurped from her sweet tea. The radio twanged half-heartedly.

"So, Aub," Emma said eventually, "did anything happen with Asa?"

Candor waggled her eyebrows. "We saw him follow you up to the house."

Aubrey gave a tinkling little laugh, the kind my grandmother used when she didn't want to answer a question. "No, nothing happened."

"Whaaat? He didn't even ask you out?" Candor wailed.

"Nope," Aubrey said definitively.

I frowned. Why was she lying? I had distinctly heard Asa ask her to dinner. If she truly was seeing someone, why wouldn't she tell Emma and Candor?

"What a bummer," Emma said. "He is *beautiful*. I mean, that jawline could cut glass."

"It could cut a whole fucking window," Candor enthused.

I swallowed against the discomfort in my throat. I knew they didn't mean to be hurtful, but it stung that Emma and Candor were happy to gush over someone who had goaded me about my sexuality. Without meaning to, I glanced at the rearview mirror. Aubrey was watching me with a careful look in her eyes.

"Let's get going," she said, clearing her throat. I tried to catch her expression in the mirror again, but she stared determinedly through the windshield.

Ten minutes later, we rolled softly into Emma's driveway and parked in the same spot I'd taken the other night. I half expected Aubrey to make some snarky comment about it, but she was preoccupied with getting Emma and Candor safely out of the car. Together, we walked them to the door and ushered them inside.

There was an awkward pause before Aubrey turned to me. "So are you calling an Uber, or . . . ?"

"Yeah," I said, already pulling out my phone.

Aubrey hesitated. She seemed to be deliberating about something. "I can take you."

I looked up in surprise. "That's okay, you don't have to."

"I know I don't *have* to, but it's stupid to waste money on an Uber when I already have a car."

I clenched my teeth and stared her down. She gave me a challenging look back. I couldn't tell if she was just trying to win the argument, or if her insistent Southern manners were rearing up again. But I really *didn't* feel like waiting on an Uber, especially because I doubted there were many drivers still on the road this late. And I was definitely not going to call my dad.

Reluctantly, I followed her back to the Audi. But when I reached the passenger-side door, I paused.

"What?" Aubrey asked impatiently.

"It feels weird to take Candor's seat," I said, circling around the car. "I'll just sit where I was before."

"What? No."

"Yeah, it's fine," I said, sliding into the back and buckling my seat belt. "It's a short drive."

Aubrey scowled in the rearview mirror. "I'm not about to play *Driving Miss Daisy* with you, Scrooge. This is weird. Get in the front seat."

"Why does it matter?"

"It's just weird! It feels, like, off-balance. Like straightening one side of your hair but not the other."

"Oh my god, you are *unhinged*." I huffed and made a big show of unbuckling my seat belt and stomping back to the passenger side. I plopped into the front seat, jammed my seat belt into the buckle, and threw her an impatient look. "There. Are you happy now?"

"*Happy* isn't the first adjective that comes to mind."

Adjective. Of course she would employ the correct fucking part of speech when she was arguing with me. "Has anyone ever told you how annoying and overbearing you are?"

"Every day," she said easily, making it clear that I couldn't wound her. "Has anyone ever told you how impossible and entitled you are?"

"Every day," I parroted.

She rolled her eyes. "What's your address?"

I told her. She punched it into her sleek little console, then backed the car out of Emma's driveway. When she clutched my headrest to make a reverse turn, I caught a whiff of her floral perfume and scowled at how good it smelled.

"You don't have to turn your body around," I pointed out. "You have a camera."

"Oooh, do I?" she asked sarcastically. "Thanks for the tip."

"I'm just saying."

"My dad taught me how to drive," she said, turning back to the front and thrusting the gearshift forward. "He was *very* adamant that I always look behind me, even with the back-up camera."

I snorted. "Yeah, I'm sure your dad expects the whole world to follow his rules."

She faltered the tiniest bit, then tried to pretend she hadn't. "Well, yeah, of course he does."

I couldn't decipher her tone. There was something defensive about it, but there was resentment there, too.

"Do you like him?" I asked.

She shot me a look. "Excuse me?"

"Do you like your dad?" I repeated clearly, and I was surprised to find that I genuinely wanted to know the answer. Not only because I considered Rhett Calhoun and his football agenda a threat, but because I couldn't understand what made this girl tick.

Aubrey was quiet for a long moment. I expected her to tear into me for asking such an invasive question, but instead she seemed to deflate. "No one has ever asked me that before."

"Seriously? Even with your dad being Mr. Hotshot?"

"That's exactly why no one asks."

I waited, but she didn't continue.

"Wow, you *don't* like him," I said quietly.

"I didn't say that."

"You didn't have to."

She sat up straighter, gripping the steering wheel with both hands like she was trying to grasp for every last ounce of control. "Forgive me if you're the last person I want to have this conversation with, Louisa."

I registered the use of my actual name but didn't call her on it. Instead I nodded and said, "Okay. Fair."

We lapsed into silence again, until I could no longer ignore something that had been bothering me for the last hour. "Were their feelings really hurt? Emma's and Candor's?"

Aubrey didn't seem put off by the segue. Instead, she looked over at me like she was searching for something. "Wouldn't yours have been? If they had come up to Connecticut, made plans with you, and then blown you off?"

I knew she was right. The truth of it cut through me like a hot knife, searing against the shame I already felt from what had gone down with Hatch earlier.

"I feel like I can't do right by anyone lately," I said quietly. The shame grew stronger, because why was I admitting this to *her*?

"Not to be rude," Aubrey said, "but are you really trying that hard?"

"Excuse me?"

She gave me a look. "Are you?"

"Yeah, actually, I am," I croaked, caught somewhere between anger and hurt. "I'm trying *extremely* hard to roll with all the chaos life has been throwing my way. I just came out, like, two months ago, and then I got called down here because my uncle died way before I was ready to face everyone, and my whole family is acting like being gay is some kind of fairy-tale thing I made up, and I somehow inherited a real live business that people depend on to feel safe and included, and now I have to figure out how to save it—"

"I, I, I, I, I," Aubrey rattled off. "Do you hear yourself? 'Oh, poor me, my uncle died before *I* was ready to deal with people.' Do you truly think everything revolves around you?"

"Don't you dare judge me for—"

"I *am* judging you," she said, jerking the steering wheel onto Main Street. "You have all these people who care about you, you've got nothing stopping you from living out and proud all summer, you're on this cool new adventure with the bar, and yet here you are feeling sorry for yourself. I get that you're going through a hard time, but so is everyone else at any given moment, and you're choosing not to see that because you're too wrapped up in your own shit. You may think I have a stick up my ass, but I'll tell you what, I'd rather have a stick than my own head."

I fell back against the seat, my mouth open in protest. I wanted to retaliate, to scream and yell and put her in her place like I'd done in the kitchen earlier, but the words got stuck on my tongue. Suddenly I was flipping back through every conversation from the past week, with Dad, with Hannah, with Hatch, and I was seeing things in a new light. My body felt molten, like I had no choice but to sit there in the cushioned leather seat and digest what Aubrey was saying, even if I hated her for it.

"Well?" Aubrey said after a heavy minute. Her voice was shrill, almost self-conscious. "Aren't you going to throw some vicious response my way?"

"I . . ." I blinked over at her, still reeling. The question rushed out before I could sit with it. "Am I a selfish person?"

Aubrey swung the car into Dad's driveway. She thrust the gearshift into park, lowered the music, and looked intently at me. "You're not selfish, you're self-involved. There's a difference." She paused. "You can't see past your own nose, Scrooge. It's what I was trying to tell you earlier."

We fell quiet. I understood that she was letting me have my reckoning, and I took it, slumping back against the headrest with my eyes on the stars.

"I'm probably going to regret saying this . . ." I began, "but I think you might be right."

"Yes, I usually am," she said, like it was obvious.

"I don't mean to be self-involved. It's just . . . ever since I came out, and especially since I came back here . . . it's like everything has felt so *raw*. Like I've scooped out my innards and laid them on the table, and everybody can walk up and take a look, and I just have to stand there and hope they'll be kind about it."

The car was absolutely silent. Bullfrogs croaked in the distance, playing off the cicadas. Aubrey bent her head and twisted a ring on her finger.

"I'm sorry you feel like that," she said finally. The porch light reflected off her eyes: a slash of seashell blue. "Have you told Emma and Candor?"

"No. I don't know if they'd get it. I mean, you heard them fawning over Asa tonight."

"Yeah . . . ," she said, biting her lip. "I'm sorry about that."

I looked at her. "Why did you lie to them?"

She blinked. "What?"

"About Asa asking you out. You told them nothing happened."

Even in the dark, I could see the blush settle high on her cheeks. "It wasn't a lie. It was just . . . an omission."

I thought of my family, omitting the truth about Uncle George's sexuality. Hatch, omitting the truth about the football program buying the land. "An omission is still a lie."

Aubrey looked away from me. "There are just . . . some things I'm not ready to talk about yet."

I studied her. What kind of secrets was this girl holding close?

"It's late," Aubrey said pointedly.

I recognized the dismissal for what it was. "Right. Well . . . thank you for the ride." I looked sideways at her. "See? I do have *some* manners."

"Even Satan was an angel once," she quipped, and despite myself, I laughed.

10
HAIR OF THE DOG

"Well, look what the cat dragged in," Hannah said when I entered the bar the next day. "Because you'd have to be dragged, for sure. Certainly the cat couldn't make you do anything unless it was your idea."

"Good afternoon to you, too."

She smiled. "How are you feeling?"

"Better." I swallowed and met her eyes. "Thank you."

She winked, then shook what looked like a seasoning packet. "Wanna learn how to make a Bloody Mary? Rook is in dire need of one."

Rook raised a lone palm from where they lay face down on the bar top. They were clearly hungover as all hell.

"Yikes," I said sympathetically. "Rough night, Rook? Too much line dancing?"

They merely groaned in response.

Hannah and I mixed Bloody Marys for Rook and a few other patrons who trickled in. Then I went about my chores as diligently as possible, scooping the litter box, sweeping the hallway, and breaking down boxes from the morning's delivery. When I couldn't find anything else to clean, I walked along the walls and straightened each and every picture on the wood paneling.

"Any idea when Hatch will be in?" I asked eventually.

Hannah looked up from her personal laptop. She was taking advantage of the afternoon lull by catching up on wedding tasks from Baker's color-coordinated spreadsheet. "Not sure. Why?"

I shrugged. "Just wondering."

The truth was I'd been thinking about Hatch all day, picturing the rage on his face when he'd caught me holding his photo of Uncle George. I kept hearing Hannah's voice in my head: *You don't know what it cost him*. Her voice was followed by Aubrey's: *You can't see past your own nose, Scrooge*.

What was it about Hatch that I wasn't letting myself see?

The hours went on. Hannah got bored and popped an old VHS tape into the box TV, and we watched *Steel Magnolias* as patrons filtered in and out. Every time the door opened, I braced myself to encounter Hatch—but he never showed up.

Midas stomped in just before the evening rush, gracing us with a bad mood because he'd slipped off his bike. Hannah fetched the first aid kit and dotted antibiotic cream on his knee while Midas whined and cursed at her.

"You are an evil, pain-inflicting daughter of darkness!" he squealed.

"You're welcome, sweetie," Hannah replied, slapping a My Little Pony bandage over his torn skin.

Much later, after Hannah had clocked out and it was only Midas and me behind the bar, I got tired of waiting for Hatch and decided to pick Midas's brain about the matter. Maybe hearing his perspective would shed more light on the parts of Hatch and Uncle George that I didn't understand.

"Can I ask you something?" I muttered during a lull. "Did you know George well?"

Midas's hands slipped on the oranges he was peeling, but he pretended they hadn't. "I wouldn't say *well*. Not like Hannah and Hatch knew him." He paused. "But yeah, I knew him."

"What was he like?"

Midas frowned. "I thought he was your uncle."

"He was. But I didn't know him in this context."

Midas allowed that to settle. He became pensive in a way I hadn't seen before, his hands intent on the orange peeler.

"He was cool," he said finally. "I only knew him for a year or so, but I liked him."

I waited, hoping for more.

"I'd heard stories about him, you know, like he was this big persona who thought his shit didn't stink, so I kinda went into this job thinking I wouldn't like him. But he surprised me. He genuinely wanted to know me. He was like that with everybody, really. Wanting to know their stories, their situations. He *really* loved RuPaw. He used to bring her little Ziploc baggies of chicken bits he'd cooked at home."

I glanced at RuPaw, who was curled up in Edge's lap while he graded papers in the corner. Had she curled up with Uncle George like that? Did she miss him?

"He wasn't always good with trans stuff," Midas went on, popping discarded peels into the trash can. "Like he'd ask ignorant questions or forget to use inclusive language. But he'd always listen when I pointed it out. He tried to get better. He liked to learn." He paused, then tapped the trans flag pin on his collar. "He, uh.

He bought me this pin on a trip to Boston last year. Said he was in a bookstore and thought of me." Midas swallowed. "I haven't stopped wearing it since he died."

I gave him a moment. His body had gone very still, his palms spread over the counter as if to steady himself.

"It seems like you and Hannah have kept things going so seamlessly," I said softly. "It's hard for me to picture where Uncle George fit in here."

"Oh, definitely not. Losing him was like losing our compass. If we make it look easy, it's because we're trying to hold it together for Hatch. He acts like he's covered in armor, but he's not."

I heard the protectiveness in his tone. "You care about him."

"We *need* him. George might have been the beating heart of this place, but Hatch is the brains, the backbone. The Cricket would fall apart without him."

"What do you think about him selling this place?" I asked tentatively.

Midas shrugged. "He needs to do what's best for him."

"But what about you? Where would you go?"

"Eh, I'll land on my feet. I always do." He rinsed his hands and looked sideways at me. "Why all the questions?"

I sighed. "I don't think I've given Hatch a fair shake."

Midas shrugged. "To be fair, he hasn't given you one, either."

"I just . . . I thought I understood what Uncle George wanted me to do here. I thought he saw himself in me and wanted me to keep this place going. Keep the legacy going. But then Hatch is, like, completely uninterested in that."

Midas's brow furrowed. "What makes you say that?"

"He basically told me. Last weekend, when I met him. And it's not like I see him engaging much when he's here. He stays holed up in his office the whole time. It's hard to believe he cares."

"First of all." Midas held up a finger, and I could see that I'd pissed him off. "You've been here for, like, a week. And it's the week following his husband's funeral. I mean partner. Ex-partner. Whatever, you know what I mean. His *person.*" Midas gave me a hard look. "So you don't get to make that judgment."

I swallowed and forced myself to meet his gaze. *You can't see past your own nose, Scrooge.* "Okay. You're right."

"And you don't see a lot of the invisible work Hatch does. Payroll, taxes, liquor licenses, health codes, vendor relationships . . . the list never ends. And then there's all the stuff with this shitty old building: plumbing, internet, electric, even the garden out back—"

"Electric," I said, seizing on the word.

"Yeah, I just said that."

"No, I know, I . . ." An idea was forming in my brain, a simple thing I could do as a gesture of goodwill toward Hatch. "Midas, you're brilliant."

He blinked, clearly confused by the conversational whiplash. "I mean, yeah," he conceded. "I'm not just a handsome face. Anyway, let's talk about something else. Lecturing people exhausts me. I don't know how Hannah gets off on this stuff."

"Okay. How'd you get into bike racing?"

Midas's eyes lit up, and he chatted away until the moment we locked the doors.

It wasn't until Monday that I finally saw Hatch.

"Good morning," I said in my sunniest voice, greeting him the moment he stomped through the door.

Hatch narrowed his eyes. "It's two P.M."

"Right. Right. I just meant . . . hi. It's nice to see you."

He grunted and shoved past me, barking a quick hello at Hannah before he shut himself away in his office.

"Fuck," I said under my breath.

"It was a good try," Hannah said sympathetically. "Give him an hour, then try again."

I shook my head. "No, I need do this now." I marched after Hatch, drew to a stop in front of his door, and took a deep breath. Then I knocked.

"What?" he yelled.

I knocked again.

"Jesus Christ, come in already!"

I opened the door carefully. "Sorry, I just didn't want to barge in—"

"Oh, suddenly you care about privacy?" he asked cuttingly. He leaned back in his chair and swiveled to face me. "What is it you want, Wade?"

I took another deep breath and steeled myself. "I owe you an apology."

Silence.

"I shouldn't have gone through your . . . things," I went on. "It was disrespectful, and it wasn't my place, and I'm sorry."

Hatch stared at me, his chest moving slowly up and down, his piercing blue eyes going right through me.

"And also . . . I called the electrician. About their overdue visit. Three times, actually. I didn't get anyone, but I left messages, and I'll try again when—"

"You didn't call your grandfather?" Hatch interrupted. He didn't sound angry, but somehow the question felt like a test.

I chewed my lip. "I don't exactly . . . *like* my grandfather. And I don't trust him."

Hatch folded his hands over his stomach. He regarded me thoughtfully. "Something you and I have in common. And something George and I disagreed on. He always saw the best in people."

I nodded. "I, um . . . I'll keep calling."

Hatch gave me a curt nod of his own. "You do that, Wade." He paused. "And, uh. Whatever you're doing to make the staff and patrons like you . . . well . . . keep it up."

I tried in vain to tamp down my smile as I went back to work.

The week settled into its usual rhythm. We ordered more decorations for the upcoming Pride party and Midas fixed the office printer while Hannah tested a potential Bacardi cocktail. When Hatch arrived each day, he grunted hello and asked about inventory, but otherwise he left us alone. I considered it a win that he occasionally looked in my direction without his eyes popping.

"We had a dunk tank for Pride last year," Midas told me. "George's idea. He kept going on about how everybody would have so much fun, but I think *he* had the most fun. He refused to go in himself but kept throwing every time Hatch or me was in there. It was literally the only time I've seen his quarterback skills."

"He wouldn't let me sit up there," Hannah said with a roll of her eyes. "Kept saying it was rude to 'dunk a lady.'"

"You weren't exactly pushing him on that," Midas pointed out.

"Well, my hair looked good that day."

"So did *mine*."

"Yeah, but mine looked better."

"Shut up and go work on your wedding invitations before I tell Baker you've been slacking."

"You wouldn't dare."

"Of course I would."

Baker had been frequenting the Cricket more often lately. Hannah claimed it was because they had so much wedding coordination to do, but I suspected she was just trying to show emotional support for Hannah and Hatch in the wake of losing George. Every time Baker walked in the door, I immediately poured her a Diet Coke with lime over ice, which I'd learned was her preferred drink. Hannah noticed and told me I was an incorrigible little suck-up who was angling for an older woman.

"Yeah, yeah, she gets it, Louisa, stop mooning over her," Hannah griped as I handed over Baker's drink one afternoon.

I met Baker's eyes over the top of Hannah's head. "For the record, I'm not into you," I said matter-of-factly. "No offense."

Baker took this in stride. "I know," she said, rolling her eyes like Hannah was a particularly unruly pet that we shared custody of. "Hannah thinks everyone has a thing for me."

"Well, *yeah*," Hannah said emphatically, brushing a strand of hair from Baker's eyes. "Have you seen you?"

Baker patted Hannah's knee and went back to focusing on the list in front of her. "Okay, what about Nathan?"

Hannah grimaced. "I love your brother, but he doesn't have the same gravitas as George."

"Rude," Baker said flippantly, but she crossed Nathan's name off her list.

They were talking about a replacement for their wedding officiant. Hannah seemed rather morose about the whole thing, which was probably why she kept snarking at me; Baker, on the other hand, was businesslike about it. "We can't change what happened, honey," she kept saying, rubbing Hannah's back. "George would want us to keep going."

"I know, I know," Hannah grumbled, rattling the ice cubes in her Coke.

When Hatch entered the room, he greeted Baker with a stiff hug. "What's wrong with her?" he asked. My back went up, assuming he was referring to me, but then I saw he was focused on Hannah.

"Trying to choose our wedding officiant," Baker said meaningfully.

A shadow passed over Hatch's face, but he quickly got hold of himself. "Hmph."

"Maybe you should do it, Hatch," Baker said in a lightly teasing voice. She glanced at Hannah, clearly hoping the joke would rouse Hannah from her somber state.

"No chance in hell," Hatch said. "I'm not donning a penguin suit and giving some cheesy speech."

Hannah popped up, a spark coming back into her eyes. "A penguin suit? What on *earth* makes you think we'd have a black-tie wedding?"

"I met Baker's mother," Hatch said, jerking a thumb at her. "That woman screams *black-tie event*."

"You're not wrong," Baker mused.

"We're going for an outdoor, sundresses-and-chinos kind of vibe," Hannah went on. "You can wear a fishing shirt for all I care."

"I'm not doing it," Hatch said with finality.

"Fine, you grouchy old gremlin," Hannah said, sinking onto her stool again.

"Hannah," Baker said, with a tender hand on her neck. There was a sudden no-bullshit ring of *you knew this was coming* to her tone. "We can keep going through the motions here, but we both know the solution is to ask Kate."

Hannah groaned. “But she’ll totally know she was second choice! We’d already told her about asking George!”

“Yeah, and she loved that idea.” Baker paused. “And now she knows he’s gone, and I’m sure she would be honored to step up and do this for us.”

Hannah pulled her hands down her face. “You’re right. I know you’re right.”

Baker kissed her temple. “I’ll call her tonight.”

“Ughhhhh,” Hannah whined. “Thank you.”

“You’re a good partner, Baker,” Hatch said unexpectedly.

Baker looked at him, touched. “Thank you, Hatch.”

Hatch seemed to realize everyone was looking at him fondly, because he squirmed and retreated behind the bar top. “I just figure, you know, it takes a special lady to put up with *this* one.” He jabbed a finger in Hannah’s direction.

“I love you, too, asshole,” Hannah shot back. “Now how ’bout you pour my *lady* another Diet Coke?”

11
SLEEPOVER

That Friday, I left the bar early so I could spend time with Emma and Candor before the weekly field party. I felt a pang about missing Frisky Friday—and I really wanted a redo from the previous weekend—but I knew it was more important to prioritize my friends, especially in light of my reckoning with Aubrey.

We grabbed a late dinner at the barbecue joint on Main Street. I was the first to arrive, tucking the Cadillac into a parking spot out front, shaking my hair loose from the messy bun I'd worn while bartending. My feet were aching from a long shift, but the coral sunset sky took my mind off the discomfort.

Emma, Candor, and Aubrey arrived together. I didn't even protest Aubrey's presence this time; I had expected it and, to my surprise, I was getting used to it. Emma slid into the booth first, facing me. I fully expected Aubrey to take the spot next to her, but she pivoted to my side of the table.

"Scoot over, Scrooge," she said bossily, already sliding in next to me.

"I didn't hear a 'please,'" I said, just to be a pest.

"*Please*," she said with a pointed look. Her eyes popped against her blue linen shirt. The V-neck cut showed off the freckles on her chest. I pretended not to notice.

We ordered pulled pork plates with baked beans, fried okra, and sweet potato soufflé. Emma downed three sweet teas while Aubrey and Candor got into a heated debate about whether tomato- or mustard-based barbecue sauce was better. I splurged on pecan pie for dessert and couldn't decide what was more delicious: the pie or the look on Aubrey's face when I told her she could have a bite only if she said the word *fuck* in public. She hemmed and hawed before muttering "I'm not fucking doing that," and we all laughed as I slid the entire dessert plate her way.

We swung by Dad's house so I could drop the Caddy off, and then we piled into the Audi and drove out to the farm with the top down. It was another clear, cloudless night and the sky stretched ahead of us in every direction. We parked at the bonfire, drank our way through a box of cold beers (and in Aubrey's case, seltzer water), and squeezed Candor's arm when one of the County High boys came over to chat her up. When Asa tried to catch Aubrey's eye, I turned my body to block him from view. Aubrey noticed and gave me a deep, searching frown like she was recalculating everything she understood to be true.

Later, when we were drunk, we made a group trip to the bathroom and locked ourselves inside, shrieking and giggling at the sight of an inflatable lawn decoration that one of the Waldron boys had posed inside the bathtub. It was the Rustin mascot, a tiger wearing a straw hat, and Candor grabbed him and pointed him toward us until Emma screamed and threatened to pop him with her teeth. I laughed so hard that my chest muscles hurt and I wondered how I could even explain this moment when I was telling Hannah about it later.

It was nearly one o'clock in the morning by the time we left, plopping into the Audi with bloated bellies and spinning heads. Aubrey nursed a fresh seltzer as she drove us down county roads, the wind in our hair and the moon glowing white high above us.

"Scrooge," Aubrey said at the first stoplight. Her voice swam toward me through my tipsy haze, clear and controlled and admittedly pretty. "Do you want me to drop you off, or do you wanna just hop on the sleepover train?"

I wasn't sure if I'd heard her right. I knew Emma and Candor were spending the night at her house, but I had assumed I wouldn't be invited. "You mean . . . with you guys? At your house?"

"No, with the inflatable tiger in the bathtub," she said flatly, and Candor squealed with laughter.

"You're such a dick, Cotillion," I said with a smile in my voice. "Sure, I'd love to."

For the second time this summer, I found myself in Golden Hills, Uncle George's old neighborhood. The gate attendant waved us through before Aubrey had even stopped, and we drove quietly past the looming wealthy houses with their gas lamps and waterfall features wasting money in the middle of the night.

The Calhouns' house looked stately and imperious in the dark. It wasn't the kind of home I felt peaceful coming back to, and I remembered what Aubrey had said outside Uncle George's house just last week. *Mansions have a lot of empty space.*

"All right, listen," Aubrey said as she parked the Audi. Her voice was jagged, caught somewhere between a whisper and normal volume. "My dad's probably still up and y'all are too tipsy to pull one over on him. We're gonna have to use the trellis."

"Yes!" Emma said, fist-pumping. "I love when we get to climb the trellis."

"It's gonna be harder when you're tipsy, Em," Aubrey said seriously. She turned to Candor. "Are you sober enough to help her?"

"Am I my Emma's keeper?" Candor asked solemnly. "The answer is yes, yes, I am."

"That's my Candie," Emma said, patting her knee.

Aubrey turned her eyes to me. "And what about you, Scrooge?"

"I'm fine. I can do it," I said truthfully.

"Okay. I'll get out first and disable the cameras, then I'll wave before I close the front door. That will be y'all's cue to sneak over to the trellis."

"I love being your dirty little secret," Emma said. "It's so titillating."

"Em, seriously. Be cool."

"I'm cool, Aub. I'm good."

"Just know that if y'all screw this up and get me caught"—her eyes blazed with sudden fire as she looked from Emma to Candor to me—"I will thoroughly dismember each one of you until the pieces are small enough to send in the mail."

"Jesus, Cotillion," I said with a shudder.

"That is an oddly specific threat," Emma said thoughtfully. "Do you watch a lot of *Dateline*?"

Aubrey slipped out of the car without answering. We waited for her signal, and then I followed Emma and Candor to the front-left corner of the house, where the garden trellis leaned against the wall. Candor and I popped Emma up first, then followed suit. We scampered clumsily across the roof of the garage and over to a brightly lit window, which Aubrey opened mere seconds after we reached it.

"Phew," Emma said, stumbling inside. "I thought I was gonna die, y'all."

"How'd it go with Coach?" Candor asked.

"Fine," Aubrey said in a clipped tone. She busied herself with taking her jewelry off at the vanity. "He's down there pounding bourbon and watching *Duck Dynasty*. He'll pass out in the study soon enough. Magnolia wanted to come with me, but he made her stay with him."

"Nooooo," Emma whined. "We have to save Magnolia!"

"We have to stay quiet," Aubrey said pointedly.

"Yeah, yeah." Emma yawned and flopped backward onto the canopy bed. "Whose turn is it for the air mattress?"

"Y'all can have the bed. I'm not tired yet." Aubrey caught my eye in the vanity mirror. "You can share with them, Louisa, if you don't mind squeezing. I actually kind of enjoy the air mattress."

"Oh," I said, surprised by the offer. "Thank you."

"Thanks, Aub," Candor said, hugging her from behind. She spun to give me a hug, too, nestling her head into my shoulder. "Lou, can we come to the Cricket soon? It's been months since you took it over."

I laughed into her hair as a warm glow spread over me. "It's been, like, two weeks. But yeah, I'd love for you to come."

"Marvelous," she mumbled sleepily. And without further ado, she tugged off her shorts and sandals and burrowed into the bed with Emma.

"What are you gonna do?" I asked Aubrey, watching her yank her fancy European sneakers off and line them up by her closet.

I was curious about what she did to wind down at the end of the night.

"Probably sit on the garage," she said routinely.

I blinked. "Wait. Really?"

She must have realized how strange it sounded, because she laughed self-consciously and glanced away. Her voice fell to a whisper. "Yeah, no, it's kind of my favorite thing about this house." She chewed her lip before looking me in the eye. "Did you want to join me?"

And without waiting for my answer, she grabbed a box of High Noons from a hiding spot in her closet and disappeared through the window.

We sat side by side on the roof of the garage, gazing out over the treetops, our bare feet splayed in front of us. Aubrey's pedicure was rose-pink and perfectly maintained, whereas mine was UConn blue and chipping from neglect. The difference was all too fitting. Aubrey pulled two High Noons from the box, handed one to me, and cracked hers open with the air of someone settling in after a long day.

"I thought you didn't drink," I said.

"I don't drink in public," she corrected, as if nothing more needed to be said.

"Why not?"

She looked at me like I was being deliberately obtuse. "Don't you ever worry about losing control? Revealing parts of yourself you don't want other people to see?"

I studied her intently, not caring that I was being obvious about it. "You keep a lot of things hidden, don't you?"

"Doesn't everyone? Don't you?"

I thought about it. "Not anymore."

Aubrey took a long swig of her drink. "Tell me about the bar," she demanded in a tone that meant she was tired of my probing questions.

"The bar," I repeated, smirking. "I thought you were against the bar."

"I'm not *against the bar*, I just thought your plan was half-baked and impulsive."

"Right, right, thanks so much. To answer your question, the bar is amazing. Better than I even thought it would be."

Aubrey looked expectantly at me, waiting for me to say more.

"Well . . ." I went on, feeling slightly self-conscious beneath her gaze, "the people are just . . . I mean, it's humans of every size, shape, skin tone, personality . . . but they're all just so *themselves*. The other day, this real tough-looking old butch stopped me on my way to the bathroom, and I thought she was ready to run me over with her motorcycle, but she just grabbed my wrist and asked, 'Can I fix that tag on your shirt, honey?' and it was just—it was really sweet."

Aubrey smiled. It was the first real, unguarded smile I had seen from her, and I wondered if this was the Aubrey my friends were used to being around. "I imagine the outfits are pretty great."

"Understatement. Just incredible style choices all around. Nail art on people of every gender. Wigs and tutus and glitter everywhere. This one guy that I work with, he has a tattoo of an oak tree winding all the way up his arm." I could almost feel Midas sitting there, glowing with pride. "And it's just so welcoming. Like, sickeningly welcoming. A fucking chimera could stroll in and they'd all line up to hug them."

Aubrey snorted. "I used the word *chimera* a few weeks ago and Emma was like, 'You mean those grumpy little dogs?'"

"She has an amazing brain."

"She does."

"Anyway, it just . . . it feels like I can be *me*."

When I looked up, I caught a hint of longing on Aubrey's face, but she quickly straightened her expression and took another long gulp of her drink.

"What?" I asked.

"No, nothing, just . . ." She shook it off, but I could tell she had let her veneer slip without meaning to. My stomach gave the tiniest flip, as if it recognized something I hadn't consciously identified yet.

"I just wish I had a place like that," Aubrey finished. "That's all."

"You should come sometime. With Emma and Candor."

"Oh . . . I don't know. I have to be really purposeful about where I go, which local businesses I support . . ."

"You sound like a politician."

"I know," she said wryly. "But it matters, you know. Where people see me. How they see me."

I read between the lines. "Your dad doesn't like queer people, does he?"

The set of her mouth told me the answer. "He likes to use that classic line, like, 'It's none of my business what adults do behind closed doors, but I don't want to hear about it.'"

"Charming."

"He *is*, actually. At least to other people. That's the problem."

I took this in. "Did my uncle like him?"

She shrugged. "Impossible to say. He was always nice to my dad, but, like . . ." She trailed off, her eyebrows knitting together in thought. I could see the alcohol starting to take effect: Her cobalt irises had gone dark and her accent was becoming more Southern by the second.

"What?" I prompted.

"Nothing, just . . . obviously I didn't know George well, but I found him hard to read. I could never figure out his real feelings. He always seemed like he was playing the part of who people thought he should be."

My neck prickled. "You have no idea."

She turned to face me. "Do you miss him?"

I met her eyes, then looked quickly away. "You want to know something awful? I *don't* really miss him. Not properly. I don't think I'm grieving, like, at all. All these people . . . They worshipped him. They *loved* him. And I barely feel that way at all. It's almost like he's a concept in my head. Like, I can remember the smell of his aftershave, and I can list off facts like *Yeah, he liked martinis* or *He swam laps at the YMCA every morning*, but I don't feel like I *knew* him like everyone else did. I'm almost jealous of them. Of you."

Aubrey took this in, her eyes still steady on me. "I don't think it's awful."

I looked at her, surprised.

"It's honest," she said softly. "And maybe the only real way to honor someone when they're gone is to be honest about where it leaves us."

A lump rose in my throat. I chugged my drink to try to swallow it away. "Um. Thank you for allowing me to spend the night."

She laughed through her nose. "I didn't *allow* you, I invited you."

"Same thing. I just . . . I'm sorry I was such a dick to you. When we met."

Aubrey shifted, wrapping her arms around her knees. "Yeah. That was . . . not what I had hoped it would be. I really wanted to be your friend."

"You did? Why?"

She ignored the question. "I'm just glad we've gotten to know each other since then."

"Yeah, me too."

We lapsed into silence, the nighttime sounds filling the space between us. I finished my drink just as Aubrey finished hers. She put both empty cans back in the box and explained she would throw them away tomorrow.

When we slipped back through the window, Aubrey didn't even bother to set up the air mattress. She grabbed an old fuzzy blanket from the closet and curled up on the floor. I crawled into bed next to Candor, quietly pushing her toward the middle, and turned on my side so I could just see the silhouette of Aubrey's hair in the moonlight. I had the strangest urge to tuck it away.

12
PRIDE

"Enough standing around—we have party prep to do. Can you run out to my car and grab the streamers?"

And that's how our prep for the Pride party started. It was only too perfect that the anniversary of the Stonewall riots fell on a weekend this year. We scrubbed the bar top to bottom and hung rainbow streamers from every free surface. Midas even painted a giant watercolor portrait of Marsha P. Johnson that we mounted next to the bathrooms. It wasn't *good*, exactly, but it was so earnest and reverent that it took my breath away.

"Special delivery," Baker said on Saturday afternoon, breezing into the bar in her veterinary scrubs. She pulled a package from her tote bag and shot an excited look at Hannah. "Look what came."

"Finally!" Hannah said, dropping the broom. "Louisa, c'mere a sec."

I joined them at the bar top, where Baker had placed the beaten-up plastic package. It contained something lumpy and soft. "Go ahead," she said, gesturing to me.

"It's for me?"

"Just a silly little something," Hannah said, but I could tell from her tone that she was chomping at the bit for me to open it.

I ripped the package open and pulled out the cloth item inside. It was a big navy T-shirt. I flipped it around to see the front and—

"Oh my god. You *didn't*."

It was a sketch outline of a state that I assumed to be South Dakota, but the caption read SOUTH DAQUEERTA in bold, rainbow lettering.

"This is the stupidest, most amazing thing I've ever seen, you assholes. Where the hell did you find this?"

"That's a trade secret," Hannah said.

"Etsy," Baker said over her.

I pulled the shirt over my head. It was snug with my button-down beneath it, but I knew it would fit perfectly on its own. "How do I look?"

"Absurd," Hannah complimented.

"I'm gonna wear it tonight."

"Yes, I was hoping you would!" Hannah high-fived Baker like it was the best thing they'd ever done together.

"Thank you so much."

"You're very welcome," Baker said warmly.

"It was four hundred dollars," Hannah said dryly. "We'll take cash."

Baker elbowed her so she'd shut up.

Hatch rounded the corner and drew up short at the sight of us. "Am I interrupting a lesbian convention?"

Hannah didn't even look up. "No, that's at Home Depot later. What do you think of Lou's shirt?"

I turned and spread my arms wide for Hatch to see, too giddy to care what he thought.

"What am I looking at," he asked in a flat voice.

"Da-*queer*-ta. *Queer*-ta, Hatch! Come on," Hannah said in a put-upon voice.

"Otis is on his way," Hatch said, rolling right over our conversation. "He wants to help set up."

I raised my eyebrows. "You two made up?"

"Don't push your luck, Wade."

"Not to be rude," Hannah interjected, "but how exactly is *Otis* going to help us? He'll just get in the way."

"He's bringing a piñata. Won't shut up about it." Hatch flicked his fingers over the three of us. "Just help him however he needs."

"You're pawning him off on us?"

"I'm *informing* my *employees* about another *task*."

"Not an employee," Baker pointed out, though she rounded the counter and poured herself a fountain Diet Coke.

A few minutes later, Otis Penny burst through the door with the biggest piñata I'd ever seen. It looked more like a parade float than a party accessory.

"The fuck," Midas muttered under his breath.

"Party City!" Otis yelled, as if we were all dying to know. "Did you know such a business existed?"

"Yes," we said in unison.

"Here, Lou-ella, take this," Otis said, pushing the gigantic piñata into my arms. "Hatch, how about a Mule before we get to work?"

"I already made it, Mr. Penny," Midas said, dropping a lime on the finished concoction.

"Thank you, handsome," Otis said suavely. I wondered if he had any clue what Midas's name was.

"Well, Otis," Hatch said, "I'll leave you to it. The girls and Midas can help with the piñata."

"Don't you want to help me get it up?" Otis asked sincerely, and Hannah snickered into her hand.

Hatch ignored her. "One more thing. The mechanical bull will be here in forty-five minutes."

Hannah, Baker, Midas, and I froze.

"Ex-*cuse*?" Midas asked.

"I told y'all that," Hatch said cagily.

"You very well know you did not," Hannah said.

"Be on the lookout. They're coming from Atlanta, big truck, big trailer. Make sure there's room in the parking lot."

I was still digesting this sudden information, but Hannah was jumping with questions. "How big is this thing, exactly? Where are we supposed to put it? And why are they coming from Atlanta? Nobody closer had a mechanical bull?"

Hatch gave her a hard look. "These things come with mandatory attendants. Nonnegotiable, for safety reasons. I wanna make sure we're getting attendants we can trust. If we're gonna have fun, it better be safe."

I understood what he meant by *safe*. It wasn't liability Hatch was worried about: It was bigotry. He wanted his patrons to know beyond a doubt that they could be their full authentic selves in front of the attendants.

"And we can trust this company?" Midas asked warily.

"A guy I know vouched for them," Hatch said vaguely. "Owner has a trans daughter."

"It's all in the family, then," Hannah said. She and Baker gave him a fond, appreciative smile.

Hatch seemed to recoil from it. "Get back to work," he grumbled, marching back to his office.

Forty minutes later, with the piñata successfully hung up in a far corner, we stood outside and watched for the mechanical bull. Hannah kept dithering about the parking spaces, worrying she needed to move her car again. Baker had scooped a glass full of ice cubes into her watered-down Diet Coke and was pressing it against her heat-flushed face. Midas bounced on his tiptoes and rolled his shirtsleeves under his armpits. Even Otis had come outside to join us, though he seemed ready to sneak back inside, judging by the way he kept mopping his bald head with his embroidered handkerchief.

At last, a monstrous navy truck slowed and pulled into the driveway, towing a gigantic metal trailer that rattled and clanged as it made its way to our front door. Two white men jumped out of the cab, a ruddy-faced young one and a hound-like older guy with a belly that hung low over his jeans.

"This the Freaky Cricket?" the older man asked, adjusting his waistline.

Hannah rushed to shake his hand. "Frisky! Yes! Welcome!"

The younger guy blinked in the sunlight, his cowboy boots scraping against the pavement. Both Otis and Midas eyed him with interest.

"Are you Marion Hatchet?" the older man went on.

"No, he's in his office, I'll grab him—"

"Just show me the layout of the place, if you don't mind, and we'll figure out how to get the old girl inside."

It was a long process. Our doors remained open, letting the sweltering heat inside as the two men hurried back and forth to the trailer, bringing tools, tarps, all kinds of equipment. Hatch emerged from the office to shake the owner's hand and sign the paperwork, then disappeared again. The rest of us tried to stay out of the way and busy ourselves with other tasks, except for Midas, who kept asking if any extra muscle was needed.

"I've been doubling down on arm day," he told the younger guy, whose named we learned was Brian.

An hour later, the mechanical bull was finally set up and ready to go. She took up so much space that I worried our patrons would resent the loss of the dance floor, but Hatch didn't seem bothered. His blue eyes were bright in a way I'd never seen before.

"What's her name?" Hannah asked, running a hand over the bull's fake hide.

The guy named Brian squinted at her. "She dunn have a name."

"Well-she-needs-one!" Hannah said in a rush. She raced across the bar and grabbed Baker by the shoulders. "Babe. The mechanical bull. What's her name?"

"Am I supposed to know?"

"Help me think of one!"

I found myself caught up in Hannah's giddiness, but Baker must have been used to it, because her countenance didn't change. She furrowed her brow, considering the task, looking more like an analyst than a bar patron.

"Bull-bra Streisand," Hannah rattled aloud. "James Bull-dwin. Katharine Hep-bull."

"Let's give the puns a rest," Baker said easily, and Hannah rolled her eyes.

"She never had a name before," Brian said uncertainly.

"A travesty," Hannah muttered.

"Be nice," Midas said through his teeth, shooting a clandestine look at Brian.

"All right," Baker said finally. "Her name is . . . Shane." She paused. "Because everyone gets a ride."

There was a shimmer of a moment while the joke registered for Hannah, and then she burst into raucous laughter and shook Baker delightedly. "Oh my god, I love you. Genius. No notes. Marry me?" She kissed Baker and twirled away.

"What is she *on*?" I asked.

Baker shrugged. "Vibes."

"Who is Shane?"

Baker took a leisurely sip of her fresh Diet Coke and smacked her lips before she answered. "You need to watch *The L Word*, kiddo."

In the opposite corner, Hatch was propped on a step stool with more rainbow streamers in his hands. He seemed oblivious to Hannah's hyperactivity, or maybe just immune to it. He was trying to juggle the streamers in one hand and the adhesive tape in the other.

"Here," I said, appearing at his shoulder and ripping off a strip of tape.

"I got it, thanks," Hatch said gruffly, ignoring my proffered piece of tape.

I clucked my tongue. "Otis Penny is right. You are one stubborn old queen."

"Skedaddle," Hatch said, shooing me. "Let the grown-ups work."

"I want to help *somehow*."

"Is Ru's litter box clean?"

I grumbled and shuffled off to empty Her Highness's bathroom, but not before Hannah called, "Oh, and while you're at it, see if you can wrangle her into her dress!"

The evening went on like that, a series of tasks that seemed to roll together. Otis kept offering to buy Brian a drink while the rest of us worked. Midas one-upped him by hand delivering a beer to Brian and assuring him it was on the house. When Baker announced she was dipping out to change her outfit and walk the dog, Hatch slipped her his credit card. "Mind to pick up dinner for the whole staff?"

Baker smiled. "You got it."

"Hannah, go on and get everyone's orders. You can text them to your better half."

Hannah strode over and peered at the credit card in Baker's hand. "Ooh, AmEx, fancy. Bake, make a copy of this so we can extend the bar at our reception."

"Very funny," Hatch gruffed. "Ralph?" he asked the older guy. "Brian? You want dinner, on me?"

"That'd be nice," the older man answered.

By the time Baker returned—now wearing a cream lace tank top that Hannah couldn't take her eyes off of—we had finished setting up and were ready to open. We sat haphazardly on the freshly polished floor and passed around the takeout cartons from Tambrie's, digging our hands into fried chicken, potato salad, fried okra, and corn bread. When Midas ended up with stray mayonnaise on his cheek, Brian leaned forward and swiped it away with his thumb. Midas froze, his face flushing all the way to his hair. Otis Penny scowled.

It was the best night of my life.

Our patrons showed up with full wallets and eager grins. Their eyes lit up when they spotted the mechanical bull, and already there was a waiting list to have a turn riding Shane. People were dressed in every style imaginable, with as much or as little clothing as possible, in every color, texture, pattern, and gender-bending form. A group of Rustin students, living in town for the summer, passed out glitter on the dance floor. Soon everyone had shimmers of blue, green, and orange across their eyelids and down their cheeks. The music pounded with a mix of crowd pleasers from every decade, everything from Donna Summer to Sabrina Carpenter. Midas mixed drinks with the speed of a New York bartender on cocaine. Hannah actually stepped away from her duties to dance with Baker in the middle of the crowded room, her hands wandering, her eyes glassy from the two Aperol spritzes she had already downed.

I assisted Midas behind the bar, trying to anticipate when he would need a lime wedge, a clean glass, a scoop of ice cubes. We fell into an easy rhythm as more and more patrons poured into the space, until the room was so crowded that it felt like a sauna. My temples were sweating and dark rings appeared on my new T-shirt, but I couldn't get enough of this moment, this wild, pulsing heartbeat of community and joy. Even RuPaw seemed happy, perched on the old TV stand high above the bar top, her rainbow dress sparkling in the dim light.

When Midas announced he needed a break—which I suspected had something to do with Brian taking five for a cigarette—I stepped up to take his place at the bar top. The night had settled into an easy, predictable thrum and patrons were coming for drinks one at a time. Most people were hung up on the person currently riding Shane—a lanky, attractive Middle Eastern grad student with a streak of pink dye in their hair. They had managed to ride the bull for a full minute now, and the crowd's delighted screams had reached a fever pitch.

I was catching my breath when a gorgeous, dark-eyed Latina approached the bar, hastily stuffing a vape into her pocket. I recognized her as one of Hannah's best friends, Maria Paula. Next to her was her fiancée—Brooke, if I remembered right—who had the pretty, approachable girl-next-door look of everyone's favorite babysitter.

"So Hannah said there's fresh coffee so I was thinking I'd have an espresso martini," Maria Paula said in a rush.

"Oh," I said, taken aback. "Um. Yeah, I don't know how to make—"

"I've got it." She skittered around the bar and went straight for the vodka without waiting for my response.

"I don't know if—" I began, but her fiancée interrupted me.

"She'll do it whether you want her to or not," Brooke said, adjusting her glasses. "You can just ring us up for twenty dollars, if that sounds good. That's what Hannah usually does."

I looked at her, bewildered, then back to Maria Paula, who was already fixing two drinks in our finest martini glasses. Her massive diamond ring reflected the dim lights like some kind of homing beacon.

"Er—okay," I said uncertainly. I did as Brooke suggested and charged them $20. She handed me her credit card and waited for me to slide the receipt across the counter to her. Maria Paula seemed completely oblivious to the exchange; she was taste-testing the espresso martinis like some kind of cocktail sommelier.

"Thanks, Louisa," Brooke chirped happily. She slid the receipt back to me and I saw that she'd tipped me an excessive $10. "Hey, you should come to one of our pool parties! We call them 'coven meetings.'"

I blushed. I had no idea how these pretty older women knew my name, and I was flattered to be invited to hang out with them. My brain latched on to *Lesbians in bathing suits* for a full thirty seconds before I regained my composure.

"When are you playing Taylor Swift?" Maria Paula asked after a long pull from her espresso martini. She gestured at the ceiling to indicate the Shaboozey song booming from the speakers. "You *will* play her, right? Because otherwise I'll fight."

I stared at her small frame. She was barely five feet tall. "Um. Midas controls the music. He stepped out for a second."

"I'm on it." She zipped away with the martini glass teetering in her hand, Brooke holding tightly to the other.

I was in the middle of mixing a White Russian for Claudia when there was a sudden rush to the bar. It appeared Ralph had joined Brian outside for a break, and the resulting lull in the mechanical bull line seemed to signal that it was time for everyone to get a refill. People jostled for spots at the counter, all of them trying to catch my attention, shouting so loudly that my head spun. I had to lean my ear forward to hear them scream VODKA SODA WITH A SPLASH OF PINEAPPLE, their breath hot on my skin, their eyes glassy but keen. One impatient patron tapped the edge of his credit card on the counter over and over, a staccato reminder that I wasn't delivering at the pace he was used to. When I finally took his card and went to run it through the POS system, my elbow knocked over an entire pint glass of beer.

"Come on!" he yelled. "We're missing Whitney!" He jabbed a stubby finger toward the ceiling, where the unmistakable sounds of "I Wanna Dance with Somebody" blared from the speakers.

"I'm s—" I started to say, but then someone appeared beside me.

"That's enough," Hatch growled. "You want to be rude, you can take your business elsewhere."

The guy wilted. I slid his receipt over and let him sign in silence.

"Scoot over," Hatch told me. "Keep mixing. We'll wipe that up after the rush."

His hands began to move as fluidly as a dance: pouring, squeezing, sliding, swiping. It was the practiced rhythm of a true bartender, even down to the way he stacked pint glasses right to their tipping point, knowing exactly how much pressure they could hold. I hustled to keep up, filling orders at half the rate he was. Within five minutes, the rush had completely cleared.

Hatch let out a routine exhale and tossed me the rag to wipe up the spilled beer. He took a swig of water, wiped his mouth on his wrist, and cast his eyes on me. "Not bad," he allowed. "Call for help next time."

I nodded. "I will."

Hatch poured two lemon drop shots and handed one to me. Wordlessly, he raised his glass and waited for me to mirror him. I held my shot glass across from his, unable to tell whether I was being rewarded or hazed. We took the shots together, Hatch downing his like a champ while I choked and pawed at my watery eyes.

Then he slipped away, leaving me dazed and inordinately pleased with his feedback. I understood it was the best I could hope for.

I served the next customers who stepped up—Marc and Joe, sauvignon blanc—and when I next saw Hatch, he was lurking in the corner, transfixed by his patrons enjoying the mechanical bull, the ghost of a smile barely visible on his face.

When Midas returned, he had a shit-eating grin on his face.

"You didn't," I said.

"Oh, but I did," he singsonged. He looked across the bar and winked at Brian, who flushed red.

"Wow. You have game."

"Of course I do." He swirled a spoon around the whiskey sour in his hand. "Hatch told me you took a lemon drop shot."

I shook my head, still trying to make sense of it. "He offered it to me. With no catch. Like . . . he was *nice*."

Midas laughed. "I've told you, Hatch is a good guy." He handed the whiskey sour to me, and when I eyed it with trepidation, he laughed again. "You've already had a bite of the apple, sweetness. Might as well go all in."

I smirked and took the proffered drink.

"And now . . . ," Midas drawled with a glint in his eye, "I think it's time you took a ride on the bull."

"Dude. No way."

"Hannah's up next. At least go cheer her on."

"You just want me to keep her occupied so she doesn't notice you flirting with Brian."

"She can notice that all she wants. Doesn't mean I'm gonna stop." He waggled his eyebrows, then his tone became serious. "Come on, freshman, go have some fun."

He shoved me away from the counter. I smiled gratefully at him, took a huge sip of the whiskey sour, and ran off to enjoy the night.

Hours passed. Hannah fell off the mechanical bull three times. Baker managed to stay on for forty-five seconds while Hannah screamed to anyone who would listen that her fiancée was the sexiest woman on earth. I took two turns of my own, falling off within five seconds the first time, then fifteen seconds the next. My knee bled from where I scraped it on the bouncy tarp, but when Brian rushed to help me up, I laughed uncontrollably and assured him I was fine.

And then we danced. Song after song after song, disco lights reflecting on the walls, glitter blooming in the air like stardust. People I didn't know wrapped feather boas around my neck and shimmied me into their open arms. Edge appeared out of nowhere and did a passable impression of the robot. Brooke hoisted Maria Paula onto her shoulders and tried to chicken fight another lesbian couple until Hannah, drunk as a skunk, yelled at them to quit. I sneaked off to the bar for another lemon drop shot, and then another, until Midas had had enough and refused to serve me anything but Coke.

And everywhere I looked were beautiful people. College girls who held my gaze and smiled soft, beckoning smiles that urged me closer. Women in the prime of their lives who shook their long locks and their ample thighs. Older women in orthopedic sneakers who were completely out of fucks to give but still brimming with swagger and lust. Femmes and butches and sporty gays and fuck-bois, trans guys in muscle tanks who proudly showed their scars, bears and gym bros and skinny dancers and choirboys, enbys with gauges and cowboy boots and tattoos and tutus. And when Ralph-the-bull-guy's daughter showed up—reportedly because her dad had texted her "Come 2 Bama u can't miss this"—she literally took people's breath away in a sequined floor-length dress that shimmered like fish scales from the old children's classic *The Rainbow Fish*. As I passed by her on my way to the bathroom, another trans woman was asking her to autograph her arm "because I need some of your magic for my own."

By two thirty A.M., Hatch had had enough. The crowd had started thinning out but the remaining partiers showed no signs of stopping. We announced last call and played "Sweet Home Alabama" three times in a row until people got the message and finally spilled outside the doors. And then it was the usual suspects: Edge and Otis and a gaggle of the old guard, hanging around with the last trickles of their drinks, shouting about how Uber was taking too long and the Cricket ought to buy its own bus.

"That's it, I'm tired, get your asses in my car," Hatch grumbled, shoving them out the door. "Penny, don't you dare bring that Mule along. Edge—no, Edge, put RuPaw down!"

"Do we have to clean up now?" I asked after Hatch had taken his delinquents home.

"Hell no," said Midas. He was dazed and exhausted, but his face was bright from having scored Brian's phone number.

"We'll clean up tum-morrow," Hannah said, bleary-eyed and slurring.

"Come on, Lou," Baker said, looping an arm around my shoulders. "I'm driving you home. And we're getting McDonald's."

I grinned and followed Baker and Hannah out to the car while Midas locked up behind us. The air was still warm and heavy and the stars were sparkling in the black sky. I opened my arms wide and took a deep breath, like I wanted to soak everything up, like I wanted every night to be like this one.

Hannah stumbled into the passenger seat, giggling. I flopped into the back seat and slumped against the headrest. Baker drove, steady and relaxed, taking the back roads like she had all the time in the world. Hannah lowered everyone's windows and dialed up the music, and Baker gave her an amused smile like she'd been waiting for her to do that. Hannah screeched song lyrics in an off-key, raspy voice, and then she changed the words of every song to be about RuPaw. When Tracy Chapman began to play, Hannah yelled, "*You've got a fast claw*," and burst into another giggling fit, and Baker's shoulders shook with laughter as she gave Hannah that secret smile that she saved only for her.

The McDonald's drive-through was five cars deep. The glaring lights had me rubbing my eyes, drunk and sleepy and hungry and exhilarated. Hannah was still singing terribly. Baker propped her left leg up to rest her knee against the sideboard, and I laughed without meaning to, remembering that internet joke about how queer people were incapable of sitting properly. We inched forward in the line, and I had no idea whether we'd been sitting there for one minute or ten. It didn't matter.

We got Happy Meals, all three of us, with cheeseburgers and fries and Coca-Cola. The toy puppy that came in my box was apparently from a kid's show, and I ripped off the plastic and danced the pup across my knees, not caring that it was childish, already promising myself that I'd keep this memento forever.

It wasn't until we'd finished eating that Hannah began to cry. I wasn't sure if I was hearing right at first, but her singing had definitely stopped and she was sniffling like someone with a sinus infection.

"Baby, what?" Baker asked softly. She gripped Hannah's hand and smoothed her thumb over Hannah's palm.

"Sorry. It's the song. I miss George."

This made no sense to me, because the song that was playing was Lady Gaga's "Poker Face," upbeat and dancy and loaded with innuendo.

"I should have gotten him those tickets to see her," Hannah sniffed. "Last fall, on her tour. He would have loved it."

"Honey, you didn't know," Baker cooed.

The beat continued to thump. Hannah cried harder. In the slivers of moonlight coming through the windshield, I could see Baker's aching expression.

"I just wish we'd had more time," Hannah sobbed. "I wish the diagnosis hadn't knocked us sideways. I would have asked him so many more things."

"I know, honey. I know."

"He was supposed to marry us."

"I know."

"I'm so mad at him. I'm so mad."

Hannah's sobs were so devastating that I started crying, too. I cried because she was hurting, and because Baker was hurting, and because they had known my uncle better than I had. How strange, I thought through my tears, to be jealous of another person's grief. To yearn for the pain that was proportional to the love.

I understood intuitively why Uncle George was on Hannah's mind. Tonight had been one of the best nights of my life, and the only reason I had lived it was because of him. Because of what he'd built, what he'd given, what he'd left behind. The searing joy of tonight was inexplicably twined with the senseless grief of losing the man who had cultivated it. His legacy was stamped onto every person who had walked through the Frisky Cricket's doors.

I thought of Hatch, of the picture of Uncle George he kept hidden in his desk, and I cried harder.

Baker missed the turn for my street, and I opened my mouth to protest before I realized what she was doing. She turned left, and left, and left again, and I understood she was looping us in a circle until Hannah and I could finish crying. Even after the song changed to something I didn't know, Baker continued to drive with her hands steady on the wheel, giving us space in this long, necessary moment. It was a gift I didn't know how to say thank you for.

When our cries finally died down, Baker made a gentle turn onto my street. She lowered the music and pulled quietly into my driveway. Then she handed me a fast-food napkin to wipe my face.

"Get some sleep, okay?"

I nodded. I couldn't speak. Hannah couldn't, either. She leaned forward with her head in her hands as I climbed out of the car. I snapped the door closed and ambled to my dad's front door, exhausted in every way. The Subaru lingered in my driveway until I had safely gotten inside.

13
THE LUNCH DATE

The last person I ever expected strode through the Cricket's front door the following Tuesday.

Grandpa.

Immediately, my blood went cold and my heart dropped down to my toes. What was he doing here? How dare he have the audacity to come in? This was my waterfall, and Grandpa's presence felt like an invasion, a violation, a defilement of something sacred. I had a visceral urge to run at him and shove him right back through the door.

"Hello, good sir!" Midas chirped before I could say anything. "What can I get you today?"

Grandpa glowered at him. My pulse sped up, as I worried that Grandpa might be rude or outright bigoted—

"Hey, Gramps," I cut in, leaning casually against my mop. I struggled to make my tone sound casual and sunny. "What brings you in today?"

"Cut the Pollyanna nonsense, Louisa," Grandpa said impatiently. "I'm here because I'm taking you to lunch."

Midas glanced at me, clearly confused. "Wait—you're poly?"

I ignored him, momentarily distracted by Grandpa's invitation. "What?"

"Lunch," Grandpa repeated. His eyes swiveled from one side of the bar to the other, full of disdain. "I'll wait for you in the car."

He strode out the door before I could argue.

"Sorry—just—that was your *grandpa*?" Midas asked, shaking his head.

"The one and only," I said grimly.

"I was gonna say," Midas muttered, "he looks almost offensively straight."

"What's this about?" I asked Grandpa fifteen minutes later. We sat across from each other at Tambrie's Café, me in another one of my messy work T-shirts, Grandpa in a pair of corduroy pants and a dress shirt.

"Your father let slip that you've been . . . *staying out late*." He pursed his lips. "Working and partying at that bar."

I deflated in my seat. Why on earth had Dad told him about me working at the bar? I had thought we had a mutual understanding about keeping Grandma and Grandpa far away from my arrangement with Hatch.

"Louisa, being part of this family means there are certain expectations on you," Grandpa went on. "People in town, they look to us as examples of what it means to be from Rustin. You can't be running around, staying out late, cavorting with riffraff without someone noticing." He gave me what he probably thought was a compassionate look. "It's not an easy mantle to take up, I know. There's always someone who needs something. A donation, a referral, sometimes just peace of mind that the heavy hitters in this town are good people. It wears on you. But our family has been blessed with an abundance of talent and leadership, and it's a wasteful sin not to put that to use."

"Riffraff," I repeated. "Do you mean the people from the bar?"

He didn't answer. "Can't you hang with your other friends, what's-their-names, the dumb one and the Black one—"

I stiffened. "Their names are Emma and Candor and you've known them since I was five."

"You don't need to get snippy," he said, swatting like I was an irritating mosquito. "Anyway, I have news. The athletic foundation has invited the family to their summer fundraiser. They'll be presenting us with a plaque in George's honor. We'll all be going, and I want us to look sharp." He looked pointedly at my torn, baggy jean shorts.

I twisted my napkin in my lap. "Is Hatch invited?"

Grandpa narrowed his eyes like I had said something forbidden. "Excuse me?"

"Oh, come on. You can't start a conversation about me working at the bar and then act surprised when I mention Hatch."

Grandpa threw me a hard, scathing look. "No. That man doesn't need to be there."

"Of course he needs to be there."

Grandpa blinked rapidly, like maybe he had misheard me. "What the hell makes you say that?"

I stared hard at him. Then I spoke slowly and deliberately, like Grandpa was the one who was slow on the uptake. "Because he was Uncle George's partner."

Grandpa laughed a dark, foreboding laugh. He leaned back in his chair and widened his shoulders, crossing a leg over his thigh like he was settling in for an interesting debate. The challenge in his eyes was clear as day. "You fancy yourself Marion's protector, Louisa?"

"He prefers 'Hatch,' but I think you know that."

Grandpa sputtered out a laugh. "I would too if I had a woman's name."

"Hatch was important to Uncle George," I continued, ignoring him. "We didn't include him for the funeral, so it would be nice if we included him for this *honor*."

"George couldn't stand that man," Grandpa said, still laughing.

"What are you talking about? They were in love."

Perhaps it was my use of *love* that shut him up. "Louisa," Grandpa said in a tone that suggested how childish I was, "my brother was never *in love* with that hillbilly barkeeper. George took one look at Marion's ridiculous ultimatum and shut the door. He saw Marion for what he truly was: a pathetic hanger-on trying to drag him down."

"By ultimatum, do you mean Hatch's request that they get married?"

"'Married,'" Grandpa mocked. He threw his napkin down and sneered. "Don't be so profane, Louisa."

"Uncle George was your *brother*, Grandpa. How could his love life be so offensive to you?"

"George always intended to stay in Rustin. His whole life was here. His business, his family, his legacy! Marion just couldn't stomach all the attention George got. He was hell-bent on taking that away from him. Jealous as Cain, and I'll tell you what, I'll swear to every last soul in this restaurant that it was the stress of dealing with him that sent George to his early death."

I pictured Hatch in his nondescript clothes and jangling keys, telling Hannah that he refused to dress up and make a speech at her wedding. I couldn't imagine him wanting any attention on him at all.

"You're wrong," I said, looking my grandfather square in the eye. "And I don't want any part of your stupid little plaque presentation."

"Oh no, no, no, no, no," Grandpa snarled, pointing a shaking finger in my face, "you'll be there to represent the family, and you'll dress *appropriately* in a dress and stockings, or you can forget about that handy tuition money your grandmother and I set aside for you."

"I don't need that money anymore," I reminded him. "Uncle George made sure of that."

"Oh, did he? Because it's my understanding that you won't make money until the sale goes through." A wicked smile spread across his face. "Which it hasn't yet. And which I've heard you don't want to happen."

He had me there, and he knew it. I fell silent, my chest heaving like I'd just fallen off the mechanical bull. All I could focus on was getting away from him.

I pushed back from the table just as Ms. Tambrie arrived with dessert. Her voice was high-pitched and performative as she trilled, "All right, then! A fresh batch for you all!"

I scooted around her, shot one last glare at Grandpa, and hustled out of the restaurant.

"My family is the most evil, fucked-up, delusional set of humans I've ever met," I huffed, dropping into the passenger seat of Aubrey's Audi ten minutes later. "I swear they must be inbred."

"Hi to you, too," Aubrey said, shooting me an amused look. "Why does this feel like a prison break?"

"Because spending time with my grandfather is cruel and unusual punishment." I leaned my head into my hands and breathed. "Thank you for getting me. You're sure you don't mind?"

"I told you, I was out and about anyway." She turned around to back out of the parking lot and her arm accidentally brushed mine. Both of us jerked away.

"Sorry," I said hastily.

"Sorry," she said at the same time.

We turned onto Main Street and zipped through a green light, and I tried to ignore my tingling skin.

"So . . . what happened?" Aubrey asked.

I sighed and stretched out in the seat. "My grandpa just informed me that we'll be going to the Rustin Athletic Foundation's summer banquet to be, like, *emissaries* of Uncle George's stupid football legacy."

Aubrey's eyebrows shot up in surprise. "I'm going to that, too."

"Wait, really?" I brightened, temporarily forgetting the injustice of it all.

"Yeah, of course. My dad wouldn't miss a chance to parade our family in front of the bigwigs. Why don't you want to go?"

I drew up short, remembering she didn't know the truth about Uncle George. "I just . . . I feel like my grandparents try to capitalize off my uncle's legacy without . . . um . . . truly loving him for the person he was."

Aubrey nodded in a way that meant she didn't quite follow me, but she was trying to be polite about it. "Oh. I'm sorry."

"It's all right." I looked ahead of us, at the back roads golden with afternoon sunlight. "So . . . where are we going?"

"Dorm room shopping." She glanced over at me, those seashell eyes gauging my reaction. "I figured focusing on the next four years will be helpful for both of us."

"Both of us? Why, what's wrong with you?"

Aubrey licked her lips, seemingly bracing for something. A full minute passed before we turned into the Target shopping center and parked in an open spot—not near the door, but far off in an empty section of the lot. Aubrey unbuckled her seatbelt and thrust the gearshift into park, but she kept the car running and stared through the windshield with her jaw clenched.

I frowned at her, unnerved by the swelling silence. "What's going on?"

"The Rustin alumni magazine interviewed me today," she said without preamble. "They wanted to do a story about, you know, growing up as Coach Calhoun's daughter."

I waited.

"It was fine at first. I gave my usual scripted answers." She picked at her manicure and took a slow, gathering breath. "But then the interviewer asked if I knew any of Dad's players, and what he would do if I dated one of them."

My pulse raced beneath my skin.

"The thing is . . ." Aubrey took a deep breath. "I'm never going to like a football player. I'm never going to like a . . . guy."

I waited a long moment before I spoke. "I know."

We looked at each other, and there was a sudden understanding between us. We had crossed some invisible bridge—a bridge that, deep down, I had probably known was there all along. I unbuckled my seatbelt, shifted my body toward hers, and lowered the music without asking. This was a moment that deserved our full attention.

"Are you okay?" I asked in my gentlest voice.

Aubrey was shaking, but she was doing her best to hold her own. "You make coming out look really easy."

I held her eyes and willed every atom in my body to show her that it was okay. "It shouldn't have to be hard."

"I know it's not my business, but could you tell me the story? Of how you came out?"

And suddenly I was talking. Talking in a way that I hadn't talked in a while, excavating my own heart, handing over the pieces that I thought might mean something to her. "And then Mom came into my room the next morning, after she'd found the letter I wrote her, and she sat on my bed and just rubbed my back for a while. I woke up and she was doing this really deep breathing, like she was meditating or something, and I wasn't sure if she knew I was awake but then she said, 'I love you, honey. It might be an adjustment, but I love you.' Then she gave me a kiss and left for work."

The longing was back in Aubrey's eyes. "You're really lucky."

I nodded meaningfully. "I know I am."

She chewed her lip. "Did you know my dad is gonna be on *College Gameday* in September? It's all anyone can talk about, is how good the Reckoners are looking. People from ESPN are calling all the time. *Southern Living* is doing a feature on our house." She paused, and her voice trembled more. "And behind closed doors, my parents barely even speak to each other. They sleep in separate beds, they eat their meals at different times, and every few weeks they get into a massive, blowout fight, and then Mom leaves to stay with her sister for the weekend, and then she comes back and acts like nothing ever happened."

I swallowed. I had the sudden urge to reach for her hand, but I stopped myself.

"There's, like, this unspoken rule that we're supposed to be the picture-perfect family that represents everything Rustin stands for," Aubrey went on. "We have to look right, dress right, sound right . . . and everything comes back to football, to Dad's career, even when he's being a narcissistic asshole. The only person who gets it is my sister, but she's in grad school in Nashville, just trying to stay above it all. She only comes home when Dad makes her. Usually for some publicity stunt."

"That sounds like a lot, Aubrey."

She steeled herself, her eyes still hooked on mine. "And all the while, none of them knows I'm hiding in the closet of our ridiculous mansion."

"Does *anyone* know?" I asked, already suspecting the answer.

"No one knows." She picked at her perfect violet nail polish. "Not even Emma and Candor."

I let that settle into my bones. Here was this prim, put-together, incredibly burdened girl, and she was sharing her truth with me, even though I hadn't done anything to earn it. I wished I could tell her how much that meant to me, how much I wanted to make things easier for her, but I didn't know how to convey the gravity of those sentiments.

"Well . . . now *I* know," I said lightly, "and I'm always available to talk about hot girls and shit."

Aubrey snorted. "Thanks, Scrooge, that's such a comfort," she said, sounding more like herself. "Okay, let's get moving." And like the flip of a switch, she squared her shoulders, checked her mascara, turned the car off, and opened the door.

"Wait, what?" I asked, feeling whiplash from the sudden shift. "I'm sorry . . . just . . . pause for a second? You just came out to me in a Target parking lot, and now we're just gonna flit through the aisles like it's a chill weekday afternoon?"

"I don't *flit*," Aubrey said. "I walk with purpose. And yes, I'm obviously feeling out of control right now, so I *need* to walk those pristine, perfectly organized aisles with a caramel macchiato in my hand."

"You are truly one of a kind, Cotillion," I said with a shake of my head.

We ambled through Target with all the time in the world, nursing our coffees as we took turns pushing the unwieldy red cart. The space between our bodies felt different now. Gone was the standoffishness and tension; instead, there was an easy familiarity between us, almost like I was breezing the aisles with Emma and Candor.

Except with Emma and Candor, I didn't feel this kind of sweet magnetic pull, this urge to reach over and touch them—like I was doing with Aubrey right now.

"They're the *same thing*," I said, watching her fret over whether seafoam or sage linens was the better choice for dorm bedding. I stepped closer and tickled her side in an effort to make her move.

She squirmed and smacked my hand away, her brow still creased with concentration. "They are *not*."

"It's just green! Light green!"

Aubrey dropped her jaw theatrically. "Lord, you are so *uncouth*," she pronounced, shoving me away.

An hour later, laden down with shopping bags, we trudged back out to the car. I watched a bead of sweat roll down her neck and wanted to follow it down to her lower back. Our arms brushed as we loaded up the trunk, and I wondered if her skin was tingling like mine.

"So, where to?" she asked as we settled into our seats.

I hesitated, not wanting to make her uncomfortable. "Any chance you could drop me off at the Cricket? I left the Caddy there."

She set her jaw. Nodded. "Yes."

"You can drop me around the corner if you're worried about someone, like, seeing—"

"No," she cut in. "That's fine." She looked uncertainly at me. "Baby steps, right?"

I smiled. "Baby steps."

She punched the Cricket's address into her GPS, revved up the engine, and sped out of the parking lot with a determined expression.

"So . . . when did you realize?" I asked, picking up where we had left off.

She told me, and it was like listening to a familiar bedtime story: the spark, the doubt, the internal reckoning. "And then I dated this guy back in Arkansas before Dad got this job. It was kind of my last-ditch effort—like maybe my feelings were just latent or something, and here was this objectively hot guy who could help me unlock something. But, like, he'd hold my hand and write me these little notes during class, and I couldn't *feel* anything. Even when we kissed and fooled around, I found myself thinking about my friend Polly instead. So I went for a run one afternoon and went down to the creek and just stood there staring at the water for like an hour. And then I sat in it. Like, full-body sat. I know that sounds absurd, but it was the only thing that calmed me. And I watched this woodpecker for a while and it hit me, like, *That woodpecker doesn't give a shit if I'm gay*, and I started laughing and—I don't know—I guess that was when I came out to myself."

I smiled wryly. "The woodpecker doesn't give a shit, but plenty of other people might."

"Exactly."

"So . . . What's your plan? I mean, are you ever gonna come out publicly?"

"Of course," she snapped, her voice taking on the edge I was used to. Then her face softened. "Sorry. I mean." She took a steadying breath. "Yes, I'm going to come out. I made myself a promise right before we moved here: that I would just get through graduation, bide my time during the summer, and come out when I got to college." She took another deep breath. "I'm *almost* there."

"But you're going to Rustin, right?"

"Absolutely not," she said quickly. "Gramick."

I thought I'd heard her wrong. "What?"

"Gramick University, up in Philly," she clarified. "It's far away, it's private, they're not in the SEC, and as far as I can tell, they don't give a shit about football, which means nobody will give a shit who my dad is."

I couldn't help the smile pulling at me. "You're coming up north?"

She shrugged self-consciously. "You won't be the only Yankee around here, Scrooge."

I laughed. "I guess not."

"I did a lot of research," she said with a note of justification in her voice. "I only looked at schools that had high ratings of LGBTQ acceptance. And I just, I don't know, I liked Gramick's vibe. And there's this really neat queer bookstore in Philly that I want to see."

"And your parents were okay with that?"

"They don't know why I chose it. I gave them some line about the academic excellence or whatever. All my dad cares about is that I'll still be cheering for the Reckoners." She shrugged again. "And I mean, it's not like they don't have the money for it. They can pay the tuition, and hopefully that's the last thing I'll ever need them to pay for."

"You've really thought about this."

"I think about everything," she said matter-of-factly. We turned onto Route 29 and cruised past the familiar farmland that neighbored the Frisky Cricket. "Can I ask you something? Did you ever have a crush on someone here? Like, before you moved away?"

I laughed as I remembered. "Do you know Emily Caldwell?"

Aubrey grinned. "Of course."

"She had me in a choke hold all through sixth grade," I admitted. "What about you?"

She tilted her head back, thinking. "Probably Abbie Ziegler."

I pictured our old classmate. Sweet smile, crooked nose. "She was cute."

Aubrey blushed. "Yeah, well."

She swung into the Cricket's parking lot and pulled up right next to the Cadillac. I watched her eyes rake over the building, the Pride flag, the front door. There was something breathless in her expression.

"You know . . ." I began, "we're having another big party this weekend, for the Fourth, if you wanted to come. The theme is 'Independence Gay.'"

Aubrey smiled appreciatively. "Thanks, but I've got the Chamber of Commerce barbecue on—"

"Before you come up with an excuse," I teased, "you should know we're having the party on Friday. Hatch didn't want to compete with the fireworks on Saturday."

Aubrey lowered her eyelashes to refute me. "First of all, not an excuse. My attendance is required because the mayor and city council and alllll the important people are gonna be there." She paused, biting her lip. "But . . . let me think about it." She met my eyes again, letting me see the openness on her face. "I really do want to come. I'm, like, itching to see it. But I'm just . . ."

"Worried," I finished with an understanding nod. "I get it. Truly. But if anyone picked up on you being there, you could always spin it like, *Football is for alllll Americans and I'm here as an ambassador of that spirit*."

Aubrey laughed genuinely. "Look at you. Ever thought about a career in PR?"

"Why, are you looking for a publicist?"

We grinned at each other, and I knew what this was, knew it was flirting. My stomach wouldn't stop fluttering and the skin behind my ears felt hot.

"Well . . . thanks for the ride," I said, slowly opening the door. "And for saving me from Grandpa."

"Thanks for the conversation."

"Conver-*gay*-tion."

Aubrey rolled her eyes, but she was beaming. "Yeah, yeah."

"Tell Abbie Ziegler I said hi."

"Shut up."

I climbed out of the car and hovered there for a moment, my hand on the door. I didn't want to say goodbye to her, and I could tell she didn't want to say goodbye to me, either.

"Think about it," I said at last, gesturing behind me to the bar.

"I will," she promised. From other people, those might have been empty words, but from her I knew them to be true.

"Bye, Aubrey."

Her eyes lingered on me, sparkling blue and full of something new. "See you later, Louisa." She bit her lip, smiling up at me. "Stay gay."

14
INDEPENDENCE GAY

I was sitting on the bar counter, kicking my sneakers against the wall and reading Hannah's copy of *The Color Purple*, when she suddenly plucked the book from my hand and dropped it on the countertop.

"Hey!" I said, reaching for it. "I didn't mark my page!"

Hannah crossed her arms and gave me a shrewd look. "What's going on?"

"Huh?"

"You've been sitting there humming and smiling weirdly for, like, twenty minutes. You did the same thing when you came back from your three-hour errand yesterday." She raised her eyebrows. "So? Spill."

I felt Aubrey's name on my tongue, dancing with sparks. "Am I that easy to read?"

"For a school counselor? Yes." She leaned her elbows on the counter and stared expectantly at me. "So?"

"You are *so* annoying."

"I'm aware. Go on."

I told her about my surprising conversation with Aubrey, though I made sure I didn't use her name or hint at her identity. Hannah let me talk without interrupting, but her eyes widened in all the right places.

"So your—*enemy*—came out to you? In a Target parking lot? After rescuing you from your cartoon villain grandpa?" She looked at me. "Wait. Do you have a crush on her?"

"No!" I said too quickly. "And God, Hannah, who says 'crush'? You're so old."

"Oh, you definitely have a crush."

"I do not," I insisted. "I'm just—I don't know, *happy*—that I have another queer friend here."

"What am I, a hetero?"

"Another queer friend *my age*."

"Uh-huh."

"Stop making that face! I'm serious!"

"So are you gonna invite Target girl here, to the bar?"

I drummed my fingers on the book spine. "I tried inviting her already, but she shot it down."

Hannah saw right through my attempt at disinterest. "Oh shit, you've got it bad."

"Will you stop?"

"Why did she say no?"

"She's not comfortable, like, being out in Rustin. I'm the only person she's told."

That was enough to make Hannah stop teasing me. She took on her compassionate elder expression and clucked her tongue. "I hate that for her."

"I know."

"Well, give her time. All you can do is be her friend."

I nodded. "Yeah, I know."

That Friday, for our Independence Gay party, I stole one of dad's denim shirts and tied my hair back with a red bandanna to look like Rosie the Riveter. Hannah showed up wearing a navy Y'ALL MEANS ALL T-shirt with shooting star earrings and an American flag cheek tattoo. Midas put us both to shame with his full Uncle Sam costume, complete with a top hat and an elastic white beard. Hatch, of course, made absolutely no effort and defaulted to his favorite maroon polo, which prompted Hannah to berate him for a quarter of an hour about how *maroon* and *red* were not the same. I tried to tamp down my smile, thinking of sage and seafoam linens, until Midas jammed his top hat over Hannah's head to make her shut up.

"We need more blue food coloring," Midas said just before the doors opened. "Lou, can you get it from the back?"

"I can create some, if you'd like," said a mild voice. Edge had arrived early and was now sitting at a two-top, twirling his USA drink stirrer around his martini glass. He had opted to dress down in a Hawaiian print shirt and khaki pants, but he still brought his briefcase and handed it to Midas to stash behind the bar. Hatch sat across from Edge, sipping his own martini while he counted money from the cash box. He had acquiesced to Hannah's request that he wear a Fourth of July headband, which sat ridiculously on top of his sleek white hair.

"That's okay, Edge, thanks," Midas said good naturedly. "Lou, can you—?"

"Go get it, Louisa," Hatch barked without looking up.

I scowled but went to the storeroom and found the food coloring Hannah had picked up from Piggly Wiggly. When I returned, Otis Penny had joined us, fresh from the barber and wearing *suspenders* of all things. They were bright red with spangled silver stars, and I could tell from the way he puffed out his chest that he thought he was the cat's meow. Until the actual cat jumped on his back and set him screaming.

"God *damn* it!" Otis yelled, throwing RuPaw off his shoulders. She clung to his pressed shirt, ripping a tear in the fabric, while Hatch roared with laughter and made no effort to help him. "Damn cat! Can't you put her up for the night?"

"She's an American, too, Otis," Hatch said innocently. "She deserves to celebrate."

"Yeah, and she'd better wear that patriotic bandanna Hannah forced me to track down," Midas added.

"There's a snag in your suspenders, Otis," I said, fingering the catch in the fabric that had clearly attracted RuPaw's attention. "She wanted to play with it."

"I swear it's George egging her on," Otis said darkly. "He was always jealous of my style."

Midas coughed into his shirtsleeve. Hannah clearly struggled to keep a straight face. I whipped up a Moscow Mule for Otis while RuPaw scampered away, clearly determined to avoid her patriotic bandanna.

By nine o'clock, the bar was packed and thrumming. We weren't as full as we had been for Pride, but the crowd was certainly thicker than a usual Frisky Friday. I poured drinks, wiped tables, and took over the music when Midas needed a break to fix his fake beard. All the while, I kept an eye out for Emma and Candor, who planned to make their Frisky Cricket debut tonight. They hadn't said whether Aubrey was coming with them, but a small flicker of hope buzzed inside my chest.

I was on my way back from the bathroom, where Hatch had dispatched me to mop up spilled beer, when someone started shaking my shoulders.

It was Emma and Candor, screaming in my ear. Their arms were suddenly around me, their purses scratching my skin. "We've been looking everywhere for you!" Emma yelled above the music. "That bossy blonde lady legit told me to *take a chill pill*—"

I stopped listening, because standing next to Emma was—

"Aubrey!" I shouted, forgetting myself and pulling her into my arms. "You came!"

Aubrey smiled the widest smile I had ever seen from her. Her long, shiny hair was covered by a navy baseball cap—an attempt to fly under the radar, I assumed—but she was *here*, at the Frisky Cricket, standing so close to me that I could smell her perfume.

"I figured I could use a girls' night out," she said, biting her lip. Her eyes lingered on my hair. "Cute bandanna."

I blushed. "Trying to be, you know, *riveting*."

"Love it," she replied with a silly grin, and I couldn't look away from her.

Emma and Candor stared back and forth between us. "Um. Why are y'all suddenly cool?" Candor asked.

"What? We're fine," I said, trying to arrange my face into a casual expression.

"No, there was definitely tension before," Emma said.

"We had a come to Jesus talk," I admitted. Then I played off my own name and muttered, "Come to Ouis-us."

Aubrey collapsed into giggles and shoved me like I was too much for her.

"What is happening," Candor stage-whispered to Emma.

"I don't know, but I feel like my soul is leaving my body," Emma whispered back.

"Oh, shut up," Aubrey said with a bright laugh. "We don't hate each other anymore, shouldn't you be happy with that?"

"I guess?" Emma said. "It just seems like you're—"

"*Anyway*," I said forcefully, wanting to redirect the conversation. I swept my arm across the bar, focusing intently on Emma and Candor so I wouldn't get hooked into Aubrey's eyes again. "What do you think?"

"It's awesome!" they chorused. "The music, the outfits, oh my god!"

"Come on, I'll give you the tour! You have to meet RuPaw!"

"RuPaul's here?!" Candor screamed.

We made the rounds, the four of us grabbing each other's hands as we slinked through the hot, sweaty bodies. I showed them every small perfect touch that made the Cricket what it was, and their delighted smiles soaked into me like nothing I had ever felt before. But it was Aubrey I couldn't stop looking at, her face glowing like someone had just switched on the light, her mouth slightly open in wonder as she took in this place that was made for people like us.

I led them to the bar top, where I quickly mixed whiskey-Cokes without caring whether Hannah, Hatch, or anyone else saw me. I paused before grabbing the fourth glass, but when I caught Aubrey's eye, she nodded to indicate she wanted whiskey, too. She felt comfortable enough to let her guard down. The realization made my heart sing.

We spun into the middle of the dance floor, flouncing around absurdly like we had in middle school, belting out song lyrics with everything we had. Candor and Emma pretended to tango, and Aubrey snorted into her whiskey drink, and I took it all in, my heart fit to burst.

Until someone bumped into us and sloshed an entire beer down the front of Aubrey's shirt.

For a moment, Aubrey could only stare. I couldn't tell whether she was more shocked by the sopping liquid or the fact that the person hadn't apologized.

"It's okay," I said, grabbing her arms. "I've got extra shirts in the Caddy—come on—"

Without waiting for the others, I motioned her to follow me through the packed bodies. A second later, I felt her warm hand clasp mine, our fingers twining together. *It's so she doesn't lose me*, my brain said reasonably, but the pitter-patter in my heart made itself known.

There were only a few people in the parking lot: a group of middle-aged friends smoking cigarettes and a young couple grabbing every inch of each other's skin as they made out against the brick wall. I led Aubrey to the Cadillac and dug through the back seat until I found one of the clean T-shirts I kept in there for situations like these.

"Here," I said, handing it to her.

"Thanks," Aubrey said, stepping under cover of the tree in front of my car. And without further ado, she set her drink on the car's hood and peeled her tank top off in one smooth motion.

"Oh . . . ," I muttered.

If she knew what she was doing to me, she didn't show it. She simply hung her beer-soaked shirt from a tree branch and shifted the new shirt around to stick her arms through. I tried not to linger on the smattering of freckles across her chest, but she caught me looking.

"What?" she asked breathlessly. Her eyes dropped to my mouth.

There was a moment where I couldn't speak, where all I could do was look at her mouth, too—

And then one of the cigarette smokers squealed with laughter, and the moment was ruined.

"Um," I said. "Let's . . ."

"Yes," she said hastily.

I wasn't even sure what she was agreeing to, but when she took my hand again, I moved without thinking and led her to the empty backyard. I took a seat on the same steps where I had first encountered Hatch and gestured for Aubrey to sit next to me.

"So . . . how are you feeling? Being here?"

Aubrey gave me a deep, searching look. "Can I tell you something? I feel like I'm actually in my skin when I'm with you."

My heart raced. My palms were sweating. I couldn't stop looking into her bold, vulnerable eyes. "You're really pretty, Aubrey."

The loveliest blush bloomed on her cheeks. Her gaze dropped to my mouth, and I knew what was coming next. "I'd like to kiss you, Louisa." Her eyes ticked between mine. "Please."

I tried and failed to tamp down my smile. "You and your manners."

Aubrey leveled me with a look. "Scrooge," she said, like the stupid nickname held all the weight of the world, "for once in your life, shut up and use your mouth for something else."

So I kissed her.

It was a short kiss, gentle as a butterfly finding purchase on a petal. Just enough to make contact, to know her lips were warm and smooth and tinged with whiskey. She pulled back and we looked at each other, breathless, and then I leaned forward and kissed her again.

And suddenly we were making out right there on the steps,

all sense of decorum forgotten. Aubrey yanked her baseball cap off in a rough, impatient motion and tilted her head to kiss me harder, her hands knotting into the hem of my denim shirt, her tongue hot in my mouth. It was like every small string that kept her in place had been cut unceremoniously, and she was unapologetically hungry for every last inch of me. She let out a low whine, almost poignant sounding, as I steadied her waist with my hands.

"Okay, okay," she said, pulling back suddenly. Her skin was flushed and her eyes were bright. "You're a really good kisser," she panted, "and if you keep doing that, I'm gonna . . . I'm just gonna . . ."

I grinned and tugged on her hand. "You're gonna what?"

"Don't look all pleased with yourself."

"I am, though."

She shoved me. I grabbed her hand and kissed her again.

"I'm torn," she said breathlessly. "Part of me wants to keep making out with you, and the other part of me wants to go back inside and suck up every detail of this place."

I smiled. "I told you it was amazing."

"I had no doubt."

"Can you imagine if the whole world was like the Cricket? We wouldn't need safe places or stolen moments. We'd have the whole earth. We could roam anywhere, kiss anywhere."

"Maybe that's the dream," she said softly. "But for tonight, I'm just really glad we have the Cricket."

"We do," I said, glowing with pride. "And I think we should dance."

* * *

When I looked back on it later, a few things stood out about the end of that night. The first was the smell of Aubrey's perfume and the shine of her hair beneath her baseball cap. The second was Emma and Candor's joy as they danced their hearts out to the point where Emma's shirt was dark with sweat. And the third was the sweet, warm thrill in my belly when "Stars Fell on Alabama" began to play and Aubrey pulled me close to slow dance.

I didn't care that our friends were watching. I didn't care that Hannah and Midas were posted up in the corner beaming at me like a couple of gushing parents. All I cared about was the heat of Aubrey's body against mine, and the absolute freedom she felt to finally be herself in a public space, and the soft press of her lips on my cheek right as the song came to an end.

"I did *not* have this on my Bingo card," Emma whispered to Candor, but I ignored them and kissed Aubrey full on the mouth, right there in the middle of the dance floor, with my heart swelling and swelling until it could have popped open the ceiling. The music played, and the people danced, and I thought inexplicably of Uncle George, wondering if he'd gone to heaven, and if it felt like an infinite moment of this.

15
THIRTY DAYS

"All right, freshman, I need a favor," Hannah said a few days later.

"Step into my office," I said breezily from my spot at a high-top table.

"Not you, the *other* freshman."

Aubrey looked up across from me. She had started dropping into the bar during the day, usually accompanied by a puzzle or Sudoku book that she used to pass the time while I worked. Today she had brought an old game of Guess Who?, and we were locked in a fierce battle while I took my thirty-minute break.

It was a long, languid afternoon, the kind that only happened in the dead heat of summertime. Hannah was zooming about the bar, chattering up a storm and busying herself with unnecessary tasks, which likely meant Baker had packed her an extra-large cold brew that morning. Our only patrons at the moment were Maria Paula and Brooke, clacking away on their laptops as they ordered one espresso martini after the other, apparently devising a new online business that they swore would make them filthy rich.

"And what is this business?" Hannah asked suspiciously, bringing them fresh waters in a not-so-subtle attempt to sober them up. She held up a finger to Aubrey and me, indicating she would be right over to make good on that favor.

"Proprietary goods, specializing in alternative health, kind of like an online pharmacy but with a distinct human touch that will deliver straight to the consumer—" Maria Paula rattled off.

"Weed," Brooke cut in. "It's weed."

"Sign me up," Midas singsonged from the bar top.

"Will you ship to Pennsylvania?" Aubrey asked.

"Oh, sweet little moon child, weed is already legal in Pennsylvania," Maria Paula said, her eyes never leaving her laptop screen. "But sure, we'll ship to you." She finally looked up. "Also, who are you?"

Aubrey laughed the bright, relaxed laugh that meant she felt safe and happy. I was starting to see it more and more, especially after kissing her the other night. She didn't bother answering Maria Paula, just gave me a secretive, flirtatious look across the top of the game board.

"All right, so," Hannah said, appearing next to us. "I hear you have a dog."

Aubrey raised an eyebrow. "Yes . . . ?"

Hannah scooted my game board aside, leaning her elbows on the table and completely invading my space. "Baker is taking me to Atlanta in a couple of weeks, for my birthday, and we need a dog-sitter. Are you game? We'll pay you, obviously, and you're welcome to stay at our house."

"Stay at your house? Like, the whole time?"

"Yeah, if you want to. That might be better so you can get the mail and everything."

Without meaning to, I looked at Aubrey. The spark in her eyes told me she was thinking the same thing I was.

"Oh no, not so fast," Hannah said. "You are house-sitting *alone*. I don't need a couple of horny teenagers taking up residence in—"

"Hannah!" I interrupted, blushing to the roots of my hair. "Oh my god, shut up, we get it."

"Just sayin'." Hannah shrugged like she hadn't just embarrassed the hell out of us. "I remember that summer after graduation—looking for stolen moments, empty beds—"

"*Stop talking*," I hissed.

"I'm gonna use the restroom," Aubrey said, scooting out of her chair. Patches of burgundy had settled high on her cheeks.

The moment she turned the corner, I smacked Hannah on the arm.

"Ow!"

"I will kill you," I said darkly.

"Oh, come on," she replied easily, but before she could say anything else, the front door swung open and two men strode across the threshold and into our sacred space.

My grandfather, and behind him—

Coach Calhoun.

My blood went cold. Immediately, I reached for my phone to text Aubrey a warning, but she had left her phone on the table.

"Well, ain't this a fun little gathering on the island of misfit toys," Grandpa said. His eyes narrowed on Hannah's LIVE LAUGH LESBIAN T-shirt.

Hatch appeared out of nowhere, almost like he had sensed the invasion. "Nice to see you, Amos," he said in a tone that was the exact opposite of nice. "I hope you're here to finally look at that breaker box?"

"Easy now, Marion."

"We've been calling you for weeks, Amos."

"I've got a long list of clients, Marion, and we have to prioritize."

I read between the lines of what he was saying: that it was important to *prioritize* non-LGBTQ businesses.

"What is this about?" I said loudly, my neck prickling.

Just then, Aubrey returned from the bathroom. She took one look at her father standing there in the bar, and her face went white as a sheet.

"Aubrey Lynn?" Coach Calhoun said weakly. He was momentarily back-footed, and it would have been delicious to see if I hadn't known Aubrey would become collateral damage. "What the hell are you doing here?"

Aubrey swallowed. "I—uh—"

I scoured my brain for something, *anything*, that might explain Aubrey's presence here, but Hannah beat me to it.

"Oh, you two know each other?" she asked in a fake-bright voice. "What a small world! Coach, are you an animal lover, too?"

Coach Calhoun cocked his head at her. "Excuse me?"

"I read about Aubrey's pet-sitting services online," Hannah went on blithely, like we were just a group of gals at a mimosa brunch. "I asked her to stop in and interview before I hired her. Is that how you two know each other? Do you have a dog? Would you recommend her as a pet-sitter?"

Coach Calhoun looked from Hannah to Aubrey, clearly trying to get a handle on the situation. "Aubrey, is that right? You've started a pet-sitting business?"

"Yes, sir," Aubrey said, rolling seamlessly with the cover story. "A few weeks ago. I, um, didn't tell you because—because I didn't want you to feel obligated to help with finding clients. You're busy enough as it is."

Coach chewed on the lie. I couldn't tell whether he bought it.

"So this is your first time in this . . . business?" He looked around, eyes narrowing on Midas's trans flag pin and RuPaw's rainbow tulle dress.

"Yes, isn't it cute?" Aubrey said in a passable impression of naivete. "It's so quaint and authentic."

"Honey, go on home," Coach said. "We'll talk later."

"But I—"

"Aubrey Lynn."

Aubrey bit her tongue and nodded. "Yes, sir."

She left the bar without looking at me, and I was very careful not to acknowledge her in front of her dad. I looked at Hannah instead, trying to thank her with my eyes. She gave a subtle nod.

"The young'uns are always susceptible," Grandpa told Coach. "You were right to send her home."

Coach shot him a cursory glance but didn't reply. He stepped farther into the room and switched back to business mode, moving in to shake Hatch's hand. "Good to see you again, Mr. Hatchet."

Hatch frowned and clasped his palm only briefly. "Hatch." He glanced subtly at the rest of us and said the next part more quietly. "And I thought you were coming alone."

Immediately, my heart started racing. I looked at Hannah and Midas, who met my eyes with bewildered expressions.

"Amos is a big investor in our program," Coach Calhoun said smoothly.

"Is he now," Hatch muttered darkly.

"That's right. He wanted to see the property. So what do you say you show us around, Hatch? This"—Coach Calhoun looked around—"*space* is nice and all, but as you know, we're keener on the rest of the land."

"Why?" I interjected, rising from my seat.

Coach Calhoun blinked in the manner of someone who wasn't used to pushback. He gave a polite chuckle to save face. "Well, that's between us men, sweetheart."

Fury coursed through my veins. I swore I could hear Hannah's jaw clench.

There was a prolonged pause.

"Right this way," Hatch said stiffly. He turned and led the way past Hannah, Midas, and me, refusing to meet our eyes. I tried in vain to stop my shoulders from shaking. It wasn't until the men had exited through the back door that I realized I'd been holding my breath.

"It's okay," Hannah said, putting a steady hand on my shoulder. "We're okay. We'll be okay."

"What did you tell them?" I rounded on Hatch when he returned, alone this time. "What did you promise?"

Hatch looked like he was about to teeter over. He dragged himself to the bar top without his usual speed. "Nothing," he said without looking at me.

"Bullshit."

"Louisa," Hannah said.

"He knew Coach Calhoun was coming here today. He definitely knew," I ranted, pointing an accusatory finger at Hatch.

Hatch settled on his stool. He still looked like someone had hit him with a truck, but he accepted the glass of ice water Midas placed hastily in front of him. He chugged it without seeming to notice he was doing so.

"Well?" I prompted.

"I'm just keeping my options open, Louisa," Hatch answered.

"They said RU had nearly reached a deal—"

"Louisa, we're on the same team as you," Hannah interjected. "Please stop shouting."

"I am aware of what they said," Hatch huffed, finally meeting my eyes. His voice had gotten stronger and the color was returning to his face. "That doesn't mean it's true. Of course they're putting that narrative out there."

I closed my mouth. Only then did I realize how fast my chest was rising and falling. Midas placed a barstool beneath me, the expectation clear: Sit down and chill. He slid a glass of ice water in front of me, which I held against my face until the heat receded.

"I have not spoken with the university," Hatch repeated. He was speaking calmly, but there was a note of finality in his tone.

I exhaled. In my bones, I believed him. But I was still too wound up to respond, so I busied myself with sipping my water.

"So they're stunting," Midas supplied.

"It's July," Hannah said before I could respond. "I'm pretty sure they—the university—run on a July first to June thirtieth fiscal year. I don't think it's coincidental that they're coming out swinging early on in the month."

"Stupid greedy businessmen," I spit, "with their stupid politics and their—"

"It's business, Louisa," Hatch interrupted.

"Don't patronize me."

"I'm not patronizing you. I'm trying to manage your expectations."

"Oh, now you want to act like a mentor?"

"That's enough!" Hatch yelled, slamming his hand upon the table. The sound was loud as a cannon and sent RuPaw's fur standing on edge. We all froze. "Don't speak to me like that. This is my business and I'm doing my best to accommodate you."

The three of us withered in the silence. I wanted to fire back, but Hannah shook her head subtly in my direction.

"Now, listen," Hatch said, struggling to regain his composure. He took a deep belly breath and exhaled. "We're having a good summer. Let's hold it together a little while longer and see what happens."

See what happens. Those three words held the entire fate of the Frisky Cricket, but I realized with a jolt that they weren't necessarily negative. Was Hatch saying there was a chance he would keep the bar?

"I'm sorry," I managed to say.

Hatch cleared his throat. He glowered at a spot on the wall and said, "I apologize for losing my temper."

There was a pressing silence as we figured out what to say next.

"What I'm hearing . . . ," Midas began, "is that maybe we should throw another party?"

Hannah laughed in spite of herself. She smacked Midas and said, "I hate you, you little monster."

I ignored them. I was watching Hatch. His eyes had cleared and his expression was tinged with something close to regret. Wordlessly, he stood up from the two-top and retreated to his office.

16
THE BUNGALOW

The following night, Aubrey texted me at work. I was on my hands and knees, scrubbing up RuPaw's latest revenge vomit (*She's mad because I didn't let her knead Rook's cape*, Hannah had quipped), when my phone buzzed in my pocket.

Aubrey Calhoun: Hi . . . are you off work soon? If so, is there any chance you could come over?

Me: Is everything okay?

The text bubble appeared, disappeared. And then finally:

Aubrey Calhoun: Not really.

My pulse tripped. I clambered to my feet and anxiously approached the counter. "Hannah."

Hannah looked up from the closing checklist. "What's up?"

I showed her Aubrey's text messages. Her brow furrowed with concern, and I could tell she was thinking the same thing I was: that something had happened between Aubrey and her dad after he'd caught her at the bar yesterday. Had he laid into her? Punished her? Had her plan to escape to college gone off the rails?

"I'm sure she's fine," I said, trying to manage my racing brain. "I'll check on her after we close."

"No," Hannah said, giving me a deep look. "I'll handle closing. Go now. And please let us know if we can help."

I didn't need her to tell me twice.

When I pulled into the Calhouns' driveway fifteen minutes later, a lone figure leapt up from a rocking chair on the porch. She skittered to the driveway like a nervous squirrel, her face white beneath the floodlights. I climbed out of the Cadillac and steeled myself.

"Hey," I said, "are you—?"

Before I could finish the question, Aubrey was in my arms, clinging to me so tightly that it physically hurt. I could feel her shaking against my rib cage.

"*Oh*," I said softly, rubbing her back on instinct. "It's okay. You're okay."

"I can't do this," she said, her voice tight.

"It's okay," I repeated, trying to steady her shaking body. "Breathe. Just breathe."

When she finally pulled away, she looked stricken and off-balance. Her eyes were vacant and lighter colored than usual. She was dressed in an old cotton T-shirt and running shorts with her hair twisted up in a messy topknot. It was the least put together I'd ever seen her, the polished veneer completely forgotten.

"Thanks for coming over," Aubrey said, not meeting my eyes. She jabbed her bare toes against the concrete driveway.

"Where are your parents?" I asked.

"Mom went to visit Aunt Kathy." Aubrey's voice cracked the tiniest sliver, and I understood that her parents had gotten into another bad fight. "Dad is . . . Who the fuck even knows where Dad is. I disabled the cameras just in case."

"Let's sit down and talk, okay?" I said gently, nudging her toward the rocking chairs.

We sat side by side on the stately front porch, and for a moment there was no sound except the insects and birdcalls. I snuck a sideways glance at Aubrey, who was staring out over the treetops, her eyes still vacant.

"My dad had words with me today. About catching me at the Cricket."

I waited.

When Aubrey turned to me, the pleading in her eyes was so naked that it took my breath away. "How did you do this, Louisa?"

I didn't know how to answer her, or whether she wanted an answer at all. I simply looked at her, and when she began to cry, I let her.

"I'm sorry," she said between sobs.

"Please don't say that." I leaned over and pulled her head onto my shoulder. "Just let it out. Let it out."

Aubrey coiled in on herself, but then she let go, crying into my shoulder, her sobs muffled by my T-shirt.

"You're okay," I said softly, brushing a hand down her face.

"The past year, I just kept telling myself, *Just get to college*,"

woman. I wanted what Uncle George had never allowed himself to want.

Hannah leaned her elbows on the counter and started chatting like we had dropped in for a normal visit, telling us how the house was built in the 1930s, how they were planning to redo the backyard, how the real estate agent had asked if they were sisters when she first met them. Baker busied herself with steeping the tea bags, fetching the cream from the refrigerator, stirring the honey in a way that seemed routine. She let Hannah talk in what I had come to realize was their usual arrangement, Hannah filling the silence with words, Baker creating the hum in the background. They seemed for all the world like they were used to having a couple of anxious teenagers in their kitchen in the middle of the night.

"I'm so sorry for disrupting your night," Aubrey said eventually.

"Yeah, huge disruption," Hannah said dryly. "Totally threw us off our rhythm of lying in bed, eating tortilla chips, and watching *Criminal Minds*."

"You weren't sleeping?" I asked.

"Pssshh. We're so young and vibrant, always partying, never sleeping."

Baker set our tea mugs in front of us. Tendrils of steam swirled up to cradle my face. "You never have to apologize for needing a safe space, Aubrey." She turned to me. "You either, Louisa."

"So tell us," Hannah said gently. "What's going on?"

Aubrey crossed one leg over the other and cupped her hands in her lap. She seemed determined to appear put together even in the midst of everything. "Well," she started, using that clean, proper voice I assumed she used on the alumni interviewer, "I'm . . . I'm gay."

Her words landed in the silence. For a moment, no one spoke. Then Hannah nodded vigorously and said, "Same."

I snorted and shook my head while Baker rolled her eyes, but we could both see that Hannah's stupid joke had done the trick: Aubrey's shoulders visibly relaxed, and the hint of a smile crossed her face.

"Have you ever said that before?" Baker asked kindly.

Aubrey glanced at me. "Only to Louisa."

"How does it feel?" Hannah asked.

"Scary. And also like I'm not doing it right."

"Is there a right way to do it?"

Aubrey bit her lip. "Sometimes it seems that way. I just, um . . . I'm having a hard time, like, getting my arms around it." She lowered her head. "My dad had words with me after he caught me at the bar yesterday and I just . . . I wanted to tell him the truth, to stand up and be like, *This is who I am*, but I—I don't think I'm brave enough."

She began to cry again, burying her head into her arms, her whole body shaking against the counter. I got off my stool and hugged her from behind, squeezing tight against the racking sobs, drying my own hot tears on her sweatshirt. When Aubrey finally settled, I let go of her to find that both Hannah and Baker had reached across the counter to rest a hand on her arm.

"I'm sorry," Aubrey said thickly.

"Please don't apologize," Baker said softly, handing her the tissues. "We've been where you are. We know how much it hurts." She reached for Hannah's hand. "Coming out was excruciating for us."

"It was like being in a choke hold," Hannah agreed. "On fire. With lice."

I looked between them. "What happened?"

Wordlessly, they searched each other's expressions like they were deciding who would answer first. Finally, Baker began to speak, her voice thin but practiced as she told us the rough edges of their story: the pining, the fighting, the crying. I watched everything settle over her face, how she still seemed completely in control even as pain was leaking through her façade.

"It was terrifying," Hannah went on. She was watching Baker with such a tender look that I felt like we were intruding. "Like being outside of my skin. Every single person I met was another chance to be accepted, or to be shunned. And every time I came out to someone new, it was like holding my breath and jumping into the deep end."

"The breathing," Baker said, pointing like she could see the very word shimmering on the air between them. "That was a whole thing. I literally started breathing differently after I came out."

"Oh, for sure," Hannah agreed. "Even after we finally got together, it wasn't quite . . . *happiness* that I felt, even though I was euphoric inside. The most palpable feeling was that ability to breathe again. Like I'd been in a pressure tank, running out of air, and someone had finally opened the door." She paused, considering her words. "Or rather, I opened the door. I was terrified, and felt all these eyes on me, and of course my coming out was very intertwined with Baker's, so I was always worrying about her, too—but through all of that, at least I could breathe."

"I'm sorry you went through that," Aubrey said quietly.

"Thank you," Baker answered. "I'm sorry you're going through it now."

Aubrey swallowed. "Does it actually get easier?"

"Yes," Hannah said immediately. "You have to remember that nothing you're going through is new. That's not to say it's not hard, because it is. But so many people have been in this exact situation and come out just fine on the other side. It's clichéd to say it, but the only way out is through."

Aubrey hung her head. "I just . . . I want to know that I'll be happy."

"We can't promise you that," Hannah told her. "We can't promise a straight or cisgender kid, either. But I *can* promise you that there is space in the world to be your fully queer self. Even if you can't see it right now."

"Are you happy?" I asked them.

"Oh, absolutely," Baker said, like it was as easy as answering two plus two. "In my daily life, I don't really think about how long it took to get to this point. Maybe that sounds weird. But I'm more preoccupied with the same things my friends are—my career, the wedding, the next project we need to take on with the house. I'm happy and I'm living the life I want, but it's in a regular, ordinary way. There's no jumping out of bed each morning feeling 'euphoric' that this is my life, but when I do stop to think about it, I'm overwhelmingly grateful." She shrugged. "And then our dishwasher leaks and I'm back in everyday reality, but I'm doing it with my best friend, and I get to fall asleep with her every night."

"That sounds like the dream."

"It is," Hannah said, "but what we're trying to tell you is that it happens slowly, one day at a time, one coming out experience at a time."

I believed her, and I could see on Aubrey's face that she believed her, too. I had a sudden awareness of myself, of how small I was in the vast order of things, but it was a pure and comforting kind of smallness, the kind that made me feel like I was standing in the midst of a giant cathedral and watching the sunlight pour through the stained glass.

"Thank you," Aubrey said quietly. She wiped her sleepy, red-rimmed eyes. "I wish we didn't have to leave."

"I'm not sure I want you leaving this late, anyway," Baker said. "You need sleep. Both of you. If it's okay with your parents, our guest room is free."

The guest room was small, simple, and dimly lit in a way that invited burrowing. The curtains hung high over the windows and nearly touched the old wooden floor. A well-worn rug tied the room together and looked as soft as something from a preschool classroom; I longed to rub my bare feet against it. The bed was neatly made with a patterned quilt and long, soft pillows. A small white desk was pushed against the far wall, covered with papers, billing statements, and wedding invoices.

"Sorry about the desk," Hannah said as if reading my mind. "Most of our wedding vendor contracts end up here."

"We keep our overflow books in here," Baker added, "if you like to read before bed."

"There are two fans in case you get hot. My sister is kind of a diva when she comes to visit."

"Do you need anything else?" Baker asked. "If you get hungry or thirsty, feel free to help yourselves. Don't be shy."

"We'll be okay," I assured them, "but thank you. Really."

"All right," Hannah said, clicking on another lamp for us. "Sleep well, and don't be afraid to knock on our door if you need anything."

"Good night, Aubrey. Good night, Louisa," Baker said with a kind smile.

"Good night."

And then they had shut the door, and Aubrey and I were alone in the room.

"Are you all right?"

"I'm all right," she assured me. "I feel better."

We slipped under the covers and stayed on our respective sides of the bed, but it was comfortable and normal. Aubrey rolled on her side to look at me.

"Thank you for being here."

"Thank you for letting me be."

"Do you think we could be happy like this someday?" she asked. And my heart skipped, because I wasn't sure who *we* was: if she meant the two of us together, or just us as queer people in a bigger way.

"Yes," I told her, and I believed it in my bones.

The fan overhead circled in a steady, calming way. Beyond my door was the distant sound of Jolene's nails clacking happily on the floor. I closed my eyes and listened. I smelled the faded laundry detergent on the pillowcase. I sent up a prayer that I could hold on to this feeling of coming to shore when I awoke.

It was the fastest I'd ever fallen asleep.

17
THE SUMMER BANQUET

The pavilion lot was packed with Bentleys and Mercedes. I parked the Cadillac and made my way inside, past the golden balloons neatly tied to the handrail and the laminated poster board welcoming me to the Rustin Athletic Foundation's summer banquet.

It was my first swanky cocktail party, and it looked exactly as I imagined it would. Servers in uniform shirts flitted around the room, offering shrimp cocktail and glasses of champagne to every guest they passed. The attendees were impeccably dressed in sport coats and Lily Pulitzer dresses, leather loafers and strappy heels. Flashy diamonds sparkled on the women's hands and necks. Expensive aftershave clung to the men as they ambled past me. Nearly everyone was white, and if I had to guess, probably all of them were straight. *As far as you know*, said an inner voice that sounded like Hannah.

Sponsorship boards lined the perimeter of the room: everything from Coca-Cola to the local plastic surgeon's office. Burt

LaMott from LaMott Cadillac laughed uproariously in a corner, surrounded by a gaggle of middle-aged women. Officious people wearing gold-plated Rustin University name tags swiveled from guest to guest, chatting them up, thanking them for their support.

"Champagne?" someone asked, and I turned to find a young server standing next to me: an attractive dark-skinned Black boy with dyed yellow hair and an ear piercing. He looked familiar, and I could tell from the way he was appraising me that I was familiar to him, too.

We realized it at the same time: He was a regular patron at the Cricket.

"Wow," I said, smiling at him, "we really are everywhere, huh?"

He laughed in a sweet, surprised way. "We are." He leaned in closer and whispered to me. "Let me know if you want something stronger. These events can be . . . A Lot."

I grinned. "Thanks. See you at the bar."

"See you at the bar. Or as my friends call it, *church*." He winked and strode away, proffering the champagne tray to an elderly woman bedecked with pearls.

Feeling more at ease, I wound my way along the perimeter of the room, searching for familiar faces. I spotted Grandma and Grandpa in the middle of the crowd, holding court with several couples whose eyes glinted with power. Dad wasn't with them. I kept walking, searching for him, until I was distracted by a pretty girl in an emerald green jumpsuit.

Aubrey.

Her eyes were on me, giving me that soft, secret smile I had come to know in the past couple of weeks. There was a thrill of intimacy between us, even as we stood ten feet away. I made my way toward her, one hand in my dress pocket and the other balancing my champagne flute, trying to affect a casual air like I had run into an old school friend and was simply checking in.

"Fabulous party," I said loftily, coming to a stop just before I reached her. I positioned my body next to hers like we were surveying the crowd, making sure to keep a safe distance between us.

"Oh, just the loveliest," she said, playing along.

I lowered my voice. "You look really pretty."

She kept her eyes on the crowd, but she blushed the tiniest bit. "I wouldn't mind if you wore that dress again," she said under her breath. "Please."

I chewed down my smile and tipped my head toward the sea of people. "Do you think they're actually having fun? Like, is this their big night out on the town?"

"A chance to see and be seen." She looked sideways at me. "They don't know the real party's at the Cricket later."

I glanced around to make sure her dad wasn't passing by, then turned my body toward her the tiniest bit. "How are you?" I asked meaningfully.

"I'm all right, actually." She took a deliberate breath. "Just trying to make it through the spectacle."

"That makes two of us."

We lapsed into silence, simply watching the crowd. My dad stepped into view on the side of the room, nursing a glass of whiskey. A university administrator had his ear, but I could tell Dad wasn't truly listening. He nodded his head every few seconds, but his mind was elsewhere.

There was the tap of a microphone, a sudden break in the cocktail music. The conversation fell away as everyone turned their attention to the stage at the front of the room.

"Thank you, everyone, thank you," said a striking blond woman in a violet dress. She had that tough-as-nails, pretty-as-pie aura about her like she would eviscerate you in the boardroom and then stop for a manicure on the way home. "Welcome to the RAF's summer banquet. We are so grateful for your support. It's been a busy summer gearing up for a fresh year of Rustin Athletics, and we can't wait to tell you everything we have in store . . ."

I zoned out, surveying the room again. My grandparents had a pompous, expectant look on their faces. Dad looked pale and apprehensive. My server friend from the Cricket wove silently between the guests, collecting empty flutes. A businessman tapped him on the shoulder and crumpled a cocktail napkin unceremoniously onto his tray.

"—but first, we'd like to introduce one of our special guests this evening: the head coach of Rustin Football, Rhett Calhoun!"

There was an uproar of applause. Aubrey stiffened next to me. I inched closer and brushed my arm against hers.

Coach Calhoun was businesslike as he stepped forward to the microphone. His tie was knotted impeccably, his shoes so shiny that stage lights gleamed off of them. His thick hair was combed precisely, with one cowlick styled to fall forward.

As the crowd continued to applaud, Coach Calhoun raised one large hand to silence them. They hushed immediately.

"It's the honor of a lifetime to lead this program," he began. "When my family and I first moved to Rustin, I knew this was a special place . . ."

Aubrey was still holding her breath, her body tight like she was contracting every muscle. Her mother stood at the front of the room, beaming at Coach Calhoun, and I wondered how long it had taken her to perfect that look.

". . . We're ready for Media Day on Monday, and a week from then, we'll start camp. These boys are ready to step up and deliver. They know what this town expects of them, what I expect of them, and we're taking every measure to ensure they have the support and resources they need. Speaking of . . ."

Coach paused to let the silence swell around him.

"Some of y'all know what's coming next tonight. I gotta tell you, this is probably the worst-kept secret since my lovely wife sniffed out my marriage proposal all those years ago. But I ain't mad about it. Secrets leak when people are excited, and the wave of excitement about this next investment is something a head coach could only dream of . . ."

My skin prickled. Restless whispers filtered through the crowd. Grandpa puffed out his chest.

"Now, now, Coach," the striking blond woman said, stepping hurriedly up to the podium again. It was clear she wasn't about to let anyone take her announcement away from her. Coach Calhoun laughed good-naturedly and graciously stepped back to give her space.

"Let's get to it, then, Rustin," the woman said with a Cheshire cat smile. "On behalf of the Rustin University Athletic Foundation, the board of trustees, and our unstoppable Rustin football program, we are thrilled to unveil . . . the George Wade Football Performance Center!"

Suddenly, a gigantic draped curtain was pulled aside behind her, and every eye fell upon the image: a dazzling, colorful rendering, as large as a movie theater screen, showcasing a state-of-the-art facility with a bright green practice field. The crowd gasped, roared, applauded so loudly that the glass chandelier vibrated above the room.

"This eighty-five-million-dollar investment is a testament to RU's belief in our growing football program, and in *your* incredible support—"

But I wasn't listening anymore. My body had gone cold as ice water. My ears rang and my heart drilled against my chest. *Where is it*, my brain pleaded with the woman to tell us, *where is this facility going to—*

"It was a long, extensive search to find the right location for the center, but after months of scouting, we settled on an expanse of land out on Route 29—"

No, I thought. *No, no, no.*

"—Without further ado, please allow me to introduce Mr. Amos Wade, brother of the late George Wade, and his darling wife, Martha, both of whom are longtime supporters of—"

I wasn't processing anything. My hands were cold with sweat and a sour, nauseating feeling spread across my stomach. I felt Aubrey's eyes on me, and when I turned to her, I saw the terrible confirmation in her gaze.

Grandpa was at the podium now, his voice coming to me as if through water. The crowd cheered, clapped, pulsed with energy. My dad remained silent and still at the edge of the room, his mouth set in a thin line. I stared at him until he felt my gaze. When he turned to look at me, an infinite conversation passed between us. He looked sadder than he had on the day of Uncle George's funeral.

"And I said to my brother," Grandpa went on, enjoying the shine of the crowd, "I said, 'Georgie Boy, now just you wait and see what your legacy will mean to this town—' "

"Don't call him that!"

My own shout surprised me, and I flushed with the sudden attention from the crowd.

Grandpa froze for a fraction of a second, then continued on like the interruption was a fluke. "And I know George would be proud to—"

"What about the bar?!" I shouted, louder this time. I felt reckless, untethered, detached from my own body. The familiar mantra rose up in my head, but this time I felt it like a battle cry. *I am gay . . . I am here . . . I am HERE I am HERE I am HERE.*

The crowd rustled, officially disturbed now. Their necks craned to look at me; their murmurs zipped through the air. Aubrey distanced herself with a subtle step away.

"We'll speak later, Louisa," Grandpa said in a low, terse voice. "As I was saying—"

"WHAT—ABOUT—THE BAR!" I shouted again. I was scaring myself now, feeling completely out of control, and yet I couldn't have stopped myself if I'd tried.

There was a whine of feedback as Blond Lady moved the microphone and shuffled my grandfather aside. "Honey, I understand people have attachments to different things, but this really is the best thing for the university, and your uncle would have—"

"It was HIS bar!" I screamed.

The crowd reached a fever pitch, not bothering to lower their voices anymore. Women scowled at me; men widened their eyes like I was disturbed. The server from the Cricket stood stock-still on the perimeter of the room, watching me anxiously.

"Louisa!" Grandma hissed. "Be quiet!"

"No!" I was on the edge of a precipice, my throat thick with fury and grief, my emotions threatening to boil over. "I'm tired of staying quiet! I'm tired of you erasing us!"

"George *wanted* his football legacy to—"

"*You* wanted that!" I screamed. "He was more than just a football player! He was the owner of that bar!"

"Sweetheart, you're confused," Blond Lady said patronizingly. "The bar we're talking about is . . . well, it's . . ." She licked her lips, clearly trying to figure out how to put it, and a dark, slithering satisfaction came over me as I watched her struggle. "It was a *gay* bar," the woman whispered finally, trying to tell me without the ears of the crowd. "You've got it confused with some other place—"

The dark rage swallowed me up, and my body shook against the restraints I'd been feeling all summer, and my voice was ringing out before I could stop it—

"George Wade owned that gay bar! He was a gay man, and you can't just erase that part of him!"

The crowd went unnervingly silent. Their shock was so sharp, so palpable, that I felt it in my lungs.

Suddenly, Dad's hand was on my shoulder. "Louisa, enough," he murmured into my ear. "Let's go outside and—"

I wrenched away from him, slammed my champagne flute on a table without seeing it, and bolted for the patio.

Outside, I gulped down the air, my body heaving as if I'd been drowning. My senses returned to me slowly: the screaming insects, the cramping in my hands, the filmy aftertaste of champagne. My heart thudded violently and an itchy hot rash spread across my neck and shoulders.

"What the *hell*, Louisa?!"

Aubrey was there, gripping my arm to get my attention, her eyes blazing in the glow of the string lights.

"Uncle George," I whispered, still reeling.

"Yeah, Uncle George," she said heatedly, "the man you just outed."

"I didn't out him," I muttered, dazed.

"You just fucking *did*!" Angry tears pricked her eyes, but she didn't bother to wipe them away. She glowered at me like she had never seen something so repulsive in her life, but the longer I stared back into her dark, raging eyes, the more I saw her wounds and her fear.

"People need to know," I managed at last. I shook my head, cleared the rushing from my ears. "They need to know who he *really* was, how they're distorting his—"

"That's not for you to decide!" she yelled. "I can't believe you. I can't believe—after all the stuff Hannah and Baker talked about the other night—"

"Is this about him, or about you?" I yelled back. I swelled with anger again, felt it sink me like the rush of water through a boat. "He's *dead*. He's dead, but we're alive, and they can't keep acting like we're not *right fucking here*!"

The sound of jarring metal—the patio door banging open—and then Coach Calhoun was descending on us like a ferocious predator who'd been deprived of his kill. Aubrey made a jerky movement, turning her body completely away from mine.

"What the hell was that?" he demanded, stalking toward us. For one fleeting second, I thought he was screaming at Aubrey, and my sudden anger evaporated as I moved to stand in front of her. Then I realized his rage was directed at me, and the unchecked wildness of it knocked me breathless.

"The *hell* was that, hmm?" he screamed. "What was that ridiculous, childish, selfish tantrum you just threw in the middle of my party?!"

I steadied myself and looked up at him, kept my eyes trained on those scathing blue eyes, the eyes he'd given Aubrey. In that moment, I loathed Rhett Calhoun like I had never loathed another human being before; and deep in my psyche, in my heart of hearts, I was shocked and ashamed to realize that I could understand it suddenly, this white-hot hatred of another person, this molecular impulse to silence them, to cage them, to remove them from the table at all costs.

"It's not *your* party," I said with as much disdain as I could muster.

He towered over me, his voice spitting with rage. "Do you realize you just ruined years of careful planning—fundraising—leveraging—you just hijacked the focus from our program and players to make it about *you* and your precious *specialness*—"

"Back off, Rhett!" yelled a new voice. The door had banged open again, and my dad was rushing toward us with a fury I had never seen in him before. He looked like he wanted to tackle Coach Calhoun to the patio stone and rip his limbs off one by one. "Don't you dare talk to my daughter like that—"

"This answers the question, doesn't it," Coach Calhoun interrupted, sweeping an arm over us. "You're the one indulging her, coddling her, letting her run sideways—"

"As opposed to you?" I yelled. "What kind of dad do you think *you* are, *Coach*?"

"Louisa, *stop*," Aubrey hissed through her teeth.

I whirled on Aubrey. "You knew about this, didn't you? That the deal had already gone through?"

Aubrey gawked, unable to answer me, her petrified eyes darting to her dad.

"I'm out of here," I said with as much disgust as I could muster.

I stormed off the patio, down the back steps, and away from the sickening cocktail party happening inside.

"Louisa, wait!" Dad shouted after me, but I kept my back to him and swept into the night with a dark, blistering feeling like I was ready to watch the world burn.

18
THE SILENT PARTNER

I went to the Cricket and barreled my way inside, ignoring all the people calling hello. There was only one person I wanted to unleash my crackling rage on.

He was in his office, shut behind the closed door, hiding from the world. I shoved my way inside without bothering to knock and found him sprawled back in his chair, Hannah hovering above his desk with unmistakably worried eyes.

"Well," Hatch said, blinking up at me. He seemed entirely untroubled by my whirling rage. "If it isn't our little shit-stirrer."

"Louisa, please tell me you didn't," Hannah said beseechingly. There was a desperate expression on her face.

How had they heard, and so quickly? It had been no more than half an hour since I'd erupted at the banquet. The speed of gossip in this suffocating town only added to my fury. "Which one of your little spies was it this time?" I demanded.

Hatch leaned back and settled his hands across his stomach. "Otis," he said simply, like it was the most obvious answer in the world.

I snorted derisively. "Of course. Just another fly trapped in your sticky web."

Hatch regarded me warily. "It seems you have something to say."

"Oh, there are *many* things I'd like to say. Starting with, why the *fuck* did you go behind my back with the university?"

The door banged open, and suddenly my dad was standing there, breathless like he'd sprinted from the parking lot. "Louisa," he said, his worried eyes latching on to mine. He slammed the door behind him and strode into the room, his eyes flickering from Hatch in his desk chair to Hannah prowling near the wall. "Well, good," he said with barely restrained emotion. "We'd better air this out all together."

Hannah lurched forward, still watching me desperately. "What did you tell them, Louisa? What did you do?"

"I told the truth!" I shouted. "They were going on and on about this wonderful new facility, and how Uncle George would have been *so* proud, and they were completely fucking up his legacy, and I couldn't take it anymore! I told them the truth about who he was!"

Hannah jolted away with a noise like a hissing cat. Gone was any trace of affection she had for me, any proof that she had taken me under her wing and mentored me through the last few weeks. Now her scorn sliced through me like a hot knife.

Hatch was the complete opposite. He merely tapped the arms of his chair, regarding me like an unforeseen problem that complicated his evening plans. This lack of response got under my skin in a different way, making me itch with madness. I wanted nothing more than for him to explode so it would justify my own explosion. I wanted to rail and scream and shout everything I'd been holding in all summer.

"You had no right to do that, Louisa."

It was my dad who spoke. His voice was dead quiet. He hovered behind me and I could feel his eyes burning into the back of my head, daring me to turn around.

"Whose right was it, then?!" I spit back, half glancing at him. "Who was going to stand up and tell everybody that their precious hero wasn't who they thought he was?"

"He wasn't who *you* thought he was, either," said a new voice.

We all turned. Grandpa was leaning against the door, wearing an expression of disgust and dismay that matched Hannah's. He took an arrogant step into the room, taking up all the space as if he owned it. "The two of you rushed out without so much as a good-bye," he said, looking between Dad and me. There was a hint of relish to his tone, like he was excited to eviscerate us. "Once again leaving Martha and me to clean up your mess."

"You don't belong here," I said, doing my best to hold my own against that scary gleam in his eyes. "This was Uncle George's sacred place."

"Oh, sure, very sacred," Grandpa baited. "You would know, because you knew him better than anyone, didn't you, Louisa?"

"Amos," Hatch said in a warning tone.

Grandpa pretended to look around, as if he hadn't noticed Hatch before. "Well, hello there, Marion."

"Nice of you to show up, Amos," Hatch said, unnervingly calm. "I wish you would come when we actually *call* you."

Grandpa ignored him and set his sights on Hannah. "And who are you? Another one of George's disciples?"

Hannah stared him down with more hatred than I had ever seen on her face. "I'm George's family."

Grandpa flat out laughed in her face. "It seems we have different definitions of family, sweetheart."

"Indeed we do, *sweetheart*," Hannah shot back.

"Enough pleasantries," Grandpa snapped. "I'm here for damage control. I've talked with the foundation board and Rhett Calhoun, and we're going to issue a statement that Louisa was confusing George with an uncle on her mother's side—"

I roared with outrage, but Grandpa plowed over me.

"—and, Louisa, you will speak to the press and apologize for disturbing the fundraiser—"

"Like hell I will," I spit, staring up into his pompous face.

Grandpa laughed again, almost like I was paid entertainment. "Louisa, you still don't get it, do you? George was the mastermind behind all of this."

"Dad—" my father began.

"What are you talking about?" I asked through gritted teeth.

"Oh, honey," Grandpa said with a deep, affected sigh, "George was the one who arranged for the university to buy this land *and* to name it after him. Before he got sick, when he was still on the board of trustees, he was the one who suggested this exact spot."

All the blood drained from my face. "You're lying."

"The board didn't even know he owned this place," Grandpa went on, relishing every word. "You see, back when Marion tricked him into opening a business together, George at least had the good sense to ensure that Marion was the only listed owner. His own involvement was protected by a DBA pseudonym. Otis Penny was the one who advised him."

I looked around wildly. My dad's face had gone completely white. Hannah looked as shocked as I felt. But Hatch—Hatch had the audacity to lower his head, hiding his face from me.

"Is this true?" I asked, my voice smaller than I wanted it to be.

Finally, Hatch lifted his head. There was a darkness in his eyes that could have ravaged the earth. "You remain a stand-up human being, Amos," he said in the ugliest growl I'd ever heard.

"Louisa deserves the truth," Grandpa said, unfazed—even delighted—by the crackling tension in the room. "You've had her dancing like a monkey all summer, thinking she understood who my brother was."

"Hatch," I said, not caring that my voice caught, not caring that my armor of rage was slipping off. "Hatch, please—"

Hatch gripped his chair so hard that his knuckles were white. "The thing about a silent partner, Louisa," he began, his voice softer than I'd ever heard it, "is their silence typically buys them a minority percentage of ownership."

My body seemed to understand before my brain did. A sickening prickle ran down my spine. "What are you saying?"

"I'm saying George owned forty-nine percent to my fifty-one, and this sale only required the majority owner's signature."

My heart stopped. "So you never needed me? You just let me believe we had a deal?" I gritted my teeth and poured as much loathing into my voice as possible. "You *asshole*. When did you do this? When did you sign the paperwork?"

Hatch set his mouth. "Three days ago."

"The day after my thirty days ran out," I said breathlessly. "But—but that afternoon that Grandpa and Coach Calhoun came—the thirtieth day—you told me we could still sit down and talk about it—"

"He hoodwinked you, Louisa," Grandpa said. "There was never a 'thirty days.' The sale—the naming—it was the endgame all along. Marion was stringing you along the same way he did to poor George—"

"Get out," my dad said.

Grandpa blinked in surprise. "Excuse me?"

Dad raised a shaking arm toward the door. "Get *out*, Dad. You've said your piece, you've laid your ruins. You can gloat somewhere else. *Out*."

Grandpa's nostrils flared. He took one last look around the room, then cocked his head like he was satisfied with the damage. "I'll see you later, *son*," he snipped at my dad. And then he was gone.

It was like all the oxygen had gone from the room. I couldn't breathe. I couldn't think. Hannah was bent over, her hands on her knees. My dad and Hatch made eye contact, and the whole of the universe passed between them.

"Why," I said flatly. It was all I could manage.

"Louisa . . ." Hatch sighed. "You've got to understand that the truest love of George's life was his persona."

"Hatch," my dad said sadly. "That's not why—"

"It *is* why," Hatch insisted. "George loved me, but never as much as I loved him, and never as much as he loved himself. We both knew it. The best thing he ever did for me was agreeing to finally sell this place, but in my heart of hearts, I always knew it was because of the land opportunity, the legacy opportunity. I didn't stand a chance against that, so I took what I could get."

I looked from Hatch to my dad. "But—but you let me think this place meant something to him. That he wanted me to know it because of the connection between us."

"And that's true," my dad said in a pained voice. The pity in his eyes nearly cut me at the knees. "He *did* love this place, Lou. He *did* want you to know who he was. But he wanted all those other things, too."

"He wanted them even more," Hatch said.

"I don't . . . I don't understand how he'd want to be remembered for one part of himself, but not the other."

"He was a complicated man," Hatch answered. "He wasn't good and he wasn't bad, he was somewhere in the middle."

"'Complicated,'" I repeated. My skin began to prickle again, the anger spreading across me like a toxin. "No, I'm starting to think he wasn't complicated at all. I think he was just as bad as Grandpa, taking whatever he wanted without putting anything on the line. He wanted the spotlight, but only if he could control where it landed. Never on the parts of him that were like *me*, right? And you two, and everyone here, you all made excuses for him, you protected him, you let him do whatever was easiest without ever having the guts to say, *Hey, George, maybe you can't have it both ways, maybe you should use your influence to make things better for other people—*"

"You don't know what it was like to be George," Dad started warningly.

"Neither do you! You have no idea what it's like to walk around wondering if people hate you because of something at the very core of your—"

"Stop making this about you!" Dad screamed.

I flinched, staring at him in shock.

"You didn't even care about his death until it became about you!" Dad went on, his eyes widening maddeningly. "Even now, you only want to hear about the parts you can understand!"

"I want his legacy to be known! His *real* legacy!"

"Football was his real legacy, too! Being an arrogant asshole was his legacy! Having a heart as big as the sky was his legacy! You can't cut those parts of him away!"

"The dead don't belong to just one person, Louisa," Hatch

interjected, still unnervingly calm. "George belongs to Rustin as much as he belongs to the rest of us."

I clenched my jaw and stared from Hatch to my dad. "I'm not sure I want Uncle George to belong to me at all anymore."

"Fine, then!" Dad said, sweeping his arm over the room like he was ready to do away with me forever. "Rid yourself of him! Rid yourself of the whole town! Sell the bar and get back to your life in Connecticut and—"

"Yeah, Connecticut is damn right, because there's nothing left for me here!"

"I think you've proven that this summer," Dad said with a final cutting breath. He turned, chest heaving, and bolted out of the office.

Immediately, all the fight went out of me. I wanted to sink to the floor, to collapse into a sobbing heap until all the bad things leaked out of me. But Hatch was still sitting there, silent in the wake of my family's rupture, so I grabbed for the wall and stumbled my way out to the back porch, to the spot where I had first encountered Hatch, where I had kissed Aubrey, where I had gazed at the treetops in the morning light and wondered if Uncle George had reveled in the same glory.

I had believed this place to be a sanctuary, but that wasn't true, was it? It was merely another way for Uncle George to exercise his significance in this small, suffocating town. And what had I been to him? An opportunity to live vicariously through younger blood, braver blood? Was I one last dig at Hatch, a chance to hurt him even in death? Or did I mean something to him, did he think of me, did he pray for me, did he want the best for me, did he believe I could do it, did I matter? What did he expect from me when he'd never had the guts to articulate it to my face, when instead he'd died and left me a half-baked legacy to figure out, thrusting me into this world of people who loathed him and worshipped him and pitied him and owed him?

Who had he been, really, and what did that mean for who I was?

19
THE CLOSET

For two days, I slept, played on my phone, and trundled back and forth to the kitchen. There was no juice in my muscles, no heart in my actions. I felt forsaken by everyone I knew, and even worse, I couldn't blame them. I felt ugly and ashamed and irredeemable. Dad's point that I hadn't cared about Uncle George's death until it involved me kept playing over and over in my head, cutting me to the quick of my soul, breaking me open to bleed. I knew he was right. And how was I supposed to live with that about myself?

I stayed away from the bar. Hatch wouldn't want me there, and even more painfully, Hannah wouldn't want me there. No doubt Midas shared their perspective.

The other worst part was how my outburst—my *outing*, if I was honest with myself—became the talk of the town. Everyone had something to say about it.

"It's one of the things I dislike about this generation," said the radio host for the local oldies station. "They want to rewrite history and tell us their heroes were outside the norm. It's a pathetic attempt to—"

I punched the radio off, but the voices were everywhere.

"It's all noise," Coach Calhoun said on the evening news. "Just a means of distracting us from the upcoming season. But we're not gonna pay attention to that. We know what we have to do, and we're gonna keep doin' it."

Finally, on the third day of my self-imposed exile, I took a shower, slipped into the Caddy, and drove to Uncle George's house.

It was startlingly quiet inside. Sunlight fell through the slatted blinds, creating golden rectangles on the hardwood floor. Dust motes floated through the air, the one moving thing in this otherwise static tomb.

I moved slowly from room to room. My dad and grandparents had definitely returned since that day a few weeks ago, judging by how many more boxes were laid up against the walls. The vast oriental rug was rolled up in the living room, revealing a polished patch of floor. The clock had been taken off the wall like a visual reminder that Uncle George's time was up.

I lingered at the foot of the stairs, remembering Grandpa's resistance to cleaning Uncle George's bedroom. Did *I* want to see his bedroom? What if I didn't find proof of him there? And equally as scary: What if I did?

The door was slightly ajar, as if someone had entered just recently. Had my dad been back to tackle this room on his own, or had Uncle George himself left this door open that day he'd gone to the post office and collapsed outside his car? I knew from Dad that once he'd checked into the hospital, he had never come back. He'd died in the hospice ward, away from home.

There on the bed was a thin pile of shirts, laid out like someone had started to sort through them but given up. So Dad *had* been here. I smoothed a hand down a worn navy polo shirt, then picked it up and breathed in its scent. Immediately, it was like Uncle George was there, ready for a conversation, his aftershave swirling all around us. I closed my eyes and pretended he was standing there next to me. Amazing how it was impossible to be angry with him when he no longer felt far away.

I roamed the room, stopping to absorb every detail. A small wooden cross hung next to the bed. A watercolor painting of a beach hung opposite the window. Tellingly, there was no football memorabilia anywhere; the only hint of his Rustin legacy was a bold, glinting class ring gathering dust on top of the dresser.

A pair of foam earplugs lay haphazardly on the nightstand. Next to them, on a corkboard coaster, was a forgotten glass of water. It was still half full. I picked it up and held the glass up to the sunlight, revealing the imprint of a person's mouth right there along the rim. He had been alive so, *so* recently.

His pill cutter and toothbrush were laid out on the bathroom counter. Several prescription bottles were cluttered against the mirror. A threadbare green towel hung forgotten on a hook. The shower was riddled with soap scum, but the sight of a yellow loofah made me laugh.

I went to the closet last. The pile of shirts on the bed had been just a small selection of his wardrobe. I began to pull the hangers off one by one and categorized each item into a donation pile or a keep pile. There were a few great T-shirts that my friends at the Cricket might want for sentimental value—especially a vintage cream *Rustin Homecoming 1993* T-shirt, with holes in the underarms from wear and tear, that I knew Midas would cherish.

I had just pushed aside the dress shirts when something caught my eye.

It was a hidden set of shelves in the back of the closet—a vestige from years past when many people had a personal safe. I pushed the dress shirts farther along the rack and stepped closer to the wooden shelves.

My heart lodged in my throat.

There, in the center of three shelves, was an old framed photograph of Hatch.

He was standing on a city sidewalk, leaning with one hand against a pole, grinning into the camera. His hair was russet brown, almost spiky in the style of the early 2000s, and his jean shorts and ruddy skin hinted to summertime. The piercing blue eyes were the same, but they were crinkled with something I had never seen before: unbridled happiness.

"Hatch," I whispered longingly, taking the picture frame off the shelf. I brushed my fingertips across his young, beaming face. It was a face that had the unmistakable shine of new love. Grief ripped through my body like a flash in the pan, realizing this version of him had been lost. Just like with Uncle George, I had never gotten to know the real him.

I set the picture frame back on the shelf, and that was when I noticed the ring box. Every hair on my arm stood up.

"No way," I said aloud.

I reached for it, rubbing my fingertips over the velvet coat. Then I snapped the cover open and gasped.

It was a ring. A thick, silver band for a finger much larger than mine, inlaid with tiny diamonds that wrapped like a belt. This wasn't something Uncle George had bought for his own vanity. This was an engagement ring.

I plucked the ring carefully from the case and examined it closely—and sure enough, engraved on the inside of the band, was all the proof in the world:

MH + GW

* * *

For close to an hour, I sat in the Caddy outside the Cricket, sweating in the nighttime heat. I watched people come and go. A group of friends smoked cigarettes near the front door, their laughter crackling on the sweltering air. Two men lingered by a truck, one of them pulling on the other's belt straps until he leaned forward for the inevitable kiss. A rowdy group of college girls flocked from their cars, two of them holding hands in a shy, nascent way. All the while, the blinking Frisky Cricket sign kept watch over me. I stared at it long enough to count the dozens of tiny light bulbs that made up its magic.

Grief was a strange phenomenon. I hadn't felt it for my uncle himself, but I felt it now for the dingy old building he'd left to me. It was the grief of something never fully realized, a yearning, choking thing, nostalgia for an ideal that never existed. I sucked in a breath like maybe I could swallow everything whole: the bar, the parking lot, the vast overgrown yard and tree line. I understood on some deep, unconscious level that I was here to say goodbye to this place. And what was this place, really? It was the dirt and the pavement, the delineated parcel on the map, the GPS coordinates that brought your Uber driver to the exact drop-off spot. It was the pothole that never got fixed, the county road that whisked people past as they craned their necks, the beer can tabs that told stories of nights with friends and lovers and chosen family. I was here to say goodbye to a meeting of lives, a sacred waterfall, an Eden for people who were never supposed to see Eden in the first place. And

I was here with the feeling of surrender, of giving up the fight, because I realized, finally, that it was beyond my control, and all I could do was pay my respects and my gratitude.

At last, I got out of the car. RuPaw met me at the front step, sniffing around my legs. Where would she go when this place was sold? I couldn't picture her in some hoity-toity house somewhere, laid up with catnip and string toys. She needed the freedom of the Cricket, the chance to come and go as she pleased, the ear scratches not from one devoted person, but from a parade of people who whispered nonsensical things while they slipped her treats from their pockets.

By the time I walked inside, it was closing time. Hatch looked up from the bar with a watchful, wary eye. He clearly expected me to throw another tantrum, to accuse him of a betrayal that he never had a choice in. I took a deep breath and stepped toward him.

"Can I speak with you?"

He leveled me with that intense, searching gaze. I let him.

"Wait in my office. I'm nearly finished closing up," he said finally.

RuPaw followed me into the back room. When I sat down in the chair across from Hatch's, the cat settled in my lap and purred happily. The smell of coffee wafted from the main room. Hatch must have made a pot. I wanted to pour myself a cup, but I no longer felt it was my place to help myself. I scratched my fingernail into a groove in the old, worn wood of Hatch's desk.

When Hatch finally joined me, settling into his chair with an expectant look, I had a hard time finding the words I'd just practiced in the parking lot. My throat was suddenly thick. It took everything in me not to lose control, because Hatch deserved steadiness for this conversation.

I couldn't do anything except pass the ring box across the desk.

Hatch took it warily, as if it was a jack-in-the-box that might spring up and pop him. When he met my eyes with a hesitant look, I gave him an encouraging nod.

He opened it, stared at the ring, and gave me another doubtful look—but the quickest flash of hope was there, too. "What is this?" he asked gruffly, clearing his throat. "Where did you find this?"

"In Uncle George's closet, on the hidden shelf." I steeled myself. "Hatch, it's engraved."

He blinked rapidly, rotated the ring in his fingers, and inhaled like someone bursting the surface of the ocean. "Jesus Christ, George."

I gave him a moment. He wiped his hands down his face and pushed away from the desk, as if taking space from the ring might help him gain control of himself.

"Did you know?" I asked. "That he was proposing?"

Hatch swallowed. "I didn't take him seriously. He made a passing remark about 'after the sale goes through,' but I'd stopped believing him a long time ago."

I gave him a wry smile. "I guess he was serious this time."

And what was there to say? Neither one of us understood Uncle George's motivations at the end of his life, but here was incontrovertible proof that during his final days, he had been thinking of Hatch. He had been reaching toward beautiful things for him and Hatch *together*.

"Hatch, I owe you a gigantic apology," I said. "We've been talking about how Uncle George made everything about himself, but I've done the same thing. I ignored your wishes—everything you'd been through—because I was so caught up in fulfilling my own. I guess I felt . . . that if people really saw Uncle George, they'd somehow see me."

Hatch looked me in the eyes. His were piercing, striking. "I knew on Pride night," he said suddenly. "I knew I was going to sign the papers. Ask me why."

I took a deep breath. "Why?"

"Because I saw how happy you were that night, how much you came into your own, and I knew it wasn't going to get better than that. I tried to do this without him, Louisa. The Pride party was his favorite day of the year, right up there with the Rustin home opener. He looked forward to it for months, always coming up with some scheme to make it better than last year's. The big surprise, he called it." Hatch chuckled, his expression drifting away. "Last year he got a dunk tank for the back. We had all these old queens, ten drinks deep, out there throwing the ball at the bull's-eye."

I already knew this from Hannah and Midas, but I kept quiet and listened.

"I wanted to keep it going this year," Hatch continued. "For our patrons' sake, but also for his sake. It's what he would have wanted." His chin trembled as he cleared his throat again. "So voilà . . . the mechanical bull. And it was a hit. I could see how happy everyone was. How happy *you* were. I thought, *This is it. This is the best I can do. I've got nothing left in me.*"

"Hatch," I whispered, and we simply looked at each other, and I felt I was seeing this man for the first time, the way Uncle George must have seen him.

"You were wrong the other night, you know," he said softly. "When you said I never needed you." His eyes flickered to meet mine. "For the sale, no. But I needed you this summer in ways I didn't expect."

I swallowed. "I needed you, too, even if I didn't want to admit it. I needed everyone here."

Hatch sniffed suddenly. At first I worried he was crying—but no, he was smelling something. And then I smelled it, too.

Something was burning.

Hatch was out of his chair in a heartbeat. He clasped the doorknob, feeling it for a moment, then wrenched the door open. Thick, black smoke filled the air.

"Oh my god." I jumped up, my brain short-circuiting and my body revving with adrenaline. "Fire extinguisher. Where's the fire extinguisher?"

I tried to rush into the hallway, but Hatch shoved me backward and slammed the door against the invading smoke. "Too late for that, Louisa. We've got to get out."

"No! We've got to stop the fire!"

"The smoke inhalation will take us down first," he said, hurrying toward the window. He snapped the lock open and tried to heave it upward, but it was sticking from the heat. My stomach bottomed out.

"Grab"—Hatch heaved—"the cat—"

RuPaw struggled in my arms, writhing and scratching with primal fear. I clasped her to my shoulder and tried to comfort her through the pressure of my hand on her fur. Hatch was still shoving at the window with all his might, his face flushed and quickly perspiring.

"Look around," he grunted through his teeth, "find—something—to break it—"

I flew wildly around the room, my eyes darting over everything and nothing. Smoke started curling under the door, creeping toward us like the bringer of death. I coughed and tucked my face into my arm. "There's nothing!" I joined Hatch at the window, panic clogging my throat, RuPaw clinging to me so tightly that her claws were drawing blood. "Let me try!"

"I tried it already!"

I shoved uselessly at the window, my palms aching from the exertion. It wouldn't budge. I shifted RuPaw on my shoulder and felt along the window sashes. "It's the paint!" I shouted. "Where's your utility knife?!"

Hatch dragged the knife out of his pocket and began to saw along the window sashes, digging into the paint. We were both coughing, and the smoke was getting closer and thicker, and Ru was nearly crushing my windpipe. Hatch's blade cut and moved, and I shoved upward again, and the window's resistance gave way. Together, we wrenched the whole thing upward until the open air flushed against our skin.

RuPaw sprang off my body, darting through the window and into the night. I felt Hatch's hand on my back, urging me to follow her.

"Wait," I said wildly, moving back to the desk. It was so dark I could hardly see it; I had to feel for its shape, feel my way to the drawer, and then I could hardly pull the drawer open because I was shaking so hard. I dug my hand into the drawer like a crab into a sand burrow and scuttled through the contents, feeling for the right texture.

"LOUISA, NOW! LET'S GO!" Hatch screamed.

At last, I felt that glossy material I was searching for. I plucked the old photo of Uncle George from the drawer, went sprinting back to the window, and heaved myself onto the sill. I tumbled onto the grass before I could think twice about it, coughing and sputtering, my throat ripped raw.

"MOVE!" Hatch yelled, and I scrambled backward, clearing a landing space for him. He shimmied over the sill and crumpled down next to me, and I reached for his arm and tugged him away from the building.

"Call 911," he panted, struggling to turn over.

I dug my trembling fingers into my shorts pocket, pulled out my cell phone, and dialed the emergency line. A woman's clear, tinkling voice asked me a question, but I couldn't process what it was, and my ears felt clogged and my eyes were burning, and where had RuPaw gone? What was she going to eat for breakfast tomorrow if her food burned?

You're not thinking straight, said a dull voice in my head. *Ha. Or gay.*

I rolled onto my side, lolled my head against my shoulder, and passed into nothingness.

My first thought, sometime later, was that heaven sounded screechy.

My second was that I'd finally get to talk to Uncle George.

Something was strapped to my face, steadying my breathing. An oxygen mask. I pulled it off and sat up on the stretcher.

"Hold on, now," said the EMT. She was a hefty white woman with an auburn ponytail, and I recognized her immediately. I'd served her drinks a few times. Rosé over ice. How did I remember that? Her face was pale, but her eyes were red-rimmed like she'd been crying.

"The bar," I said, sitting up straighter.

The EMT wrestled the oxygen mask over my head. "You need to rest. Focus on your breathing."

I acquiesced to the oxygen mask but sat farther forward, trying to get a glimpse of the Frisky Cricket. It was impossible to see around the fire truck blocking my field of vision. The police were here, too. Flashing red lights bounced off the trees, the cars, the endless black sky.

"Is it okay?" I asked desperately, bracing myself for the worst.

The EMT steeled herself. "It's gone, honey."

Gone. Her voice cracked on the word.

"How gone?"

Her wet eyes met mine. "Miss Wade, it's ashes."

It seemed impossible that I was still breathing. "But I never saw the fire. I never saw the fire. How can it be gone if I never saw the fire?"

The smoke. That was all there had been. The all-consuming smoke that settled in my throat and nostrils, so that for days afterward, I'd find bits of soot in my tissues. The smoke was so pervasive, so overwhelming, the one thing that spread and could not be contained. *Where there's smoke, there's fire*, as the saying went, and so many of us had seen the smoke around Uncle George's life but refused to see the fire.

Dad raced over, his face white as a sheet. He yanked me into his arms and held me tight. "Louisa," he croaked. "Louisa. Thank God you're okay." He started sobbing, and I was too shocked to do anything but hold him, my hands sticking to the moist sweat on his back.

"Dad," I said, my voice breaking, "it's *gone*."

"I know, jellybean, I know. I'm so sorry."

"Where's Hatch?"

Dad pointed to a stretcher a few yards behind me. Hatch lay there with an oxygen mask of his own, his hands folded over his belly and his eyes on the stars.

"Is he okay?"

Dad pawed a hand over my hair. "Fit as a fiddle."

"He got me out," I told him. "He got the window open."

Dad swallowed gravely. "Of course he did."

And then Hannah and Baker were there, wearing old T-shirts and drawstring flannels just like that night I'd taken Aubrey to their house. Hannah was crying without bothering to wipe away the tear tracks. Baker had an arm around her.

"You're all right?" Hannah asked, setting a hand on my arm.

I couldn't answer the question. "RuPaw," I said instead, and Hannah's eyes showed a moment's terror, "she ran off somewhere. She was trapped in there with us. I'm worried—"

Before I could even finish the sentence, Baker was hurrying away with a determined look in her eyes.

"She'll find her," Hannah assured me, sniffling.

The minutes passed in a whirl of flashing lights and scraping voices, and the police taking statements from Hatch and me, and Dad gripping my arm so tightly I thought he might cut off the circulation. At long last, the fire chief made his way over to our group. "Still too early to know for sure . . . ," he began, and in some strange, preternatural way, I knew the cause before he even said it.

"Faulty breaker box," he said solemnly. "You shoulda had an electrician out here."

20
ASHES TO ASHES

Dad sat me at the kitchen table and draped a blanket over my shoulders. For just a moment, he wrapped me tight and squeezed like he'd done when I was a little kid with nightmares. The sudden tactile memory caused me to cry again. My tears flowed freely while Dad dabbed a wet paper towel across my face, wiping away the smoke and soot. He had never been so tender with me before.

He made me a bowl of chicken noodle soup, straight from the can. "It's hot outside," I said feebly, but he insisted it was good for my smoke-riddled sinuses. I spooned the soup into my mouth, and Dad brought over crackers and ice water, and we sat there with a lone lamp on as the earth continued its dark slumber. For a while, all was silent except for the occasional flickering of the lamp.

"You've been through a lot this summer," Dad said eventually. He was slumped over the table with his chin in his hand, watching me carefully.

I looked blearily into his tired face. "So have you."

Dad seemed to be a world away. "How many times did you call for an electrician?"

"At least three," I said, watching his expression. "I think Hannah called once, too. And Hatch mentioned it to Grandpa in person."

There was a hard line to Dad's jaw. An angry flush mottled his neck. "Louisa . . . I've never been a violent man, but I'm just about ready to run him down in the street." Dad's muscles trembled. "I could tear him limb from limb for putting you in danger like that."

I reached for his hand and gripped it tight. "I'm tired of wasting oxygen on Grandpa. He's cut so many parts of us away. I think it's time we cut *him* out. For good."

Dad breathed deeply through his nose. "I agree with you." He rubbed his thumb over my fingers. "I'll get you that tuition money, even if the RU sale falls through. I'm not gonna let him hold the strings anymore."

I nodded. We lapsed into silence again.

"Dad . . . I really am sorry about Uncle George. Not just what I did, but . . . I'm sorry you lost him. I'm sorry he left you here alone. I know he was your favorite person in the whole world—"

Dad laughed in a jarring, disruptive way. I stared at him as he gave me an incredulous look. "Honey. You think George was my favorite person? Don't get me wrong, he's up there . . . but, Louisa, *you* are my favorite person. You always have been. I'm not alone as long as I have you."

His words were a salve on my blistering heart. I closed my eyes to truly take them in. "Dad, can I ask you something? When you and Mom got divorced . . . didn't it bother you that I moved up north with her?"

"Oh, I missed you every day, jellybean," Dad said softly. "I never wanted you to leave. But your mom and I had a lot of conversations about what was best for you, and one major thing we agreed on was that giving you space from your grandparents was a good, good thing. This family was already starting to dim your light, just like they dimmed your mom's."

I stared at him. "What do you mean?"

"Your mom never liked this town. I'm sure she's told you."

"Yeah . . ."

"She wasn't meant for a small college town. She'd had enough of that growing up in Knoxville. I think she enjoyed her college years here, but she never wanted to stay long-term." He smiled wryly. "Falling in love with a local frat boy wasn't her plan."

I smiled back. "It's not your fault you were charming."

Dad snorted. "Your mom—she found Rustin too small, too stifling. She wanted to move to New York or Chicago. She even mentioned Paris once. But I just . . . I couldn't do it. We tried to make it work, but neither one of us was happy. The fact that she stayed as long as she did is a testament to how well she tried to love me."

I took this in. "That's a really sweet thing to say."

"It's the truth."

"Do you find it stifling here?"

"Yes," Dad said immediately. He paused. "But once in a while, when I'm in the truck on a warm summer's night, I swear I fall in love again. There's just something about this place, Lou. The culture. The people. Yeah, there's some assholes, but most people are good, decent humans, just salt-of-the-earth souls trying to get through the workweek and cheer for some football on Saturday." He exhaled. "This place is in my bones, Lou. It's home."

I swallowed. "It's my home, too. Even more than Connecticut, I think."

Dad nodded. "I know. And I never wanted you to lose your home.

But . . ." He hesitated, letting go of my hand to brush his fingers across his mouth. "From the time you were young, I worried this place might suffocate you. My instincts said you weren't gonna be going to debutante balls or bringing home boyfriends. Maybe, deep down, I was worried you'd end up like Uncle George. Twisting yourself to be different things to different people. And I didn't want you to struggle through that here. Your mom said Connecticut, not far from the city, and I thought, *That will be a place she can breathe*."

I went stock-still. My heart thumped in my neck so forcefully that it hurt. "You knew I was gay?"

Dad looked into my eyes. "Probably? I mean, I had an inkling. And I knew how my family was, how poisonous they could be, and I didn't want you folding in on yourself and thinking it was your fault. I didn't want you trapped here."

"Dad." I was crying again, but it didn't hurt: It felt good. It felt cleansing. "The way you tried to protect me from them—I wish you would do that for yourself, too. I wish you would love yourself."

He hung his head, sniffling and swallowing. "When did my daughter get so wise?"

"When I started working at a bar."

Dad laughed a wet, watery laugh. "All right, give your old man a hug."

I let myself be swept up in his bear hug. He smelled like *him*. Like home.

"Get some sleep, jellybean. We'll talk more in the morning."

"I love you, Dad."

He rubbed my back and kissed my hair. "I love you, too."

* * *

When I woke midmorning, Candor and Emma were sitting on my bed.

"Oooh!" Candor said softly. "You're awake!"

I rubbed my eyes and sat up, Emma scooting over to give me space. My friends had anxious expressions as their eyes roved over me, taking me in. "Hi," I said croakily. "When did you get here? What time is it?"

"About eleven," Emma said, "and we got here a little while ago. Your dad made us coffee."

I smiled. *Dad.*

"Lou, we are so, so sorry about the Cricket," Candor began.

"And so, so glad you're okay," Emma finished.

My throat went tight. I couldn't do more than nod. "Thank you."

Candor scooted up the bed, wrapped her arm around me, and tucked me into her neck. She trailed her fingers through my hair while I cried silent tears. Emma held my hand, saying nothing, just letting me have my grief.

"You still smell like smoke," Candor said after a while, shifting her cheek on my hair.

"I know. I spent twenty minutes in the shower last night but it's still clinging to me." I shifted out of her arms and sat up straighter, gently squeezing her knee to communicate my gratitude. "How did you hear what happened? Did my dad call you?"

Candor and Emma traded looks.

"No," Emma said, "Aubrey did."

I drew a breath. "How did she know?"

Emma shrugged. "Small town. Someone called her dad."

"Louisa," Candor said tentatively, and I knew what was coming. "Are you okay about all that?"

I met their eyes, feeling embarrassed. "Did she tell you what happened?"

"No. Just that you had a fight."

That sounded like the Aubrey I knew. Even when she was angry and hurting, she considered it bad form to speak ill of me to my friends.

"I messed up," I confessed.

Emma and Candor sat with that for a moment. "Well . . . ," Candor said, "maybe you can apologize. I'm sure she messed up, too."

"I didn't mean to hurt her."

"We know," Emma assured me.

"I . . . I didn't mean to hurt her in the beginning, either. I was just jealous. I was afraid you guys had upgraded from me."

Candor made a soft clucking noise with her tongue. "Louisa, how could you think that?"

My eyes welled up without warning. "I guess I was worried you had outgrown me."

Emma hesitated. "And maybe worried that you had outgrown us?" she asked knowingly.

I nodded, swallowing against the tightness in my throat.

"It's okay," Emma promised. "I've been thinking about it, too. For all three of us. Especially with college coming." She glanced sadly at Candor. "But maybe we can give each other that space. Maybe we can trust that when we're growing, we're making more room, not less."

Candor started to cry. "Em," she sniffled, holding her fingers up to her eyelashes, "why are you putting me in my feelings before lunchtime?"

"We may not know you as well as we used to, Louisa Ebeneeza,"

Emma said, clasping my hands in hers, "but I like to think we still know your heart. We'll always know your heart."

Candor cried harder, wiping her eyes on my duvet cover.

"When did you get so wise?" I asked fondly, echoing my dad's question from the night before.

Emma shrugged. "I've always been emotionally astute. I'm, like, a suaveant."

I burst out laughing, hearing Hatch in my head: *Well, look at that, a business savant.*

My heart panged.

"Guys," I said urgently, swinging my bare legs onto the floor. "I have to get to the Cricket. See if I can save anything."

"Can we help?" Candor asked, surfacing from her tears. "Or is this something you need to do alone?"

I stopped, considered. What a gift, to have friends like these, who weren't directly impacted but still wanted to share in the pain, who wanted to love all the pieces of my heart. "I'd love some help."

I cleaned myself up, got dressed, and let Emma and Candor pamper me with scrambled eggs and coffee. Then Dad appeared, listening to our plans.

"I'll drive you," he said.

Emma, Candor, and I sat in the truck bed like we had when we were kids. The wind rushed over my hair, stripping the lingering smell away, as I sat with my back against the cab and kept my eyes on the blue sky. None of us talked, other than Candor advising Emma to shift her baseball cap over her pinking face. My friends seemed to understand I didn't want words right now.

As the truck rolled up to the bar, I squeezed my eyes shut and prayed for the courage to look upon the site. *I am gay . . . I am here . . . I am gay . . . I am still here.* The sounds reached me with my eyes still closed: noises of scraping and shoveling and tossing, but more than anything, the voices. There were so many voices.

I opened my eyes and turned around.

Dozens of people were toiling on the land where the Frisky Cricket had once stood. For a moment, that's all I allowed myself to see: living bodies tending to our dying home. The sight of it put a rock in my throat. I felt the totality of our loss, the weight of our communal grief. I felt the tenderness of our compassionate hearts.

The bar was a shell of itself, a corpse mangled and marred by fire. The entire front side of the building was destroyed, along with most of the left side where the bar top had been. Almost all of the roof was gone, having collapsed in on itself; a few remains hung on like gnarled, blackened tree limbs. White smoke rose up from the ruins, billowing like mist around our former patrons' feet.

I slipped out of the truck and forced myself to confront reality. Candor and Emma stood on either side of me, squaring up to face the wreckage. Emma was the one to start crying this time. Candor squeezed my fingers.

Someone approached us. It was Claudia's wife, Melanie, wearing a face mask. She handed us a package with more masks, and wordlessly, the three of us took them and snapped them on. We nodded our thanks. We stepped forward into the ruins.

I am gay. I am here. I am here. I am here.

A few embers were still smoldering where the porch had been. One of the neon beer signs lay flat in the dirt, covered in gray ash. The area beneath the porch was now exposed, revealing RuPaw's old hideout, the burnt husks of cigarettes and weeds. I walked along the right side of the building and found Claudia and Hannah, both wearing masks, pulling damaged picture frames off the crumbling wall. Claudia had on work boots and gloves. She gave me a chin nod and kept working.

Hannah stepped over the rubble to give me a hug. She pushed my hair back from my forehead like my mom sometimes did, like that might help her get a better sense of my well-being.

"You look okay," she muttered through the mask.

I nodded. "Did Baker find Ru?"

"Yeah. She slept at our house last night. On our bed, in a blanket nest, while Baker sang lullabies to her." Hannah gave me a wry smile. "Baker did her blood work and vitals first thing this morning. She suffered the indignity of having a bath, but she's otherwise thriving."

I nodded. "Hannah . . ."

She put a hand on my arm to stop me. It was soft, not dismissive. "Later," she promised.

I grabbed a trash bag from the box at her feet and kept walking. I found Midas at the back of the building where the delivery door had been, sorting through the utility hallway to see what was salvageable. His eyes were red-rimmed, his hair flat and unwashed. Rook was with him, lugging items out of the way, wearing a mask they had clearly thought to bring themself based on the cartoon pattern. I was slightly cheered to notice they were still wearing a cape.

Midas yanked me into a hug, beating his fists against my back. "This is fucked-up," he said in a strangled voice.

"Understatement," I said croakily.

"I heard Hatch saved your ass."

I laughed unexpectedly. "I saved Hatch's ass."

He shook his head against mine. "I don't want to think about Hatch's ass."

I walked on. More of our patrons could be found sifting through the ashes. Brooke and Maria Paula were photographing everything—"for insurance purposes," Maria Paula assured me, "but also because I'm useless in a crisis"—Marc and Joe were hauling trash bags to the dumpster, and a group of Rustin undergrads was handing out water. Edge was there in his standard bow tie, but he'd traded his dress shoes for Reeboks; he shook my hand and told me I was looking well, but his throat bobbed with emotion. Even the guy who'd been a douchebag that time I hadn't served his drinks fast enough came up to me, wrapped me in a hug, and thanked me for everything. I didn't have the heart to ask him what "everything" was.

My dad joined me right as I got to the bar top. What remained of it was covered in plaster, ash, and debris. I set my hand along the remains as dozens of memories flashed through my mind. Midas serving me beer that first night. Hannah snarking about my fake ID. Otis Penny blithely asking for a Mule while steam poured out of Hatch's ears. Hatch himself complimenting me on a job well done, then offering me a lemon drop shot.

A blackened metal sign lay helpless on the floor, its edges curled and disfigured. I could just make out the words:

GAY OWNED

GAY OPERATED

SO HAVE A GAY OLE TIME!!!

Dad saw me staring at it. He picked it up and gave me a sympathetic look. "You should keep it," he said, handing it to me.

I cradled it to my chest and burst into sobs.

It was around midday when a series of honks made everyone

look up. A white catering van was pulling up to the edge of the parking lot, and none other than Otis Penny was behind the wheel. He flashed a grin that was entirely inapt for the situation and jerked his thumb at the van's logo: TAMBRIE'S CAFÉ. A collective cheer went up, feeble but nonetheless genuine, at the thought of fresh home cooking.

"What on earth, Otis?" Hannah asked, leading the charge toward the van.

Otis hopped out of the cab and spread his arms wide like he was putting on a show. "Tambrie's!" he said unhelpfully.

"What, did you rob them?" Midas asked.

"Ditty's an old friend of mine. She'll be along in a minute. Go on and line everybody up now, Milo."

Midas rolled his eyes but did as he was directed. My dad handed out paper plates and silverware while Hannah moved down the line with a jug of sweet tea. Ms. Tambrie showed up in her tiny sedan, carrying two foil-wrapped containers of banana pudding that earned another cheer.

"Hey, make mine a double, Hannah!" Claudia joked as Hannah poured her sweet tea. A chortle of laughter ran through the group.

"I'll take mine on the rocks," Marc called.

"We need a tip jar!" someone else chuckled.

"A biiiiiig tip jar."

"Keep your fantasies to yourself, Marc!" Melanie yelled, and the whole group broke up laughing. It was a loosening, a reclaiming. It was a refusal to stop being ourselves.

We spread out to eat, some people venturing back to the tree line, others sitting right there among the ruins. Otis Penny ate standing up, using the catering van's hood as his table. Rook untied their cape and spread it like a picnic blanket in a manner that suggested this wasn't their first rodeo. Emma and Candor sat with me in Dad's truck bed, all three of us stretching our legs out, our sneakers covered in dust.

By late afternoon, our numbers had swelled another twenty people. They trickled in the same way they had when the bar was standing: on their own terms, when they were ready, bringing their stories to share. Someone showed up with a GET WELL SOON balloon and tied it to the mailbox. The champagne server from the summer banquet brought his mom and sister to help. A news crew arrived and interviewed Maria Paula, who gave a moving eulogy of the bar while blowing vape smoke into the reporter's face.

The sun's heat died away, but the smell of smoke increased in its absence. Soon enough, we were just a skeleton crew. Emma and Candor got a ride home from Ms. Tambrie. Most of the regulars left. Then it was Dad, Hannah, Baker, and me, half-heartedly lugging the trash bags to the dumpster. When Baker excused herself to go feed Jolene, my dad squeezed my shoulder, looked meaningfully at Hannah, and said he would wait by the truck.

Hannah sat down in one of the folding lawn chairs the college students had brought. She patted the one next to her and I sank into it, exhausted, rubbing a blister on my ankle. For a minute, we simply sat there and gazed upon the debris. I wondered if she was cycling through memories like I was.

"I'm still mad at you," Hannah said eventually.

"I know," I replied. "I would be, too."

"But I get it. I understand where you're coming from."

"Because I'm young?"

"No, because you're human." She turned toward me, her head lolling on the back of the chair. "And because I wanted to say the same thing many, many times. Shout it from the rooftops until everyone finally accepted it. And maybe that's wrong, maybe it's murky, but it's how I feel."

I steeled myself to say what I was too embarrassed to tell anyone else. "I miss him. I realize that I never fully knew him, but that makes me miss him even more. All I want is to have one final conversation with him. Something that actually counts. Something where I could say, *Thank you* and *I'm mad at you* and *Why did you never tell me?*"

"I think that makes sense."

I lowered my eyes. "It's hard to realize you feel anything but grief for a dead person."

"That's what grief is, though," Hannah said gently. "It's messy and ugly and unfinished. If we could wrap it up in a neat, tiny bow, we would just call it the end and get on to the next thing."

"Does it ever go away?"

"No," she said immediately. She waited until I met her eyes. "But it softens. It stretches. You learn to breathe around it."

I surveyed the wreckage around me and breathed.

"On a less dramatic note," Hannah said, "I *do* have an invitation for you. Book a flight for October, yeah?"

I froze, realizing what she was talking about. "Wait. For your wedding?"

"No, for Indigenous Peoples' Day. *Yes*, for our wedding, you ding-dong."

A warm, sunlit feeling spread over me. "Wow. Thank you. I'd love to."

"You and Hatch can fight over who gets to be the flower girl."

I snorted and leaned back, matching my posture to Hannah's, our heads turned up toward the evening sky. "Nah. That's a job for RuPaw."

"Already asked her," Hannah deadpanned. "She wasn't interested. Said she's tired of frilly dresses."

"Get her a South Daqueerta shirt instead. See if that sweetens the deal."

"Maybe I'll get her a jumpsuit."

"Give her Hatch's gardening hat. Then she'll *really* feel powerful."

Hannah snickered, and my heart bloomed, and we went on like that, talking nonsense until the sun fell behind the tree line.

A few days passed before I gathered the courage to talk to Aubrey. I dragged myself around the house, slowly gathering my things to pack for my return flight, while I checked my phone over and over to see if she had sent me another text. I still hadn't responded to the one she had sent the morning after the fire.

Aubrey Calhoun: Louisa, I am so sorry to hear about the Frisky Cricket. Thank God you're okay. Please let me know if you need anything.

It was so very Aubrey to offer her help, even after the disastrous fight we'd had at the banquet. And I knew she meant it. I knew she would be gracious even when I didn't deserve it. It made me miss her in a way that physically hurt.

Finally, on the day Hannah and Baker left for Hannah's birthday trip to Atlanta, I responded to Aubrey's message.

Me: I heard you're dog sitting Jolene. Would it be okay if I came by?

The typing bubble appeared, disappeared, then appeared again.

Aubrey Calhoun: Sure. See you soon.

Hannah and Baker's bungalow looked even more welcoming in the daylight. I parked behind Aubrey's car and made my way slowly to the front door, my hands in my pockets, my heart in my throat. Aubrey swung the door open and stepped out barefoot, wearing a cropped Gramick T-shirt, her hair loose and long and reflecting the sunlight.

"Hi," I said breathlessly, trying my best to maintain eye contact. "Thanks for letting me stop by."

She squinted at me like she was checking for signs of illness. "You look okay."

"Just okay?" I teased.

"You know what I mean. Unscathed."

"Mostly."

There was a ruckus as Jolene, followed quickly by Magnolia, came flying through the door and jumped on me. Aubrey ushered the dogs back inside and beckoned me to follow them to the backyard, which she had decided was her favorite part of the house.

"There's just so much green space," she said, gesturing unnecessarily at the vast expanse of yard. "And look—over there—see that pond? With the fountain and the bench?"

"It's beautiful," I agreed.

"It's a sanctuary," she said emphatically.

I looked sideways at her. "Aubrey . . ."

She looked at me, waiting.

"I wanted to tell you I'm sorry. About the banquet. I messed up big time. I . . . I can't imagine how terrifying that must have been for you, watching me lose control like that. Worrying that you could be next." I cleared my throat and sniffed. "The last few weeks, I was trying so hard to make you feel safe. And then I went and ruined it."

Aubrey pursed her lips. Nodded toward the patio. "Come sit, Louisa."

Wordlessly, I followed her to sit on the back steps. It felt just like that night at the Cricket, when I'd kissed her. Or that night on her garage roof, when we'd stretched our bare legs and finally said something real.

"It's not your job to make me feel safe, Louisa. That's *my job*." Aubrey's voice was quiet but brave. "Your job is to believe in me."

I met her eyes. "I do."

"Meeting you this summer was a godsend. You showed me what's waiting on the other side. You gave me a model of how I could do this." She reached for my hand and rubbed her thumb over mine. "So yeah, you messed up. But I also understand it. I mean, I keep thinking, like, what if George *had* been out? Would it have made life easier for me? Would it have opened a pathway with my dad? Am I selfish for even entertaining that idea? George barely even knew me. He owed me nothing. He was just a human being trying to figure this shit out with the weight of the world on his back, and how can I hold that against him when I know exactly how it feels?"

I squeezed her hand. "You're a good person, Aubrey."

"I hope this goes without saying, but I didn't know about the deal. That it had gone through. I just wasn't sure how to answer you in front of my dad. I was terrified for him to see us talking at all."

I swallowed. "I know. And I'm so sorry."

Aubrey's eyes ticked over to mine. "I'm sorry, too. For not understanding how painful that night was for you. For worrying about my dad's reaction instead of yours."

I shook my head. "I would have done the same in your position. Your dad is . . . well . . ."

Aubrey smiled wryly. "The worst?"

I laughed. "Something like that."

"I came out to him."

I inhaled sharply. "You're kidding."

She released my hand and shifted to watch the dogs. "It wasn't great. But it wasn't the worst thing in the world."

I waited.

"I'll spare you the uglier parts of what he said. Most of them were wholly unoriginal." She chewed her lip, still watching the dogs. "But . . . he didn't fight me on the truth of it. That's what I was most worried about, deep down. That he wouldn't believe something I know in my bones to be true."

"Yeah. I understand that."

"Do you think he'll ever get it?"

"No," I said right away. "But maybe he'll learn that he doesn't have to."

Aubrey let that settle. She turned to me and took my hand again. "When do you leave?"

"Next Wednesday. Hannah's birthday." I smiled sadly. "She hasn't let me hear the end of it, but that was the best option for flights."

Aubrey nodded. "I don't want to say something cheesy about how I'll miss you."

I bumped her shoulder. "Are you sure? Could be cute."

She rolled her eyes, then became serious again. "Do you think—would it be okay—if maybe we met up sometime in the fall? I hear there are, like, *trains* in Philly and Connecticut?"

"There are," I said with a smile. "And yes, I would love that."

She exhaled like she had been holding her breath all day, and it dawned on me that she had been nervous to ask me. The idea of it made my face warm. I took her hand and kissed it before I lost my nerve.

Aubrey blushed but tried to pretend she hadn't. She grabbed a tennis ball and threw it long for the dogs. "So, um. Are you ready to go home?"

Home. There was that elusive word again. In truth, I had been feeling something close to grief at the thought of leaving Rustin again. Aubrey's words from that night on the roof came back to me: *Maybe the only real way to honor someone when they're gone is to be honest about where it leaves us.* Surely that applied to a place as well. I was leaving Rustin, and I was still learning where that left me.

"There's one big thing that feels like unfinished business," I said after a moment. I paused, trying to articulate. "Uncle George's urn. I hate the thought of it living at Grandma and Grandpa's house."

Aubrey's eyes ticked over mine. "I think I know the answer to this, but can you or your dad ask them for it?"

I gave her a grim, knowing smile. She nodded resignedly.

"Maybe one day, once they've passed on as well . . . ," she started.

I steeled myself to voice the dangerous idea I'd been sitting on for a few days. "Or . . ."

"Or?"

I looked straight into her eyes. "I could steal his ashes. And scatter them at the Frisky Cricket, where he belongs."

Aubrey blinked. My heart dangled on a precipice, waiting for her reaction. This was a girl who lived by niceties and pleasantries, whose notion of propriety was like something of a spiritual bedrock. Surely the crime of grave robbing went far beyond her limits.

"We'll take the Audi," she said suddenly, and my eyes went wide. "I'll be your getaway car."

We planned the heist for the one time it was guaranteed my grandparents wouldn't be home: Sunday morning.

"So church is at nine thirty A.M.," I said for the umpteenth time, "but they always get there by 9:05 to snag one of the front pews. If you pick me up around nine o'clock, that should give us a good—"

"A good couple of hours," Aubrey finished, giving me a look that meant *We've been over this seventeen times*. "I know. And you're sure that key is in its hiding spot?"

"Actually, no," I admitted, because how was I supposed to guarantee they still kept a key under the flowerpot? Grandma switched around the porch décor every season; she very well could have switched the key to a birdhouse. "Which is why . . . I'm gonna steal my dad's."

Aubrey hiked her eyebrows. "You're stealing *two* things on Sunday?"

I winked. "Let's hope Grandma and Grandpa are praying for my soul."

The first part of the plan went smoothly. I snuck out of Dad's house while he slept in, meeting Aubrey in the street so her car wouldn't make noise in the driveway. We made it to my grandparents' in eight minutes and crawled up the street until we could be sure their car was gone. We parked two houses down, walked casually down the block like we were two friends out for a Sunday stroll, and then pivoted toward their front door as if I'd had a last minute whim to visit my dear old granny. Dad's copy of the key unlocked the front door seamlessly.

"They really don't have cameras?" Aubrey whispered, following me over the threshold.

"No. Grandma thinks they're 'silly toys' and Grandpa says anyone who's man enough to rob him must be man enough to face his shotgun."

Aubrey shook her head as if to clear it. "It's no wonder they like my dad."

We went straight to the glass trophy case and gazed up at the emerald urn. It was surreal to be back here again after everything I'd learned this summer. It threw the injustice of Uncle George being trapped in this museum into sharper contrast.

"Hi, Uncle George," I whispered. "Let's get you out of here."

I went to open the cabinet door, but it was stuck. A cold, sickening feeling washed over me.

"What's wrong?" Aubrey asked.

I was afraid to look at her. "It's locked."

We looked everywhere for a key: the study, Grandpa's desk, the kitchen drawers, even Grandma's old hope chest. But it was useless. Just when I was about to call the whole operation off, there was a sudden rattling at the front door.

The knob turned and the front door opened, and my racing heart stuttered to a stop.

My dad was standing there, framed against the sunlight. "Louisa?" His eyes darted from me to Aubrey. "What are you doing?"

"Dad," I said, relieved. "What are you doing here?"

"Dropping off estate paperwork," he said, a manila envelope dangling from his hand. "Honey, what are you doing?"

It was too late to come up with a cover story, and also too late to pretend I cared about getting caught. A cool feeling of relief came over me as I decided to tell the truth. "Honestly? We're trying to steal Uncle George's ashes."

Dad stared at me. "Why?"

I stared back. "Because he doesn't belong here."

Dad gave me a long, searching look. "You don't know where the key is?" he asked finally.

"No." I swallowed. "Do you?"

Dad went oddly quiet. Then he shut the front door, dropped the manila envelope on the credenza, and marched out of the room.

"Is he getting the key?" Aubrey whispered.

When Dad came back, it wasn't a key in his hand.

It was a fire poker.

"Stand back, girls," he said determinedly. Something seemed to have come over him, and it was like he only had eyes for the trophy cabinet. Aubrey and I followed his instructions, too stunned to argue.

Dad braced the fire poker with two hands, positioning the sharp end near the lock in the cabinet door. Then, without warning, he jabbed the poker in like an ice pick. Immediately, the glass around the lock cracked open.

"Yes!" I shouted.

Dad poked the vulnerable glass until it shattered enough for him to reach inside. He wrapped his first in a dishcloth, punched out the remaining shards, and swung the cabinet door open.

"Holy shit," Aubrey muttered, apparently forgetting her manners.

"Here," Dad said, taking the emerald urn gingerly off the top shelf. He passed it to me like a newborn baby, and I took it into my hands. The urn was cool to the touch, like a marble floor, and smaller than it had looked in the trophy case. I clutched it to my stomach as Aubrey looked on.

"Thanks, Dad."

"I'm not done," Dad said. He still had that single-minded look in his eyes and a bright red flush had stolen over his neck. Without warning, he raised the fire poker like an ax and brought it crashing down on the cabinet.

SMASH.

He heaved the poker again.

SMASH.

He came at the cabinet sideways, beating the poker like a baseball bat.

SMASH.

Dad raised the poker over and over and over, brandishing it like a weapon, shattering the glass cabinet into dust while trophies and medals and picture frames crashed haphazardly to the floor. He was grunting and swearing and screaming with rage as Aubrey and I stood stock-still, watching him devolve. I had *never* seen my dad lose control like this, like every blow might purge another piece of his family from his soul, like the little boy inside of him was screaming for someone to wake up. On and on he went, a tidal wave of destruction, a chaos agent finally unleashing the pain he'd corralled for so long, until his energy finally gave out. Then he doubled over, hands on his knees, as his shoulders began to shake.

"Dad—" I started. I placed Uncle George's urn carefully on the credenza and stepped closer to my dad. His breathing was ragged and his body was still trembling uncontrollably. "Dad, it's okay—"

But when he turned around to face me, he wasn't crying. He was *laughing*.

"Hoooooo-boy!" Dad shouted, tossing the fire poker to the floor. His hair was sweaty, his face was marked up from small flecks of glass, and there was a dribble of spit stuck to his chin, but he looked younger than I'd ever seen him. He staggered to an upright stance and puffed out his chest like he'd just had the ride of his life. "That felt fucking *awesome*."

The glass trophy case was no longer standing; he had beaten it to smithereens. Thousands of tiny shards lay dotted across my grandmother's polished pine floor. The brass lock had landed at the foot of the staircase, completely useless.

"Goddamn," Dad panted, stretching out his back. "That's the best thing I've done in years. Your grandpa's gonna *shit* himself!" He laughed a great cackling laugh and ran a hand through his sweaty hair. "Imagine his face!"

I started laughing, too, not because I was picturing Grandpa, but because I had never seen my dad so loose and joyful. I wanted to bottle up the moment like a firefly in a jar.

"Sorry y'all had to see me like that," Dad said to Aubrey. "Going crazy isn't usually in my playbook."

"Mr. Wade," Aubrey said sincerely, "that was the greatest thing I've ever seen in my life."

21
DUST TO DUST

The morning of Uncle George's real funeral dawned gray and drizzly.

We had decided to meet—where else—at the Frisky Cricket, or at least what was left of it. Dad and I drove in the Cadillac together, me behind the wheel and Dad holding the urn in the passenger seat. He wore a navy PFG fishing shirt with his favorite khaki shorts and boat shoes. He hadn't shaved in a week, which I think was another form of revolt against my grandparents, and the stubbly beard rounded out his face in a way that suited him. We listened to old-school country music on the drive, Loretta Lynn's rich voice warbling through the speakers. Dad riffled through the glove compartment, popped an Altoid in his mouth, and immediately spit it out.

"Stale," he said, chucking the mint out the window. "He must've had these in here for years."

We both laughed. It was so very Uncle George.

We parked in the ruins of the Cricket's parking lot next to the other funeralgoers. Hannah and Baker stood by the Subaru, talking to Aubrey, while Midas leaned his bike against an unscathed tree. Hatch arrived last, jumping out of his Volvo. He wore one of his standard stretched polos, but the ring of keys was gone from his belt loop.

"Let's get this over with," he announced, and everyone rolled their eyes.

We gathered near the remains of the Cricket's front door, treading carefully around the loose pebbles and debris. Two weeks later and the air still smelled like smoke. Two weeks later and I still couldn't believe my waterfall was gone. The loss of it pressed on my chest like a barbell. But then I glanced at Hatch's clean belt loops, free from the weight of so many burdens, and the pressure loosened the tiniest bit.

There we were, a ragtag family trying to make sense of this man we missed, this man we resented, this man we loved. And maybe my grandparents had been telling the truth on that first night I was home: Maybe Uncle George *had* wanted a big sendoff. But I hoped he would have wanted this, too. Even if he hadn't, that was okay. The rest of us wanted it, needed it. We were taking our grief into our arms, making it our own, because it was the living who had to make sense of the legacy.

I clutched the urn to my body, pushed it right up against my sternum like the pressure might loosen the ache in my chest. Dad stood on one side of me, brushing his arm against mine, while Aubrey stood close on my other.

"Someone should say a few words," Hatch said gruffly.

We all looked at Hannah, the most expressive member of our group. She nodded, but just before she opened her mouth, someone else spoke.

"I'll do it," my dad said.

He stepped forward, cleared his throat, and folded his hands. We waited.

"We're here for George," he said after a moment. "A good man. The best man some of us knew. People out there, people who didn't really know him, they treated him like a king . . . but George knew he was just an ordinary guy who'd been blessed with a talent, not because he was anything special, but just because life works that way sometimes. He never thought he was better or worse than any other person. He simply loved people. He loved each of us."

Dad cleared his throat roughly. I put a gentle hand on his back, and he kept going.

"He was simple at his core, and he understood the simplest rules of life: Do the best you can with what you've got, and love people while you're at it, even if you don't always know how. I'll miss him every day. I know we all will. I hope he's found peace up there, and that he's doing crosswords and swimming laps and eating all the peanut brittle he could want." Dad paused one final time. "He had a big heart, big enough to bring us all together. That's what will stay with me more than anything."

He wiped his face on his hand, then looked expectantly at me. I handed him the urn and hoped he could feel my heart coming with it. Dad seized a handful of ashes, tossed them about like a farmer sprinkling seed, and stepped back into the circle. Tears streamed silently down his ruddy cheeks.

It was my turn next. I dipped my hand into the urn, rubbed the ashes against my fingertips, felt the final physicality of this person who had been so very, very real. I stepped forward and held the ashes in my fist. My throat was tight. My eyes burned. The words wouldn't come to me. All I could do was drop the ashes from my fingertips, grains of sand slipping away, meeting the earth he had built his legacy upon.

"Thank you," I managed through tears. I hoped it was enough.

Aubrey went next, quiet and thoughtful. Her eyes were dry, but there was a depth to them that knocked me breathless. She sprinkled the ashes dutifully and said, "Thank you for playing fetch with Magnolia. I wish I'd known you better." She drew back into the circle with her cheeks tinged pink. I put an arm around her waist, and she let me.

Midas was next. "George taught me a lot about what it means to be a man," he said through tears, and Hannah choked quietly on a sob. "He was tough, but gentle—strong, but fragile—confident, but also humble. All the contradictions, all the things we try to balance all the time. I loved him. I'll always love him." He grabbed a fistful of ashes and scattered them across the dirt.

Baker shook out her ashes with trembling hands. Her eyes were red and watery, but her voice was steady when she spoke. "You meant more to me than you'll ever know. In my heart of hearts, you are the person who married us."

Hannah heaved a great, ragged sob as she stepped forward, her whole body shaking with grief. "I love you, G," she said around a sob. "Thank you for—for showing us how things could be. Thank you for giving us this home. Thank you for being exactly who you were meant to be, even if you didn't always show it." She paused, scattered his ashes, and sniffed. "And I'm sorry about that time I made fun of your Minions shirt, but it really was stupid."

We laughed. Hannah stepped back, squeezed the urn tight to her chest, and passed it on to the final person in our circle.

Hatch inched forward with his eyes on the dirt. For one long, unbearable moment, I thought he was going to crumble. Then he turned the urn upside down and shook the rest of the ashes onto the ground.

"Don't be a stranger," he said tightly, and then melted back into the circle with a great, watery sniff.

The birds sang in the tree line. The morning sun broke through the clouds, warming the crowns of our heads. We breathed in the stillness, in the promise of the day.

"I brought glitter," Midas said suddenly, as if we were at a party and he'd forgotten to mention the potato salad.

Hannah laughed a great, affectionate laugh. "Glitter?"

"George added pizzazz to everything. Figured if we were scattering his ashes, we should scatter some joy, too."

Wordlessly, we took handfuls of rainbow glitter from the plastic tube in Midas's backpack. We scattered around the property, weaving between the remains of the Frisky Cricket, past patches of burnt grass where any young queer person might have had their first kiss, past barren spots where an older queer person might have had their first real one. Soon enough, Hannah and Baker were spiking glitter at each other like it was a snowball fight, and Midas was screaming at them to stop, and Hatch was traipsing off with a shake of his head and a piece of glitter caught in his bristly white beard. Aubrey held my hand as we walked in tandem through the ruins, dropping glitter in every crevice of the earth, knowing full well that try as they might, the construction crews and university henchmen would never get every last shred of glitter out of this place.

I am gay, I am here . . .

We are here . . .

We are here . . .

And someday, a Rustin quarterback might show up for his first practice on this field, wondering when he should tell his coaches and teammates, wondering if he should tell them at all, and his eyes might fall upon a stray speck of pink glitter, and his brain would not recognize it, but his heart might know on some deep, instinctive level that we had been here before, that we would always be here, that as long as the earth kept spinning and the footballs went spiraling through the air, we would never, ever be lost.

ACKNOWLEDGMENTS

This book was a long time coming, but I was lucky enough to have a whole bar's worth of people cheering me on as I wrote it.

Thank you to Marietta Zacker, Mekisha Telfer, and Connie Hsu, who were generous with their patience, grace, and faith as I figured out how to tell this story. I'm especially grateful that you helped me bring this book into the world alongside the retelling of *Her Name in the Sky*. I would give you a lifetime supply of Ms. Tambrie's corn bread if I could.

My gratitude to the team at MCPG for all you do behind the scenes: Sarah Gompper, Jennifer Healey, and Celeste Cass in production; L. Whitt and Elizabeth H. Clark in design; and Morgan Kane, Melissa Zar, and Carlee Maurier in marketing and publicity. Extra special thanks to Jackie Dever, copy editor extraordinaire, for your passionate and detailed work on both TMBTP and HNITS. Hannah and Baker would most certainly be friends with you.

A huge shout-out to Ellen Greenberg and Saribel Pages at Gallt Zacker Literary Agency for getting my work seen and acquired internationally—and to Emma Jones and the team at MacUK for bringing Lousia across the pond!

Thank you to: Jarrett Hayes, for the writing dates in VaHi and the gift of the green notebook; Dr. Tatyana Zinger, for the medical input; Malee Hogan, for answering my questions about Hannah's career as a school counselor; Megan and Bobby Trinkley, for letting me pick your brain about electrical fires; and Brooke Lalley, Cathryn Wake, Caitlin and Haley Neer, and Freida Ruane for your feedback on initial drafts.

My love and gratitude to my family: all the Quindlens, Kearneys, Bendins, Bartzes, and Ruanes. Your unerring belief in me kept me going during the roughest patches of the writing process. You are my waterfall.

I would be remiss if I did not thank my cat, Peach Marie, who kept me company while I was writing. She even contributed some sentences of her own, my favorite of which was "i≥÷÷÷÷÷÷÷÷÷÷`f." I don't know what it means, but I assume it is some kind of exquisite metaphor.

During the writing of this book, I lost several loved ones who meant the world to me: Grandmom, Grandpop, Henry, Ellie, Taco, and Blueberry. I am still learning where your absence leaves me. Thank you for the honor of loving and grieving you.

Finally: It is not an exaggeration to say this book would not exist without my partner, Mary. Your faith in me is one of the greatest blessings in my life. Thank you for showing up in all the big and small ways while I wrote this story—everything from mapping out plot points to buying me coffee to coming up with RuPaw jokes. When I need a safe place to land, you are my bungalow. Let's get married.

ABOUT THE AUTHOR

© Naomi Nielsen

Kelly Quindlen is the bestselling author of the young adult novels *She Drives Me Crazy* (winner of the Volunteer State Book Award), *Late to the Party*, and *Her Name in the Sky*. Her books have been featured in *The New York Times*, *Business Insider*, *Vulture*, and *Paste*. Kelly enjoys speaking to high school GSAs, PFLAG groups, and all manner of LGBTQ+ organizations. She lives in Atlanta with her wife and their saucy cat, Peach Marie.

kellyquindlen.com